One Summer's Night

KILEY DUNBAR

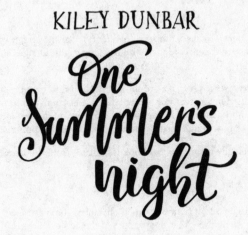

One Summer's night

hera

First published in Great Britain in 2019 by Hera

Hera Books
28b Cricketfield Road
London, E5 8NS
United Kingdom

A CIP catalogue record for this book is available from the British Library.

Print ISBN 978 1 78863 677 3
Ebook ISBN 978 1 912973 02 6

Printed and bound in Great Britain by Clays Ltd, Elcograf S.p.A.

For Nic, the love of my life

and

For Charlie, and all the lassies who loved him

Chapter One

'Love is blind, and lovers cannot see the pretty follies
that themselves commit'
(The Merchant of Venice)

Arriving by train, the Andersons had been thrilled as they
surged through the English countryside towards Warwickshire. Only a baby, Calum was too young to retain any
memories of that last perfect holiday before the accident happened. Kelsey however, was fourteen and already
hopelessly sold on Shakespeare's tragic love stories and
gossamer light poetry and would remember forever her
first glimpse of the wide River Avon and the towers and
flags of the theatres on its banks.

Having explored the maze of medieval streets all day,
their feet ached as they rounded yet another bend. Too
cool now to hold her dad's hand, but right by his side
as always, Kelsey gasped at the sudden sight of the house
where Shakespeare was born. Dismayed that it was long
since closed to visitors for the afternoon, the holiday party
stopped to gaze at the house, more of a big cottage really,
with its leaded windows and liquorice strip beams set in
caramel wattle and daub.

'Dad, can I have a go of your camera?' Kelsey asked, her eyes fixed dead ahead in wonder at the place where her hero had spent his youth and found his earliest inspiration.

'Of course. Need some help there? It's pretty complicated,' her dad responded in his soft Edinburgh burr as he lowered the strap over her neck.

Kelsey was taken aback by the heaviness of the thing, a gleaming relic of the 1970s, but soon, with her dad's calm direction, she grew used to the feel of cold metal against her cheek and on the tip of her nose as she held the camera to her eye, peering through its little viewfinder, turning the thick manual lens, focussing, breathing out, steadying herself for the shot.

'Slowly, slowly, inch it into focus. Hold as still as you can as you release the shutter. That's my girl, Kelse. You've got it.'

On tiptoe, she zoomed in on the cottage gardens, revelling in the hum of the flash recharging between pictures and the creak of the spool as she wound it on with her thumb, its clunky mechanical sounds combining with the sharp chatter of sparrows in the box hedges and the drone of the beehives somewhere deep within the grounds.

A late summer breeze swept across the garden bringing with it the scent of sweet carnations, powdery stocks, and musk roses in full bloom, filling the warm air with intoxicating perfume. It was a heady mix combined with the overwhelming emotions filling Kelsey's heart at that moment. Her lovely young dad, who she would soon come to miss so much, talked on in his kind, steady way, entrusting her with his precious camera, teaching her how to capture the images before her.

Kelsey would treasure forever those photographs taken on the day when, though she didn't know it at the time, she had found her way home to Stratford-upon-Avon.

★

The May morning sun was creeping up over Edinburgh, lighting the castle walls above the craggy rocks, turning them from grey to shining silver. It was going to be a beautiful Monday morning. Kelsey Anderson reached into her skirt pocket for the keys to The Bridges Vintage Camera Emporium. She always arrived before her boss, unlocked the heavy metal grille that covered the door and staggered inside with it. She had probably managed it once or twice without swearing. But today was different. The door was opened wide and a hunched, dejected figure was sitting behind the antique cash register, crumpled papers in his hands.

'Mr McLennan?' She never called her employer Dave; he was somehow too old-fashioned for that.

'Morning, Kelsey.' Pushing his reading glasses to the top of his bald head, he smiled weakly, nodding towards the tall stool next to him. 'Come and sit down for a minute… we need to have a wee chat.' He took a deep breath and sighed as the words formed. 'I'm sorry, Kelsey. I've had the accounts back and they're much worse than I thought. I'm sure you've noticed how quiet we've been recently. We're just not shifting cameras like we used to and we've only had a few repair jobs come in since Christmas. I'm afraid it means I'm going to have to let you go.'

Kelsey nodded slowly, trying to look pragmatic, her mind reeling. She was fond of soft old Mr McLennan.

He was no business man, that's for sure, but he was a good photographer. On wedding Saturdays and school portrait days he would dress in his ancient tweed jacket and matching bow tie and stumble off with his camera case leaving Kelsey to serve the customers – what few customers there were. Whole days could pass and only one or two art students from the college up the road would pop in for monochrome or sepia film, or one of Mr McLennan's Camera Club cronies would drop by on the off-chance of a cuppa.

'Let me go?' she echoed, aware that her pale Celtic skin was beginning to flush pink.

'Och, I'm sorry, Kelsey. You've been a great help to me here. A *great* help.'

'I've loved being here.' *Don't cry. Don't cry at work.*

Her brain raced as she glanced around the shabby old shop with its display of Hasselblads, Minoltas, and Leicas, most of them over forty years old, all reconditioned and waiting to be snapped up by the vintage photography enthusiasts who never came.

Accustomed to looking for silver linings, Kelsey felt a glimmer of optimism. 'Couldn't we turn the business around if we went digital? The shop's always needed a proper website and social media presence. I could try to sort that out. Then we could reach customers all over the world. We could get a digital photo printer, they're quite small these days, and…'

Mr McLennan was shaking his head sadly and looking down at his hands clasped on his tweedy lap. 'I'm sorry, Kelsey, it's a bit too late for that.' He scratched his head, looking utterly lost. 'The shop's closing with immediate effect. The stock will be repossessed, and all the fittings too. I'll get to keep my own camera equipment.' His voice grew weak.

Oh Lord, now don't you cry! Kelsey sprang from the stool, putting an arm around her boss, well, her *ex*-boss now.

Mr McLennan shuffled home to break the news to his wife, ready to release the weight of the business worries he'd shouldered alone for months. Kelsey noted the look of relief cross his face as he turned the key in the lock. No more secrets. With unsteady hands he passed Kelsey her pay, along with two extra weeks' money that he didn't expect her to work for. It was the least he could do, he told her. Afraid he was about to break into a fresh fit of tears, she stopped protesting and slipped the envelope into her satchel. And that was it. Kelsey Anderson was unemployed. Again.

Wandering, eyes downcast, along the Royal Mile, Kelsey felt it creeping back in: that mixture of anxiety and panic that had burdened her after her graduation when she'd been jobless and moving back to her mum's. The heaviness in her chest told her there was no way she could face the hour-long bus ride home and since everyone she knew would be at work, she nipped into a quiet café for an Earl Grey and a scone.

Above the counter, the twenty-four-hour news channel's scrolling red ticker tape paraded the same alarming stories across the screen over and over again. Kelsey turned her back to it. Sorely in need of distraction she rummaged inside her satchel for the little book that accompanied her everywhere.

Her copy of Shakespeare's *Sonnets* was a familiar old friend bound in scuffed brown leather. Just as she opened it at 'Sonnet 116' (her favourite) and began reading, '*Let me not to the marriage of true minds admit impediments. Love is not love which alters when it alteration finds,'* her phone rang.

'Fran? Shouldn't you be in assembly?' The surprise in Kelsey's voice momentarily masked her dejection. Fran hardly ever rang from work.

'Morning, you. I've got a couple of minutes. You all right?' He sounded cheery.

'Not exactly. I just lost my job! The Emporium's closing. I had no idea things were so bad. Poor Mr McLennan.'

'Aww, Kelse, that's too bad. I've always said camera shops have had their day, haven't I? It takes more than a few beardy hipsters faffing about with retro Polaroids to keep a dilapidated place like that afloat. *Everybody* uses camera phones these days; well everybody except you. You are literally the only person I know who puts actual photos in proper albums anymore. You're a dying breed.'

'I'd prefer to be called "one in a million", but I'll try to take that as a compliment,' Kelsey bristled. She'd been hoping for a little more sympathy to go with her tea.

Oblivious, Fran pressed on. 'So what will you do now then?'

'I don't know really. Maybe it was time for a change anyway? I've done nothing but work in random shops and study my arse off since I was an undergrad.'

'That's the spirit. Making that old bloke's coffee and pricing up photo frames was all right as a stopgap after the MA, but it's getting on for a year now, isn't it? Hey, it's a shame you didn't get the boot a bit earlier actually, we were looking for a new dinner lady last month. You'd look great in a tabard.' Fran was about to laugh but tailed off, sensing a scowl.

'Fran, I'm twenty-eight. Studying part time meant I was at uni *forever*. I want to do something I might actually enjoy, something I trained for.' Sighing sharply, she thought of all the work she'd put in that had gotten her precisely nowhere. 'I guess I thought the Master's degree would secure me some kind of future. I can't even keep a shop job.'

Last summer, as she crossed the stage in her graduation robes and wobbling mortar board, she'd been so full of hope and excitement. It sounded so promising: Kelsey Anderson, Master of Arts in English Literature and Theatre History. The qualifications had been hard earned, and she'd taken shop jobs to fund her studies. The second degree was supposed to set her apart from all the other job hunters, but she'd ended up falling back on her hobby.

'I might have to look a bit further afield. There could be a photographers' in Glasgow that'll have me.'

'Kelse, a photographer's assistant just isn't *a thing* any more, and the arts are very precarious, you know. Now teaching *is* a job for life, especially at a prestigious school like Greywalls. Let me know if you want me to have a word with the head, OK? Maybe there's something in admin you could do here. The secretary's retiring next year, come to think of it.'

She'd heard all this before and it never sounded any less demoralising. It was all right for Fran. Somehow – Kelsey couldn't fathom how – he'd known instinctively which career path to follow and he'd swotted and strived until he got his teaching degree, landing straight back at the school where he'd studied as a boy, except now he was Head of Maths.

Swallowing hard, Kelsey changed the subject. 'Are you remembering it's Calum's birthday tea tonight?'

'Yup. That's why I'm ringing, actually. I might be a bit late. Another meeting.'

'Well, when you do come, can you bring his present? It's wrapped up under your bed.'

Allaying her annoyance that Fran would miss the start of the party with thoughts of how excited her brother would be right at that moment as he met up with his gang of nerdy mates in the common room, she let herself smile.

Calum had been lucky, falling in with a crowd who shared his love of all things super-geek, sci-fi, and dressing up (though Calum frequently reminded Kelsey, 'it is *not* dressing up, it's *cosplay*'). He was remarkably well adjusted, if a little unconventional, for a kid who'd lost his father before he was old enough to even say 'Daddy'.

'Sure, I'll try to remember his present. Hey, what do you think he'll be wearing tonight? Maybe he'll be that wizard again?' Fran said with a laugh.

Hearing the warmth in his voice, Kelsey thawed a little. 'I caught him the other day posing like a Jedi with a plastic lightsaber. He was wearing what looked suspiciously like Grandad's dressing gown. You've got to love him. How *can* he be fourteen though? My baby brother, nearly all grown up. He'll be at film school before we know it.' Kelsey shook her head in wonder, the phone pressed to her cheek, the blue feeling returning.

Even Calum, dead set on a career in film production, knew what he wanted to do, and here she was with nothing to do for the foreseeable future but drown her sorrows in Earl Grey and try to pinpoint the exact moment when life overtook her and she got left behind.

'Don't get all maudlin on me, Kelse. Things are bound to get better.'

Kelsey wondered if Fran was talking about more than just her job situation. 'I hope so. Hey, maybe we could go away this summer, now that I'm not tied to the shop? Somewhere sunny. We haven't been anywhere nice in ages.'

Kelsey recognised the telltale hesitation.

'Remember I've got that teaching conference this summer, Kelse, and I've got the boarders to babysit on Saturdays until school breaks up in July. And then there's the expense. And you know I don't like flying anyway... or fancy food.'

There was little chance of winning this one. Fran thought prawn cocktail crisps were overly exotic so he'd never entertain Kelsey's vision of a lazy week of pool-side margaritas and tapas, but she persisted, lowering her sights a little.

'It needn't be anywhere expensive or involve taking your shoes off so some bloke can glare at you while he X-rays them. Somewhere closer to home? England maybe?' But she knew Fran wasn't listening.

'I'll be right with you, headmaster. Sorry, Kelse, assembly time. See you around eightish, OK? And chin up, yeah?'

'Don't forget Calum's pres...' she was saying, as he hung up.

Turning her attention back to her *Sonnets*, she tried to ignore as best she could the familiar feelings of not quite having made herself heard and of being somehow stung.

She was used to Fran's disappointed looks and little jibes about her earning potential, but did he really think she'd be satisfied working as his dinner lady? Maybe she didn't have a five-year career plan like some people, but her aspirations amounted to more than serving up mashed potatoes and lumpy gravy at her boyfriend's posho school.

Staring blankly at the words on the page, she resolved to come up with something sharpish that would make Fran proud of her, something that would take the pressure of him and make him smile again.

Things had been different in the beginning. Kelsey didn't like to think of the early days, but sitting in the empty café and really, truly needing to feel something, anything, other than this new low, she let her mind stray to the Student Union nightclub where she and Fran met for the first time.

She'd seen him around campus and fancied him for ages. Mirren, her best mate since primary school, had already stalked him on Facebook for her, finding out that his name was Francis Archer and that his family only lived a few miles along the coast from Kelsey's village.

Mirren had been there that night too. She had competed hard to get a place on the journalism degree at Edinburgh University where Kelsey was studying English, but Mirren always bemoaned Kelsey's decision to stay at home with her mum rather than live it up in Halls with her.

As often happened, Mirren was momentarily unable to recall Preston, her long-suffering boyfriend back home. Kelsey had watched Mirren slink off the dance floor and into a dark corner with one of the sporty lads – this time it was one of the cricket team. She could see Mirren flashing a mischievous smile at the wide-eyed bloke.

Oh boy, he's a goner! Too tipsy to feel abandoned by her friend and bolstered by the easy confidence of her youth, Kelsey had danced on by herself, eyes closed, arms raised, the music and her body euphoric.

There was a gentle touch at her shoulder. Opening her eyes she found herself face to face with Fran, tall, slim, and pale, his boy-band black hair flopping over his forehead.

'Dance with me?' he beamed. The darkest eyes she had ever seen were focused intently on her face. Without saying anything, she moved in closer towards his body. Maybe she'd had one too many lager and blackcurrants but in the white light of the dry ice he was ethereally beautiful, other-worldly even.

'I'm Kelsey,' she shouted over the music, feeling his lips graze her cheek as he leaned in to tell her the name she already knew.

Everything seemed to be slowing down. Lasers lit up the swirling smoke surrounding them as he pressed his lips against hers for the first time, holding her face in his hands, making the nightclub fade away. His low moan at the taste of her blackcurrant lips made her shiver. They spent the rest of that night dancing and kissing.

It hadn't occurred to Kelsey to mind that Fran never kissed her like that any more.

Chapter Two

'Rough winds do shake the darling buds of May'
(Sonnet 18)

Kelsey's mind was as restless as the waves beyond the sea wall that faced onto her mum's little grey stone house.

She'd arrived home to find the party preparations in full swing in the cosy kitchen, and her mum, Mari, busy skewering cheese and pineapple chunks onto cocktail sticks.

'It's all right, love, I just know you'll find something even better than the camera shop,' she'd soothed after her daughter broke the news.

Kelsey stared out the kitchen window, not willing to risk seeing the weary concern her mum was, doubtless, struggling to hide. She wondered gloomily how much longer her family could keep up the pretence that she was just a 'late bloomer', as Grandad once called her, and that it was only a matter of time before she was adulting the crap out of life like everyone else her age.

Shaking herself from her wistfulness, Kelsey cleared her throat and lifted the lid off the cake box on the kitchen table. 'Are we ready for Calum's party then? Who else is coming?'

'Let's see,' Mari replied as she plated up some mini Scotch eggs. 'It'll be us, Ted and Alex, and two or three of Calum's pals.'

Ted was Mari's best friend from way back. They had worked together at Ted's salon before Mari's husband died. After that, she couldn't face going back to work for a long time. Now she was the busiest mobile hairdresser in the area though Ted still wished she'd return to the salon to work with him.

Mari, dressed in a black tux and heels, had walked Ted down the aisle towards his husband Alex: very *Sex and the City*. Except it wasn't a glitzy Manhattan gathering of the rich and famous, more of a cold finger-buffet at the village Miners' Club. Ted had been family since before Kelsey was born, and by now Alex was family too.

Kelsey washed her hands in the cracked Belfast sink as Mari eyed her. 'Is Mirren coming tonight? Bringing Preston?'

'No, they're on a date night.'

'Very nice. They seem to have patched things up a bit, no?'

'Yeah, I think so. She seems happy enough.'

'You and Francis could do with a date night, couldn't you? When did you two last go out? He never seems to want to stay over here, either. Like I say, I'll happily get out of your way if you want to get romantic in front of the telly.' Mari tipped her head to the side with a wicked smile.

Keeping her back turned to her mum, Kelsey's cheeks reddened as she unboxed Calum's TARDIS-shaped birthday cake. 'Mu-um!' She always got flustered when Mari was playing the super-cool, laid-back-about-her-daughter's-sex-life mum.

Kelsey lowered the blue masterpiece in icing onto the chintzy china stand that used to be her granny's. *Time machines at the vintage tearoom,* she thought. The effect was a little off, but it would do.

Kelsey attempted a breezy reply. 'Fran's just really busy at the moment. And we'd rather save up than go out.'

'We?' Mari's eyebrow arched. She knew her daughter better than anyone, but Kelsey wished she knew when to stop.

Kelsey answered with a piqued, 'Yes, *we.*'

From the look of frustrated concern on her face, Mari's feelings on the subject were clear, but she chose to bite her lip. Today wasn't the day for going over old ground.

There were seventy new apartments being built on the other side of the village and Fran had already put their names down for first pick 'off plan'. Kelsey didn't want to confirm her mum's fears that she hadn't felt quite as enthusiastic as Fran when looking at the shiny brochure of the flats, all identical boxes with tiny windows and no gardens to speak of.

A hot, prickling claustrophobia started to rise at the thought of it all, so Kelsey changed the subject as she searched the cupboard for birthday candles.

'Has Ted got any vacancies at the salon?' She tried to picture herself standing behind the sinks attempting a scalp massage.

Mari was already shaking her head. 'He's got two new trainees starting this summer. I'll ask him though. You can come with me when I do my weddings. You could wash while I dry.'

'That's a nice idea in theory but do you honestly need the help? How many summer weddings have you got booked in?'

'Three so far.' Mari shrugged, and the pair nodded resignedly.

Kelsey stuck the fourteen candles on top of the TARDIS and stood back to admire her work with a wry smile. Now it really did look peculiar. 'My work here is done! I'd better get upstairs and ready for the party.'

*

Kelsey hadn't succeeded in shaking off her longing for a holiday during her wearisome bus ride home earlier and all through the party preparations. As she headed upstairs to her bedroom, the thoughts crowded in again. After ruling out the Lake District or the Highlands – places close enough to home that Fran might actually agree to a weekend away – it had dawned on her that there was only one place she truly longed to see.

'Stratford-upon-Avon,' she murmured under her breath as she dragged the box from beneath the bed and delved through its contents, a slow smile materialising alongside her memories of the place she'd last seen when she was as old as her little brother was now.

Pretty sure I've got time to have a quick look through here. Bingo! There you are. Flicking through the pages of her teenage diary, she stopped at the exact entry she'd been looking for. *August 2005.*

Glancing at the door to make sure it was closed, she started reading just loud enough to invest her words with all the drama and enthusiasm that fourteen-year-old Kelsey deserved.

'Best holiday EVER! If I died tonight, it wouldn't matter one bit because I've been the happiest I'll ever be. I'm going to write it all down now in case I forget it when I'm old. Here goes...

Does it get any better than *Romeo and Juliet* on the Big Stage at the Royal Shakespeare Theatre? It was Sold Out! We were lucky to get seats, Mum said, and they cost a fortune! The buzz going round the theatre was like electricity. And it was all so posh and so *English*! The guy playing Romeo was Completely Gorgeous!! And it was so sad. Mum cried. She didn't notice I was crying too. They're called the "star-crossed lovers", Romeo and Juliet. I love that! They'd only just found each other and they ended up on the run because their love is Totally Forbidden. Juliet's my age too and that made it even sadder. He drinks poison and she stabs herself!!! For a second I thought maybe they weren't dead after all, and that they were going to wake up and just keep on running together, but they didn't. That's when I cried.'

Kelsey smiled at the two red love hearts she'd drawn next to this with an 'R' and a 'J' inside. She read on.

'And we did loads of other stuff too! There was a boat trip on the river. And there was this massive bookshop with wonky floors and all the shelves were squinty and covered in dust and Grandad bought me a book of Shakespeare's Sonnets and Dad bought me *Romeo and Juliet*! Like I said BEST. HOLIDAY. EVER. I really missed Mirren though. She'd have loved it and would *definitely* fancy Romeo.'

Still smiling, Kelsey looked up at the sound of her mum's gentle knock. Mari popped her head round the door.

'How are you feeling now, love? I made us a cuppa while your brother gets ready for the party. I have a feeling it might take some time!'

'Usually does,' she laughed. 'I'm all right, ta. Just looking through the box. Come and see.' Kelsey handed her a bundle of photos and the pair sat side by side on the bed. They'd done this many times.

'Your dad was so handsome... and the double of Calum,' Mari said after a few moments. 'But that ginger moustache was such a mistake. And he had that checked shirt in every colour, you know? I loved him in them.'

Sipping tea and sharing memories, they stayed like this for a while. Photographs are never enough, but they are something, and they loved poring over them. Reaching into the box again, Kelsey fished out her dog-eared copy of *Romeo and Juliet*.

'It seems ages ago, Stratford. Dad bought me this, remember?'

Nodding wistfully, Mari's glance quickly returned to the pictures on her lap. 'I remember.'

Kelsey wondered how many times she had read the play since then. It was the very reason she'd gone to uni, to find out how four-hundred-year-old poetry could make her feel the way it did, like hearing voices calling her back home.

Rummaging in the box again she pulled out a theatre programme. 'Ah! Do you remember this? The Royal Shakespeare Company. It was lovely, wasn't it?'

She held the programme closer to her face, studying the image on its cover. There were white rosebuds and ivy twisted in soft tendrils like a crown around Juliet's short cropped hair. Her head rested on Romeo's bare chest, his white ruffled shirt torn open to his waist. Their eyes were closed, recreating the final scene as they die alone in the dark tomb. Kelsey remembered how she'd shuddered that night in the theatre at the eerie horror of the play's final moments and the aching romance of it all. Shakespeare knew a thing or two about passion.

'Did you know it was your dad's idea to take us to Stratford?'

'It was?'

'He saw you getting into your Shakespeare and he always tried to encourage your interests, so he surprised us all by arranging the trip himself. He used to say you were cut out for the theatre, you know?'

'Are you saying I was a teenage drama queen?'

'*Was* a drama queen?' Mari laughed, circling a palm on her daughter's back. 'He just wanted you to find your path and be happy.'

'And settle down like you two did?'

Kelsey suppressed a sigh. If that's what her dad wanted, she had sure disappointed him. Mari and Lewis had been teenage sweethearts, married fresh out of high school. They'd done everything young. Mari had been a young bride, a young mum, and a young widow. It never failed to strike Kelsey as appallingly sad and just plain wrong that her mum had been so badly treated by the universe. Just like Romeo and Juliet, they'd been ill fated.

'No.' Mari smiled, leaning into her daughter with a gentle nudge. 'I think he thought it was more important that you found a life of your own first, doing something you love.'

Bleak and tired, Kelsey looked down at the theatre programme in her hands. Her dad had dreamed of a life in the spotlight for his little girl, but here she was at twenty-eight, utterly in the dark. She hadn't cried in front of her mum for years and she wasn't going to start now. Later, she told herself. After the party.

'Hello puny humans,' came a voice from behind the door, startling them, as Calum appeared in a gold super-hero costume, his face masked.

As was often the case, neither Kelsey nor her mum had the faintest idea who he was supposed to be.

'Wow, Calum, very nice. Is this a new one?' said Kelsey, glad of the change in atmosphere her brother always brought with him.

'Yep, thanks to Grandad. Got it with my birthday money. Like it, Mum? Ooh, doorbell!'

And he was gone. There followed a flurry of excited shouts at the front door and the gold superhero, an alien, and a steampunk cowgirl shuffled off to Calum's room laden with presents and multipacks of popcorn.

'When did his voice get so *deep*?' laughed Kelsey, mimicking her baby brother's new hyper-manly tones.

Mari screwed up her face in comic pity. 'Aww, anything's better than *the squeaks!* Poor wee lamb. Right, I'd better get the sausage rolls on.' She kissed Kelsey gently on the head as she rose to go.

'OK, I'll be down in a minute.'

Alone again, Kelsey flicked through the pages of the programme still cradled in her hands, stopping at the beautiful double-page picture of the theatre taken from a distance at night. It captured all the moonlight and magic she remembered. Turning to the back pages she read through the adverts for smart Stratford restaurants and hotels. She smiled suddenly as she recognised the little bed and breakfast she'd stayed in on their family holiday so long ago, wondering how on earth she would convince Fran to fritter away some of their hard-saved flat deposit on a romantic break. Tonight at the party, she told herself, she'd begin planting the seeds, letting him mull it over for a while. He hated snap decisions. She ran her fingertips over the advertisements once more. 'Let's hope it works; we could both do with a nice holiday to look forward to,' she told herself as she glumly made her way downstairs to start the party.

★

By eight o'clock, Grandad was at his usual spot at the head of the table, the corks had been popped, and Mari and Ted were whispering conspiratorially by the sink, occasionally breaking out into wicked laughter. They'd always been like that. Nobody made Mari laugh like Ted, not even Kelsey's dad.

'So where's your man tonight, Kelsey?' asked Alex, tucking into a bowl of marshmallows with no indication that he planned to share them around, his cheeks blushing pink from the cava.

'I dunno, he's probably still at his meeting.'

'He'll be here any minute I'll bet, sweetpea.' Alex dropped his eyes to the floor knowing he didn't sound very convincing. They'd all seen Kelsey let down before.

'I hope he gets here soon; he's got Calum's present,' she replied, glancing out the steamy kitchen window, thinking about how she had scoured the internet looking for a proper professional special effects make-up set. Calum was going to be thrilled, if he ever got to open it. She swallowed down the disappointment. 'He'll have got stuck into lesson planning or something. He's really trying to advance his career, Alex. He wants to be the youngest head teacher in Scotland.'

'And I'm sure he'll do it too.' Alex smiled politely, but Kelsey could feel the sympathy and frustration behind it, prompting her to spring instinctively to Fran's defence. The last thing she wanted was for everyone to feel even sorrier for poor unemployed Kelsey.

'He's doing it all for me and our future. It's so important to get on the property ladder, isn't it? And all his hard work takes the strain off me a bit, you know, saving up for the deposit on the flat and everything.' The words tasted sickly and artificial in her mouth.

'Course it does, love. But he's a lucky man too, having you by his side.'

Is he? Kelsey wondered. *Lumbered with a girlfriend who can't pay her way, on a waiting list for a flat, perennially saving up, and never moving?* She doubted Fran felt lucky.

Suddenly sheepish, Kelsey reached for her dad's beloved Canon AE-1, long since her most treasured possession. Once again safely behind the lens, she snapped some shots.

Her grandad had been joined by Calum and his mates, all animatedly explaining their costumes and characters to him. One boy with an exceptionally well painted navy blue monobrow was holding forth.

'Actually, Nara doesn't wear this particular cape until the third part of the *Dark Sky Saga*, and *technically* he couldn't have the Maunday Stone in his possession, but...'

Wow, good on you, Gramps. Kelsey framed him in her viewfinder. *He actually looks interested.* Calum was the apple of his grandfather's eye and the reason he was so young at heart, even if his legs and his memory were beginning to fail him.

He smiled straight down the lens, wrinkling his nose at Kelsey, his eyes twinkling in the flash light. Seeing the undisguised love in his expression as he looked at her, Kelsey smiled. *OK, maybe Grandad has two apples of his eye.*

Calum was busily snapping pictures of his sister with his phone, enjoying another opportunity to tease her. 'You don't need to bother with that old thing,' he laughed. 'This is much quicker. I've Snapchatted them already, see?'

Kelsey smiled, keeping her thoughts to herself. *There's no quick arm's-length selfie (or fifty) with an old treasure like this. Photographs the old-fashioned way take a bit of skill and a lot of patience. And I don't really mind waiting for the gorgeous glossy prints to arrive in the mail from the developers, not now I've mastered the art of patience living at home waiting for my life to begin.*

Kelsey lowered the camera with a guilty glance at the clock before taking her phone from her skirt pocket. Not a peep from Fran. *And he knows how I worry about all the million awful, frightening things that can happen to drivers out on the roads at night.* She shoved the anxious thoughts away. She knew from experience he'd simply forgotten about the party. This wasn't going to be another tragic repeat of her dad's last day. No, Fran was just off doing his own thing. Kelsey let out a long breath, her shoulders dropping.

'Fran's just texted, he got stuck in traffic and turned back, sorry.' She fumbled with the box of matches and rearranged the cake stand in front of her brother, aware that everyone was watching her and falling silent. 'Shall we light the candles now, Calum?'

It was easier to tell a little white lie than face her family's sympathy and their barely concealed annoyance with Fran.

Sensing her discomfort, Ted pulled the kitchen blind closed, shutting out the May evening light, as the match flamed and smoked and the household launched into a cheery rendition of 'Happy Birthday to You' to Calum's awkward teenage amusement.

Chapter Three

'Like to the time o' th' year between the extremes of
hot and cold […] nor sad nor merry'
(Antony and Cleopatra)

It had been warm enough last night to open wide the
bedroom window but now the early morning rain was
pattering against the gently flapping blind and chilling the
bedroom.

Stretching her body beneath the rose-print duvet,
Kelsey allowed herself to drift off again, thanks to the
slowly dawning realisation that she needn't have bothered
setting an alarm last night. She had nowhere to go. No
six-thirty wake-up, no crowded hour-long bus journey
alongside the steely waters of the Forth into Edinburgh,
and no hurried coffee shop breakfast on her way to the
camera emporium. There was plenty of time to look for
jobs later; for the first time in a long time she was going to
sleep the morning away. Kelsey's dozy thoughts were cut
off abruptly by a loud buzz from her phone. She peered,
bleary-eyed, at Fran's message.

Sorry about party. Ring U at lunch. Present on step,
F xx

Lifting the blind, Kelsey stuck her head out the window into the grey May morning. Sure enough, there on the doorstep below was Calum's present in a supermarket carrier bag.

'Fran, you wally!'

Racing out to retrieve the dripping bag she wrapped the sodden gift in a towel that had been warming all night on her mum's ancient stove, shaking her head and muttering obscenities as she went.

The heat from the stove spread out across the kitchen, warming the cracked quarry tile floor. It was always so cosy in there, her favourite room in the house. Flipping the kettle on and finding a mug, a little tug of guilt troubled her. It was telling her that at least Fran had made the effort to make the round trip of forty minutes before he went to work that morning, and in this weather too. In his own way he was trying his best. And he'd known not to wake her. Although she'd have loved to pull him into bed with her this morning, just for a few minutes, or maybe a bit longer.

Distractedly taking her first sip of milky coffee, Kelsey imagined Fran heading off to his school in his suit and tie with that leather belt taut around his trim waist. He'd be freshly shaved and smelling of the expensive aftershave she'd given him for Christmas, deep citrus and spice. Bounding back upstairs, mug in hand, she grabbed her phone and tapped hurriedly:

Thanks for bringing Calum's prezzie. Am I still staying at your place on Sunday? I'll cook. You get the wine! K x

Then with a deep breath, Kelsey propped herself up on her bed, her laptop primed and coffee steaming. 'Let the job hunt begin.'

★

'Sweet Jesus, I'm in a Harry Potter movie.'

Kelsey brought herself to a sharp halt as she entered Greywalls' school grounds through the gate of the porter's lodge. She had seen pictures of Fran's school but hadn't quite realised how ancient and imposing it really was. It loomed against the blustery blue sky, turreted and impenetrable, somewhere between a castle and a military barracks.

Following the path – Fran had pre-warned her *not* to walk on the grass – Kelsey clutched the handwritten visitor's permit the old porter had given her, keeping a carbon copy on his clipboard.

'Pull the bell by the main door and ask for Mrs Craven. She's expecting you,' he'd said in a shaking voice, pointing a crooked finger across the quadrangle.

Kelsey half expected the impossibly Dickensian gent to tug at a forelock – if he'd had any hair – and put out a hand for a shiny penny. He seemed rooted to his spot by the lodge window as though he'd been there since the laying of the school's foundation stones.

'What am I doing here?' Kelsey muttered to herself as she passed the statue in the centre of the quad celebrating the stern minister who first sponsored the school. He glared down at her, blank-eyed and straight of mouth.

Her job search hadn't proven as fruitful as she'd hoped. Fran had taken pity on her and had a word with Mr Stevenson, the headmaster. An agreement had been come to that the school would at least take a look at her – Fran's words – and so here she was, nervous and dispirited and seriously wishing herself back at Mr McLennan's cosy, quiet shop.

As she reached the door Kelsey set her jaw and took a breath deep enough to get her through the entire job interview. It was cold in the shadow of the building and she found herself increasingly aware of the inappropriateness of her outfit; a simple grey jumper under her thin coat, a mustard yellow cord skirt, and long brown boots with thick grey tights, perfect, she'd thought back at home this morning, for a chilly day by the coast.

To her surprise a schoolboy opened the door and took the slip from her hand as she explained why she was here. Wordlessly, he nodded and indicated that she should step inside. The whiff of boiling cauliflower told her it was nearing the boys' lunchtime. The child, dressed in a long flowing red frock coat, walked her briskly along a corridor lined with busts of eminent whiskery men.

'Thank you, Wilson. Off you go to the refectory now,' shrilled an imperious Morningside accent when they reached the doorway at the end of the corridor. The boy scurried away, leaving Kelsey wondering what to do next.

'Miss Anderson? Step inside please,' came the voice again.

Kelsey followed it, bobbing her head around the door frame before presenting herself. A severe-looking woman of seventy or thereabouts was sitting behind the oldest computer Kelsey had ever seen. Its fan whirred noisily.

'Come in, Miss Anderson. You'll be having some tea?'

Kelsey wondered if that was a question or an instruction. 'Um, no thank you. I've just had some,' she lied. In fact, she'd have loved a cup but something in the woman's demeanour told her she wasn't truly keen on making her one.

Kelsey looked at the empty chair by the desk. She hadn't been asked to sit down yet, so she stood as casually as she could, with her hands fidgeting by her sides.

'My name is Mrs Craven. I've been secretary to Greywalls School since 1971. I'm sure Mr Archer informed you of my retirement plans. I hadn't intended to commence interviews until the summer, but here we are.' This was followed by a slight tick at the corner of her mouth. 'You are very fortunate to have a young man like Mr Archer vouching for you to our headmaster.'

Kelsey tipped her head to the side, trying to smooth her pleating brows. This sounded like some kind of accusation, as though she'd used her wiles and influence to beg a job. Far from it; she'd only agreed to come to shut Fran up.

'Umm, thanks. Mr Archer *is* lovely, yes.'

Hearing Fran referred to as Mr Archer was very strange indeed, as was the feeling that she was imposing on Mrs Craven's daytime regime in her neat little office.

The secretary seemed to snort as she shuffled papers on her desk. Kelsey quickly cast an eye over the walls, taking in the framed black and white photographs of proud and studious boys, all jutting elbows and shiny knees; row upon row and decade upon decade of privileged education, acne breakouts, and healthy Greywalls discipline.

'Tour, Miss Anderson?' The secretary suddenly stalked out of the room, taking the opportunity to run a cool eye down Kelsey's outfit as she went. Kelsey pattered down the corridors behind her, wondering if she was supposed to be taking notes.

Mrs Craven occasionally called out over her shoulder. 'Staff kitchen on the left. That's where you'd make Headmaster's tea. Milk, no sugar. Bursar's office on the right. Nurse's station at the end of the corridor. This is the store cupboard for the tuck shop stock. I keep the key for that. Any questions so far?'

'No, got it.' Kelsey wanted to sound efficient and clipped like Mrs Craven, but it came out brusque and rude instead. 'I mean, no questions, thank you.'

Mrs Craven turned to face Kelsey, her eyes boring into her. 'Headmaster likes his girls smartly turned out.'

His girls? Kelsey suppressed a shudder.

'What sort of thing do you mean?'

'Something along these lines would be suitable.' Mrs Craven swept a papery-skinned hand downwards indicating her own lemon yellow twinset and pearls and fixed hairdo much like Her Majesty the Queen's. 'No trousers, short nails, no make-up, only lipstick. Court shoes, no higher than a two inch heel. Our parents expect a certain… professionalism.'

'Will there be a regulation gym knickers check?' Kelsey clapped a hand to her mouth, but it was too late.

'I *beg* your pardon?'

'Nothing. Sorry.'

Mrs Craven turned on her heel (regulation height, of course) and marched back towards her office, shaking her head, leaving Kelsey to trudge behind her again, rolling her eyes at her own stupidity. She took the opportunity to give herself a stern talking to.

I'm more likely to get a detention than a job. Buck up your ideas, Kelse! This must be why Fran never invites me to the school Christmas parties or the kids' science fairs. I'm not smartly turned out enough. Not professional enough. And he's right too.

She turned into Mrs Craven's office already feeling utterly dejected but determined to put a brave face on it. She found the woman sitting behind her computer again. This time Kelsey was invited to sit down too.

'Your curriculum vitae was certainly... interesting.' Mrs Craven worked her lips as though wondering at a sudden sour taste.

'Thank you?' Kelsey said in an uncertain voice into stony silence.

'Degrees in theatre and history are all very well, Miss Anderson, but have you any secretarial experience?'

There it was. Straight in for the kill. She'd told Fran she wasn't cut out for an admin job but would he listen? Why had she let him talk her into this?

'Until recently I was an assistant in a camera shop. I did stock-taking and answered the phone, worked the till, and I had a key, so... lots of responsibility there.' Her voice tailed off at the sight of Mrs Craven smoothing the pleats in her skirt with undisguised impatience.

'Can you type, Miss Anderson?'

'Yes.'

'What is your WPM?'

'W...?'

'I'd expect a Greywalls secretary to type at seventy words per minute with one hundred per cent accuracy.'

'Would you?' Kelsey's voice squeaked, making her suck her lips in nervously.

Mrs Craven was on the move again. 'Take my seat, please,' she instructed.

'Oh, OK.' Kelsey shifted round the desk, perching on the threadbare cushion.

'Knees under the desk, Miss Anderson. Elbows at a ninety-degree angle, back straight. Optimum typing position.'

Kelsey glanced up at Mrs Craven who added imperiously, 'I attended the Gilmour and Bryson secretarial college. There was no such thing as repetitive strain injury in my day; we assumed the correct posture before the keys.'

Kelsey's eyes widened and just as she was worrying she might blurt out a childish laugh, Mrs Craven whisked a black canvas bag from behind her back and placed it over Kelsey's keyboard and spoke again. 'Hands inside the bag, eyes on the monitor. Please re-type the letter on the desk.'

'I'm sorry, what?'

'Touch-typing, Miss Anderson, is a necessity. Do you mean to tell me you look at the keys as you type and not at the words as they appear?'

'Um, yes,' Kelsey nodded. *Like everyone else on the planet.*

'A great typist never looks down. That was the Gilmour and Bryson girls' motto.'

'I see.' Kelsey gulped and slipped her hands into the bag, her fingertips finding the keys, but which, she had no idea. *Oh balls!*

It was only after a mortifying five minutes of jabbing blindly inside the bag and failing to recreate a single word of the letter accurately while her temperature soared and her heart pounded that Kelsey realised Mrs Craven was side-eying her from over by the book case.

'You *can't* type?'

'I can. I typed all my undergraduate essays and an MA thesis.'

The woman crossed the room and whipped the bag from the keyboard, raising an eyebrow at Kelsey's hands. 'With two fingers?'

'Possibly.'

'And *how* is your shorthand note-taking?' Mrs Craven's voice was grave and dramatic as though she'd asked, 'And you've kicked *how many* puppies?'

'Umm...'

'That good?'

Kelsey didn't bother telling Mrs Craven she could probably take dictation longhand and nobody would die as a result, or that the headmaster could stoop to taking his own bloody notes in the post Mrs Craven era, but instead she looked down at her hands on her lap.

'I thought this job would be more about running the school's social media sort of stuff and organising the boys' bassoon lessons and school trips.' Kelsey's shoulders drooped.

This is it. This is the day I'll always remember as the day I plumbed the murkiest depths of my own arsehattery and incompetence. If they were giving out medals for unemployability, I'd be a fully decorated veteran.

When she looked up, Mrs Craven was standing by the office door, smiling thinly, holding out Kelsey's coat and bag. Evidently, the interview was over and Kelsey was not destined to be a Greywalls Girl.

'Not coming back then?' asked the porter matter-of-factly as Kelsey signed herself out of the school grounds.

She shook her head as she handed his pen back. No, she wouldn't be back and she'd doubly ensured she'd never, ever be invited to the headmaster's end of term drinks party in his office. She'd never had any desire to be a staff WAG anyway, but still. Now she understood why she hadn't been asked before.

Mirren answered her phone after just two rings as Kelsey reached the bus stop. The interview post-mortem was conclusive: death by ineptitude and mortifying class difference.

'I knew Fran was from another world to me,' Kelsey lamented, 'and I knew he'd had his fancy Greywalls education and his private home tutors while me and you bumbled on doing our best at the local high school, even if it was a bit rough, but today, in that fancy school, it felt like me and Fran are from different planets.'

Mirren interjected the occasional sympathetic, 'mmm'.

'And I hadn't forgotten that while I was contented just pottering around the Sunday market or having a chippy tea with Mum and Dad he was brought up at his dad's golf club and at the cricket pavilion; but I'd never actually twigged that those differences mean I'm an embarrassment to him. Ugh, what is he going to say when he hears about this?'

'He'll say he's sorry you didn't get the job and that Mrs Speed-typist of the year 1882 is a miserable old cow,' said Mirren.

Kelsey wasn't so sure, but she was glad of Mirren's optimism. By the time the bus arrived to take her home, Mirren had Kelsey smiling again. 'Something special's waiting for you, just around the corner. I know it. Hang on in there, Kelse… and maybe don't let Fran arrange any more interviews for you, eh?'

'I can give you my word that whatever I end up doing, it'll be something a bit more… me.'

Chapter Four

'The fault [...] is not in our stars,
But in ourselves, that we are underlings'
(Julius Caesar)

'Hey, Kelsey-boo. Wake up.'

Forcing open her eyes, Kelsey made out the silhouette of a blurry Fran standing over her. 'Oh! What time is it?'

'Half six. How long have you been here?' Fran looked around his room at the empty mugs, KitKat wrappers, and mascara-stained tissues on the floor.

So much for cooking dinner. Kelsey swung her legs off the side of Fran's bed, suddenly aware that she'd been drooling and her neat braids were coming loose – and she'd been so pleased with them as she'd climbed aboard the noon bus to Fran's place. Now stray strands of growing-out fringe hung down over her panda eyes.

'I was watching *Shakespeare in Love* again and your bed was just so cosy, I must have nodded off. Where have you been?'

'I nipped round to Mum and Dad's for lunch and then headed to the gym. I didn't think you'd be coming round so early or I'd have stayed here.' He smiled, tucking a wavy wisp of her dark blonde hair behind her ear. 'It's nice coming home and finding you in my bed.' His eyes sparkled mischievously. He looked away, taking in the messy nest she'd made for herself. 'So *this* is what the life of a lady of leisure looks like, is it?'

'Fran! It's Sunday afternoon and I've only been unemployed for a bloody week, give a girl a break. Anyway, I've been searching all week, and it turns out there are only six vacant positions in the whole of Scotland and I'm qualified for precisely none of them.' Kelsey felt the tears welling again and blinked them away.

'I was just joking, Kelse.'

'I take it you heard about the interview?' Kelsey cringed, blowing her nose. It had been two days now and the embarrassment still smarted.

Fran grinned. 'Thora did mention it, yes.'

'Thora?'

'Mrs Craven.'

'She told you about the keyboard in the bag test? What a weirdo.'

'I didn't realise you couldn't type.'

'I can type. I type all the time. But I also have eyes and I don't work in complete darkness inside a bloody bag, so…'

'You could at least have practised a bit before you went, Kelse, the headmaster set up the interview as a favour to me.'

Kelsey's cheeks flamed red. 'I did my best, OK, Fran? Besides, I don't want you lending me out to your colleagues, thanks very much, no matter how many Brownie points it'll score you with the head.'

'I was trying to help you out, but if you won't help yourself…'

'All right, all right, can we change the subject please?'

Fran shrugged as Kelsey attempted to lighten the mood again.

'Anyway, I had some good news today, at least I thought I did. There was a media job going at a magazine in Edinburgh. They needed someone to do photo editing, training included. So I sent them my CV, and I got a phone interview. They were so lovely and said I was perfect, so that's good, isn't it? But then…' Kelsey shrugged. 'Then they said it was an unpaid internship. Two years unpaid! Who can afford that, Fran?'

'Of course it was unpaid. You could have taken it and worked in the evenings somewhere? Can't you go back to that supermarket you used to work at?'

Kelsey ignored him. 'How am I meant to compete with new graduates whose parents can pay for them to work for free?'

Fran, suddenly softened by the sight of Kelsey's eyes reddening again, knelt down on the floor in front of her, putting his hands on her knees.

'You'll find something, don't worry. Look, let's get some food in you. I brought that wine and I can order a pizza. We'll watch a box set or something, OK?' He was trying to wipe the mascara streaks off her face.

'Fran, did you actually *spit* on that tissue?' Kelsey smiled in spite of herself.

'I did a bit.' He broke into his lovely grin. 'What is this stuff made from? Seriously, it's like tar.'

Leaning her forehead against his chest, Kelsey sighed as Fran wrapped his arms around her. They both took a few long, deep breaths as they remembered what it felt like to be this close. Resting her cheek against his shoulder, her fingers tentatively tugged the zip on his gym hoodie.

'Let's eat later. I've *really* bloody missed you. Where do you get to, Fran?'

Kelsey tried to ignore the faintly awkward feeling as she leaned in to kiss his neck for the first time in, how long? 'I'm so fed up, Fran. Just make it all go away.'

'That I can do,' he replied in a low voice, but he was already extricating himself from her arms, placating her with one smacking kiss on her forehead. 'I'll just jump in the shower.'

'Oh, OK.' Kelsey's lip plumped petulantly, and something like embarrassment coloured her cheeks as he wandered off, phone in hand. That morning she'd cut the tags off the slinky underwear set she'd bought as a Christmas treat for Fran and never got round to wearing. They felt tight and uncomfortable under her clothes and she was beginning to wish she hadn't bothered.

Pulling the covers around her, she listened as he rang through the pizza order and started the shower running, trying to resist the urge to sulk. Fran hated when she sulked. Waiting, she unleashed her wild hair from the plaits and idly surveyed the room. It was all right, as bachelor pads went, quite grown up really, if a bit sparse.

There was a grey sofa with what appeared to be a new black fluffy blanket neatly folded over an armrest squeezed in between the end of the bed and the huge TV. *New cushions too? Bit weird.* Fran wasn't usually a soft furnishings kind of guy. Her brows gathered in consternation as it occurred to Kelsey that Fran's mum only lived around the corner. She knew that she popped in regularly to collect his laundry. *Or does she do a bit more than that?* In fact, everything, except the messy den she'd made in his bed that afternoon, looked pretty neat and tidy. *Come to think of it, there's that bowl of potpourri in the bathroom too.* Why hadn't she noticed before?

Fran wandered in, only a towel around his waist which he immediately chucked into a damp heap on the carpet. Kelsey would have wondered who'd eventually put it in the hamper if she hadn't been distracted by the sight of his lean body, which made her feel suddenly shy, and she scolded herself for it. It had been so long since she'd seen him naked, she'd have looked away if he'd glanced over at her.

'Fran? Does your mum clean up in here as well as doing your washing?'

Pulling on a faded T-shirt and trackie bottoms, Fran looked around the room. 'Uh, well yeah, I guess she does. I've never really thought about it.'

'That explains a lot. Thanks a bunch, Hillary,' Kelsey drawled in a mocking tone. 'You've got to know, Fran, I will *not* be taking over that role if we move in together. You can fold your own pants.' She lay back on the bed with a wry laugh.

'*If* we move in together?' Fran froze, suddenly defensive, a frown forming. 'What do you mean *if*?'

'I mean *when* obviously, *when* we move in together,' Kelsey spoke quickly, hiding a grimace behind her long hair. Hurriedly leaning over the side of the bed and pulling open 'her' drawer where she kept a few overnight things, she grabbed some PJs and nipped into the bathroom, all the while avoiding Fran's exasperated stare.

Soon changed, having jettisoned the fancy lingerie, she settled on the sofa next to the crestfallen Fran as he poured the wine. Kelsey knew she had to work fast if she was going to rescue their night in.

'Come on, let's get shitfaced and watch a whole season of something in one go. You can pick.'

He shrugged off the gentle hand she placed on his forearm just as the doorbell rang. Fran marched off to grab his wallet. Coming back with the huge pizza box, he placed it on the coffee table in front of Kelsey, lifted out one gooey slice and turned towards his desk.

'You watch what you want, Kelsey. I've got a ton of marking to do.'

'Don't do this. I've had a crappy week. Get over here and snuggle me up,' she implored.

It was no good. He was soon sitting in front of his computer, typing every now and then, not even touching his wine. Kelsey sank back on the sofa with a weary shake of her head.

'Can I borrow your iPad then?' It was hard to keep the conciliatory tone in her voice.

Sitting in silence staring at separate screens really wasn't how Kelsey had hoped their evening would pan out. Knowing that Fran would come round eventually, she let him have his strop, inwardly pondering if he'd always been this tetchy.

Signing into Facebook, she scrolled through Mirren's status updates. There were loads of pictures of her and Preston from their night out, their grinning faces pressed together. One was tagged, *Date night with my man #spoiledrotten #luckyme.* They looked pretty relaxed, just enjoying each other's company and what looked like two enormous steaks.

Kelsey poured another glass of wine and sullenly ran through her options for things to post on her own time-line.

Being ignored by my crabby boyfriend?

Here's a photo of me drinking wine alone?

Yep, I got this MAHOOSIVE pizza all to myself coz my BF is being a dick (Sad Face emoji. Angry Red Face)?

So, I lost my job last Monday, then totally blew an interview for a job I didn't even want (Crying Face)?

Better not, she thought, logging out.

Glancing at the cross, wounded Fran, Kelsey thought how tired he looked and she instantly regretted hurting his feelings. She seemed to be doing it all the time recently. All Fran's hard work was beginning to etch itself in thin lines across his youthful features. He'd had his gorgeous floppy fringe cut off when he got the job at the school. How she missed their scruffy, carefree days at uni when all they did was study together and go to parties, kissing under the streetlights on the nights he'd sneak her back into his Halls.

'Fran?' she asked in a quiet voice. 'Is this what we'd be like if we were living together?' He didn't seem to hear her. Suppressing a sigh, she looked back at the screen in her hands. Sharing a home together seemed like an even more distant possibility now. How would she contribute to the deposit with no job? Did Fran really want to bail her out of this mess?

Sod it, this calls for some serious grovelling.

She rummaged in her satchel for the theatre programme she'd been carrying around in the hope of enticing Fran to look at it with her.

'Fran?'

Nothing.

'Do you want to help me pick a B&B and I'll book us a weekend in Stratford, just the two of us. My treat.'

She thought of the envelope, still unopened, that Mr McLennan had given her. Two weeks' wages. What better thing to spend it on than a romantic getaway to reconnect again? The flat deposit could wait. What they really needed was some carefree time together.

Still nothing from Fran.

She flicked through the pages, turning to the advertisements at the back for fancy brasseries, cosy pubs frequented by celebrity thespians, five-star spa hotels, and… something grabbed Kelsey's attention. There at the foot of the page in eye-catching acid yellow was an advertising banner. In bold black type, it read:

> **Calling all Star-Crossed Lovers, Dreamers, Untamed Shrews, and Sweet Princes**
> **Tour Guides of Historic Stratford-upon-Avon required for the Summer Season**
>
> **Apply Now.**
>
> **Requisites:**
> **Knowledge of the Bard and his works**
> **History degree or subject expertise**
> **Acting/public speaking/teaching experience**
>
> **Full training provided**
>
> **Apply: The Norma Arden Historic Tours Agency.**

Kelsey read the advert twice and sighed.

Too bad it's from so long ago. This would have been perfect when I graduated. God knows, it would be great now.

There was no website address, only a phone number, but Kelsey was suddenly overcome by the strongest notion.

There's no harm in looking. Just a quick peek.

Already, she was typing the words, 'Stratford-upon-Avon tour guide jobs' on Fran's iPad. Eyes wide, she scrolled through the top hits – all general job sites, temping agencies, and companies offering advice on how to improve your CV.

Guess I'll be spending plenty time looking through those in the next few weeks.

But there it was, right down at the bottom of the screen: The Norma Arden Historic Tours Agency.

It still exists!

Kelsey felt a little flutter in her stomach as she glanced up to check Fran was still absorbed in his work before clicking the link.

Norma Arden Historic Tours is England's best small tour agency

Book your guided walking tours today

Choose from six historic locations:

London, Oxford, Bath, Stratford-upon-Avon,

Cambridge, or Windsor

Let our expert guides take you on a tailor-made magical journey into the past as you visit sites of historical significance and stunning beauty.

On the left side of the page there was a yellow box with the words 'Guide Vacancies' in bold lettering. Without thinking, she tapped the screen and scrolled through the list of job openings. There it was.

Stratford-upon-Avon Walking-Tour Guides. Hourly pay. 28+ hours per week. Start dates from 15 June. Contract terminates 30 August. Click here for application form.

Holy crap!

Her heart thumped in her chest. Furtively clicking on the application form, she wondered why she felt she was doing something wrong. It only took half an hour to fill in, and all the time Fran was quietly working.

Let's see – Edinburgh University, BA in History, Master's Degree in English Literature and Theatre History. Perfect. They've got to love that, right? One year's experience at the Bridges Vintage Camera Emporium. Customer-focussed… yada yada yada… Umpteen high-school and student jobs… supermarket… the newsagents and… do they really want to know all this stuff? What else? Hobbies. Photography, of course, and reading. Shakespeare addict. Bit obvious? Driving license? Well yes, but no car. Will that matter? Readiness to live and work in Stratford… no notice period to be worked… blah, blah, blah. OK. That's it. That's me. And… Send. Oh My God!

Glugging back the dregs from her glass, Kelsey stifled the little glimmer of excitement burning within her. Hearing the whirr of Fran's computer powering off, she slipped the iPad under the sofa and watched him sidle over.

'What are you smiling about?' he asked, obviously cheered up a bit.

'Oh nothing, just looking at Mirren's profile page. Looks like things got pretty messy at the bistro. She'd had a lot of vino.'

'So have you, by the looks of it. You've gone all flushed.' He pressed the back of his hand to her cheek.

For a split second she considered coming clean and telling him what she'd done, before it was too late, before it became a secret. But she couldn't face another argument tonight, not after the week she'd had.

Fran interrupted her thoughts. 'Come on. Bed time. I've got work in the morning. I'll drop you off at home before I head in tomorrow if you like, but we'll need to leave dead early.'

He picked up the barely touched pizza, carrying it off to the fridge, coming back moments later to place a glass of water by the bedside for Kelsey. His demeanour had softened even more as he climbed under the covers.

'Night night, Kelsey-boo. I'm sorry about tonight. I've got a lot on, I just…' he tailed off.

'It's fine, don't worry about it. I'm sorry too.' Kelsey slipped into bed next to him. 'Goodnight, Fran.' Kissing him quickly on the lips she curled up with her back towards him.

Within moments Fran was snoring in an exhausted slumber. Lying there in the dark, eyes open, frozen to the spot, Kelsey tried to switch off the agitated thoughts running through her mind.

What have I done? Fran won't like this at all. And just how am I going to explain it to Mum? She needs me at home. I can't just run off to Warwickshire. What do I even know about being a tour guide anyway? Where would I live? How would I afford to live? It can't pay that much, can it? No… they won't want me anyway. Of course they won't. No point worrying about it when it's not going to happen. Dreams don't come true.

And so her mind worked on and on until the early hours.

Meanwhile, deep down in the very heart of England, white swans glided silently across the moonlit Avon casting in their wake shimmering silver ripples. Kelsey Anderson could feel the impact of every wave.

Chapter Five

'We know what we are, but know not what we may be'
(Hamlet)

The delicious smell of buttery toast and strong coffee and the rub of a stubbly kiss on her cheek awakened her. Fran always made her breakfast in bed when she slept over. When she'd worked at the camera shop, he'd been the only person she knew who got up earlier than her in the mornings. He liked to be at the school before the headmaster arrived, always parking in the spot next to his to make sure his presenteeism was noted.

'You've got to stand out from your competition. Only way to get ahead, Kelse,' he always told her.

She made a grab for the coffee. 'Mmm, thanks, Fran. God, I'm still knackered.'

Fran raised his voice over the crackling buzz of his electric shaver as he ran it across his chin. 'Didn't you sleep? Lucky for you, you've got the whole day to just chill out and search for jobs.'

Instantly thinking of last night's application form with clenched jaw and tingling nerves, she didn't feel very chilled out. Hugging the hot mug tightly in both hands, she decided it was still best not to mention it. She wasn't going to push it today, not after the disappointment of last night. Another mountain out of a molehill argument. Another sexless sleepover. And it was all her fault, she thought glumly. Watching Fran getting dressed, she pensively ate her breakfast.

★

'It's almost seven, Kelse, let's locomote,' Fran called, standing at the open door tapping his key on the lock.

'I'm ready, I'm ready, let's go.' Kelsey rushed out of the bathroom as Fran eyed her impatiently, something obviously on his mind.

'Yesterday's clothes? I don't understand why you don't bring some stuff to keep at my place. You stay over often enough. I'll clear a space in the wardrobe if you want?'

Kelsey shrugged uneasily, clipping her thick wet hair up in a knot with a big tortoiseshell grip. It had never felt like the right time to bring anything from home, other than the essentials, and since Fran spent his Saturdays at the school with the boarders, she usually only slept over on Sunday nights.

'Hmm, I might bring a hairdryer next time.'

Kelsey hoped that would be an end to the conversation as Fran locked the door behind them, hustling her down the stone stairs which had been worn away to a lethal slipperiness over the last century and a half. Out in the quiet street, Fran marched ahead.

'Uh, Fran? Where have you parked? Is it on the side street again?'

Stopping dead, a sheepish grin forming, he turned to Kelsey. 'Oh! Uh, yeah… about that. There's something I forgot to tell you.'

He was standing beside a gleaming silver Golf GTI. Kelsey didn't take any interest in cars and wouldn't care if he drove a Passat or a Porsche, she only recognised it because Fran had been talking about getting one himself since they'd first met. The look on his face told her all she needed to know.

'You've bought yourself a new car. Oh! That's… nice. Wow! I… I didn't think we had any money?'

'It came up online and I just… Well, it's vintage and you like old stuff, right? And it was a steal really. I traded in the Ford and picked this baby up on Monday night.'

A moment's silence and the penny finally dropped. 'But Monday night was Calum's party… Oh.'

'I wanted to surprise you. So… Surprise!' Grinning unconvincingly, he unlocked the passenger door for her and she squeezed in, holding her satchel over her lap, leaning across to lift his door button.

'I haven't been in a car with button locks since I was a kid. It's a bit cramped, isn't it? Not very practical.'

'But it's nippy though. Great fun to drive.' He was genuinely smiling now as he climbed into the driver's seat, running his hands over the steering wheel. Kelsey sensed his nervousness; he must have known what was coming next.

'Did you spend some of the house deposit, Fran?'

'Erm… yep. Only eight grand, though.'

'Fran! Some of that money's mine, you know? It was *your* idea to get the joint account. How many years is it going to take us to save that up again?' Hot tears prickled her eyes although she fought to stay calm.

Fran was nodding and biting his bottom lip as though it had only just occurred to him that Kelsey might have a right to be mad. He turned the key in the ignition.

'I'll make it up. You're not going to be contributing for a while, so let me take the slack.'

Instantly feeling like a nag and despising herself for it, Kelsey fell silent. Fran had always earned more than her, a lot more. Didn't he have a right to spend that money? It was the car of his dreams after all. She sighed, looking around the black interior. Someone had clearly put a lot of love and care into restoring this car, and now it would be Fran's pride and joy.

'It *is* lovely, Fran. I'm pleased for you. I just wish you'd told me. That's a lot of money, you know, and I don't even *have* a car. I was putting half my pay into that account, and I know it wasn't much but it meant I had to go without a lot of the things I wanted...'

A sad sense of exasperation took away all the fight left in her. Looking out the passenger window as they pulled away into the empty road, she thought back to all those wintry mornings waiting for the bus, only for it to arrive late before it wound through the villages at a snail's pace stopping at every single bloody stop. How much easier the past year would have been if she'd felt free to spend her own wages on a car of her own, but Fran had been so set on saving up for the flat. *Breathe. Just breathe,* she scolded herself. Fran had the car he'd always wanted and she should be pleased for him.

The morning traffic was only just beginning to roll onto the A-roads. Kelsey occasionally sneaked a look at

Fran out the corner of her eye. He was smiling placidly, utterly oblivious to her frustration as they sped along the coast towards her mum's house and another day of doing nothing in particular.

Chapter Six

'The miserable have no other medicine but only hope'
(Measure for Measure)

Mari Anderson never booked in clients for Wednesday afternoons so she was free to pick up Calum from school and take him and his friends to the ice-cream parlour for their hump day family ritual. That morning she'd woken up in time to see her son off to the bus stop before making breakfast for Kelsey who was already on the sofa where she'd been firmly planted for three days now, comfy in her pyjamas and a fleecy blanket with her laptop across her thighs.

A studio debate about graduate unemployment was taking place on the TV, the kind with alarming statistics and loud men in suits warning of dire futures for arts graduates and lauding the choices of engineering and maths students. Kelsey had given up watching it ages ago and turned back to job-hunting.

'Morning, flower. What time did you get up?' said Mari as she curled up beside her daughter, putting the breakfast tray piled with jammy teacakes on the sofa cushion between them.

'Six, I think. Old habits…'

'Aww, love. Well, get some brekkie while it's hot. What are you doing today then? Coming to get a banana split with me and Team Geek at school run time?'

'That would be nice. I think I might.' She took a big bite of teacake and closed her laptop in resignation. 'I've been looking through the job sites all morning and there's still nothing for me. All the photography jobs are in London and they want computery, media types. I wouldn't have a clue how to edit photos for websites or magazines, not without lots of training.'

'What about literary stuff? Or historical stuff? Nothing in the heritage industry you fancied?' Mari persisted.

Kelsey kept her eyes glued to her teacake as she demolished it, answering between big bites. 'There were loads of teaching jobs, but I'm not qualified for them, and I saw a couple of jobs for Scottish Heritage but they wanted people with degrees in marketing or conservation. I didn't even know you could *do* a degree in conservation. I'm not especially qualified for anything, Mum, am I? I'll end up back at the supermarket at this rate.'

'Well, any job is a job. You could take something just to tide you over. What does Francis say about it all?'

'Fran? He hardly said anything about the shop closing. He wanted me to take an unpaid internship and work at night to pay for it. Not ideal, is it? Anyway, he's keeping a low profile at the moment. You know he's blown a massive wodge of our flat deposit on a car?'

Nodding sympathetically in astute silence, Mari poured out two mugs of tea from the shiny brown teapot.

'Mum… there is something I fancied doing.'

The pair sat on the sofa sipping tea while Kelsey told her all about the tour guide job in Stratford. She tried not to let her excitement show, but her wavering voice gave away her hopefulness.

'You really want this job, don't you, love?'

'I do, but...' she tailed off into silence.

'But?'

Puffing her cheeks and exhaling hard, Kelsey readied herself to say the things she'd been keeping bottled up since she first spotted the advert in the theatre programme.

Seeing her daughter's struggle, Mari placed the breakfast tray on the floor, shuffling along the sofa towards her and slipping her feet under the blanket. 'Go on, darlin', you can tell me.'

'I really *do* want the job, or a job like it at least, but I keep thinking about how you'd be alone here with Calum... and I want to stay and keep you company.' There. She'd said it, and the relief caused tears to well in her eyes.

'Kelsey, if that's all that's stopping you, then you have to know that I'm *not* alone. I've got Ted and Alex and your grandad, and Calum and his pals are lovely company, even if they are a bit weird.'

She succeeded in making Kelsey smile.

'I know, but it's always been you and me together, looking after each other.'

Wrapping her arms around her knees, pulling them in close to her chest, Kelsey thought back to the early days after her dad died, trying to coax her mum to eat or get dressed when Mari was so overwhelmed with grief, all she could manage was to feed and rock baby Calum. Kelsey had done all the shopping and housework by herself and that was on top of her schoolwork and trying to keep the truth hidden from her grandad about how bad things had become. Kelsey didn't like to acknowledge it but sometimes she felt that helping to look after her mum and Calum for so long had kept her back when all her friends were out on dates and work experience or embarking on proper careers. She'd been left behind.

'Kelse, you've always been here for me, but I don't want to be the one keeping you here, not if you've got itchy feet and need to get away. Things have changed so much in fourteen years. Look at me, I'm *almost* a normal mum now.' Flashing a daft grin and slipping her hand into Kelsey's, she persisted, 'You're always putting everyone else first, but it's your time now. You *have* to do your own thing.' Mari hesitated, before adding, 'Even if that doesn't involve Francis. You're allowed to do what you want, you know?'

Kelsey didn't have the strength to be indignant, or even to pretend everything was fine with Fran. 'I know. You're right, you're right.' Wiping the tears away with the corner of the blanket before they could fall she leaned into her mum's arms.

★

Not long afterwards, Mari had gone out to do a quick perm refresh for one of her elderly regulars. When she returned at half past two she was dismayed to find Kelsey still on the sofa in her pyjamas, pale, headachy and demoralised. The tissues crumpled in Kelsey's hand told Mari there were no new jobs this afternoon. 'Ice cream time?' she offered with a gentle smile.

'Yep, let's go. I've sent off eighteen speculative emails to the bigger shops and cafés in Edinburgh. Let's see what comes back.'

'Good for you. I think you've earned an extra scoop.'

Kelsey ran upstairs to pull on grey skinny jeans and a long burnt-orange top ready to collect Calum from school. She was slipping on her scuffed Converse when her phone rang.

'Hello, may I speak with Ms Anderson, please?' asked a woman with a clipped English accent.

'Speaking. Hello?' Kelsey faltered, trying to use her best talking-to-a posh-English-person phone voice. Without realising, she'd stood up and started pacing the room.

'Ah, perfect. Ms Anderson, this is Norma, from the Norma Arden Agency. I've got your application form in front of me.'

This is it. Why haven't they just emailed? Rejection is much easier to take when it's written down. Unless…

'Oh yes?' Aiming for casual and failing badly, Kelsey didn't know what else to say.

Having heard the ringtone, Mari eagerly popped her head around Kelsey's bedroom door just in time to see her daughter rolling her eyes in frustration and knocking her palm against her forehead.

Norma barely took time to draw breath. She launched in at bewildering speed. 'I won't mess about. You're just the sort of applicant we're looking for. In fact, I could do with five or six more of you for the summer tours. I've had two of my old regulars decide to retire this year and I'd been relying on them to start the season off. I've got groups booked in from all over. You don't say if you speak any languages?'

'I'm afraid not. Just a bit of French from school, but I doubt I'd remember much of it.'

'Hmm, well never mind. I could lump you with the North Americans, the Danes as well, and the British groups, obviously. Think you'd manage that? Tell me, how quickly could you get here?'

Kelsey's mouth fell open. 'What? I mean, I mean…' She looked at Mari with wide eyes, lost for words. *Is she actually offering me a job? In England?*

'Ms Anderson?'

'Sorry. I, uh, didn't think it would be quite this straightforward, and please, call me Kelsey.'

'There'd still be contracts to organise. You'd need to send me a copy of your passport and your degree certificates, if you have them. Oh, and I have the tour guide information packs here. They're pretty hefty but I can email them, give you a head start on memorising it all. I'll need your bank account details, national insurance number, and, of course, you'd need to find somewhere to stay. Have you looked into that at all?'

She spoke so fast Kelsey could barely keep up. No, she hadn't thought about any of that. *Living in Stratford! Actually living there! And moving all my stuff. How am I meant to do that?*

Aghast, she glanced over at Mari who was giving her an emphatic thumbs-up and mouthing the words, 'Just say OK. Say OK, whatever it is.'

'I'd need to sort out somewhere to stay, I haven't actively looked at lettings yet,' Kelsey managed.

'I'm sure we can find you a nice little garret somewhere in the town.' Norma sounded feisty and smart and like she was used to getting her way. 'A few of my guides use Mavis Thornton, she's a landlady, owns half the town. I'll email you her number, shall I?'

'Yes please. You said you needed me to start soon? How soon?' asked Kelsey, hardly believing what she was hearing, while Mari punched the air with her fists, dancing a jig in the hallway.

'I needed you yesterday, dear,' said Norma abruptly. 'My skeleton staff are managing, but it's about to get a lot busier. By mid-June we'll be run off our feet. Can you be here in a week?'

Kelsey felt the room spin, and she managed a meek 'yes' before sitting down again and cradling her forehead in her free hand.

'Good. I'll email you everything you need right away. Send the contract straight back, won't you? Let me know when you arrive and you can come directly to my office. You'll soon know the ropes. Anything you want to ask me?'

There's no messing about with this woman. 'No, nothing.' She gulped, her mind blank with shock. *There must be a million things I ought to ask.* 'Thank you, Ms Arden.'

'It's just Norma, my dear. Right, toodle-oo for now. I'll see you in Stratford next Wednesday.' With that, she hung up and Kelsey threw herself back onto the bed screaming in amazement, her eyes wide.

'Mum, they want me!'

Mari, glancing at her watch, rushed into the room, grabbed Kelsey's hands and pulled her onto her feet before crushing the air out of her with a joyous hug.

'Well done! I knew you could do it. Right, it's an extra-large banana split for you. Come on, we have to collect your brother.'

Their excited laughter trailed behind them as they rushed out the door shaking their heads in happy disbelief. How quickly life had changed its course.

Chapter Seven

'My drops of tears I'll turn to sparks of fire'
(All is True)

Mirren carried the silver ice bucket dripping with condensation over from the crowded bar to the brass-topped table where Preston was waiting with the four champagne flutes.

'Pushing the boat out tonight then, Mirr,' he said in his usual placid way.

'It's a big night for Kelse, and she might need some Dutch courage when Fran gets here.'

'She still hasn't told him then?'

'Not yet.' Mirren shook her head with a grimace, her long darkest-brown hair shimmering in the rainbow lights from the jukebox behind them. 'She said she didn't have the heart to tell him over the phone and she hasn't seen him since she heard. You know how he can be a bit temperamental. She figured he'd react better if she told him in public.'

'Well, you couldn't get more public than this. The whole village is in tonight.'

It was a typical Saturday at the Bonnie Prince Charlie, Kelsey's local, a horse brasses and pint pots over the bar kind of pub. The barman had raised an eyebrow as Mirren ordered the only bottle of champagne in the place. Mirren had been the first person Kelsey called once the shock had passed. It was beginning to sink in for everyone that in a few days she'd be in a new home in a new town with a new job. Everyone except Fran that is.

'*Such* a bad idea,' said Preston, shaking his head and sliding down in his seat, pretending to hide under the table in mock terror. 'She can't just spring information like that on the poor bloke. What's she going to say? "Sorry, babes, I'm leaving for another country on Wednesday, here – have some pork scratchings"? What if he *cries*?' Preston chuckled wickedly, his fists balled up by his temples, clearly enjoying this. He'd always tolerated, rather than enjoyed, Fran's company.

Mirren elbowed him. 'You're supposed to be here for manly moral support, so try to be nice to him. Anyway, he's more likely to storm off in a huff than cry, don't you think, going on past experience? Oh, here she is.'

Kelsey made her way through the throng. Her long hair was freshly blow-dried and flowing down her back in wild waves. She was in baggy dark jeans turned up at the ankles, her thin grey jumper and her trusty Converse. Mirren was already standing up with her arms outstretched ready to pull Kelsey in close for a congratulatory hug.

'Come here, give us a squeeze.' Mirren planted a deep red lipstick kiss on Kelsey's cheek, then smudged it away with her thumb.

Preston welcomed her with a gentle hug too. 'Congratulations, Kelsey. I'm so chuffed for you,' he said lifting the champagne off the ice. 'A little drink to toast your success?'

'Wow, bubbly! Thanks, you two.' Feeling bashful, she sat down facing the pub door.

'He's not here yet,' said Mirren, feeling her friend's anxious energy. 'Shouldn't you tell Fran somewhere more private?'

'I know! It seemed like a good idea earlier; now I'm not so sure. But it's too late!' Kelsey flinched as Preston popped the cork. 'He's going to come in here and see us guzzling bubbly and be the very last person to know. Ugh!' She buried her face in her hands. 'I'm a horrible person.'

Mirren stepped in to talk her friend round.

'He'll be fine. It's only two and a half months, not years. And it's time you did something just for you. He *should* be delighted… and I'm sure he will be.' This convinced no one.

The pub was loud with all the excitement of the weekend and the eighties pop songs that were in no way an ironic retro decision on the part of the pub management; it just so happened that 1988 was the last time they'd updated the jukebox playlist. Kelsey fiddled with the zip on her camera bag. She'd brought it with her, hopeful of capturing some nice, daft photos of the gang to take with her to Stratford.

Kelsey turned to face Preston. 'Would you be delighted if Mirren was going away for the summer?'

'Course he would,' Mirren jumped in before he could reply. 'You know how sweet he is. He'd drive me there himself and send me flowers every day…'

'Uh, I'm sitting right here, you know,' Preston butted in.

'Fair point, Mirr,' said Kelsey, ignoring Preston with a playful wink.

Mirren laughed before leaning over to kiss him. They'd known each other since they were kids and it showed. The three of them were always together at after-school drama club and all those pantos and community shows they'd performed in growing up. They'd stood side by side at her dad's funeral, they'd sipped their first beers together, and discovered the Edinburgh nightclubs at the same time. Through thick and thin, their easy camaraderie and years of familiarity buoyed up their friendship.

Still laughing, Mirren got to her feet and raised her glass towards her childhood friend. They were an unlikely pair. Mirren, tall, dark, and curvy, with the kind of huge almond eyes that made grown men swoon, always wearing black, a true rock chick; and Kelsey, shorter, and very fair, almost always in autumn colours, jeans or cute skirts – she firmly believed that *all* skirts should have pockets – and her berry red Converse. But their history bound them together.

'Here's a toast to Kelsey, flying the nest at last. Good luck, gorgeous girl, and safe travels.'

They clinked their glasses in accord and, taking a sip, Kelsey felt the rush of alcohol race through her bloodstream accelerated by the adrenalin of the last few days since Norma's phone call. She cast another furtive glance towards the door.

'I hope he turns up. I'll have to go round his place in the morning to tell him if he doesn't.'

Placing a manicured hand on Kelsey's, Mirren leaned in to make herself heard over the Wham medley blaring out from the jukebox.

'Surely if you love somebody you're meant to help them do whatever helps them become the happiest version of themselves? Listen, we all love Fran, but...' She tailed off, suddenly regretting her words.

'But what?'

Seeing how rattled her friend was, Mirren tried to use her gentlest tone of voice. 'But sometimes I think you deserve better. There, I've said it. I'm sorry.'

'You're telling me this *now*? It's been years! Don't you like him either?' Kelsey was thinking of her grandad who hadn't warmed to Fran.

'No, I do, I do.' Mirren was speaking so softly now it was hard for Preston to hear her, but he could see the sparkle of tears forming in her eyes and he reached for her hand. She continued, 'It's just that I've seen what going out with Fran has done to you. You were so happy at uni. You had the photography club and your exhibition at that gallery and all those arty friends.' Her hands shook, but she'd said this much so had to go on. 'These days you're either waiting for Fran to call or waiting for him to turn up... and you're so afraid of spending any money in case Fran gets bent out of shape about his precious savings pot.'

'Woah! OK, you have to stop.' Kelsey couldn't believe what she was hearing, and on their last night together for ages. 'He's not that bad, he's just busy with work a lot of the time, and so what if he's a planner? Somebody has to be in this relationship. Anyway, I *do* things. I have a life outside of Fran and me.' Thinking hard about what that might amount to, Kelsey slumped back in her chair. There was always watching *The X Factor* on Saturday nights with her grandad and mum, and helping Calum with his school projects – usually the night before they were supposed to be handed in – and she went to all of Preston's gigs round the local pubs, and for a while there she'd had the camera shop. *That's a life of my own, right? That counts?*

'Things with Fran might not be perfect, but I'm just waiting it out until it gets better.'

'Is he a man or an unripe avocado?' Mirren tried to joke but regretted her glib tone instantly. 'I'm sorry, Kelse, I don't want to hurt your feelings. Come on, we're going to have a lovely night,' she said consolingly, refreshing Kelsey's glass.

Mirren was right, of course, but it hurt to hear her best friend telling her she was missing out. Especially when she knew Mirren had cheated on Preston in the past, and there he was, totally clueless, gazing at his girlfriend adoringly, holding her hand, and rubbing his thumb on hers.

When did she become the relationship expert? Kelsey masked a few deep breaths. *Don't say anything. You're leaving on Wednesday. Just keep a lid on it.*

This felt like the closest they had ever come to an argument. Not that Mirren hadn't annoyed her or upset her over the years, but because she just wasn't the type to pick at her friends. Besides, Mirren had been her rock when her dad died, and she always knew how to make her laugh. Taking comfort in this thought, Kelsey leaned over and kissed her friend's cheek. She really needed her best friend right now. Especially as, at that exact moment, Fran pushed through the bar-room door, offering a weak smile as he spotted them.

Kelsey's heart sank. He obviously hadn't showered or shaved after being at work all day with the boarding kids, taking them to town on the school coach to spend their pocket money. He looked exhausted and fed up and here she was, about to break it to him that she was going off gallivanting all summer long.

'All right?' Fran nodded, looking at their grave faces, perplexed.

Mirren nudged Kelsey to her feet as Preston poured out a fresh glass of bubbly and handed it over with an encouraging nod.

'Let's go outside, Fran. I can't hear myself think in here.'

It was a beautiful early summer's evening, the first of the year where there was hardly any breeze and the sky was still pale blue and cloudless, even though it was almost nine o'clock and the evening chill would be setting in soon. Leading the bemused Fran towards the crumbling stone wall at the very back of the garden, Kelsey handed him his glass with a falsely sunny, 'Cheers?'

Fran perched on the low wall, his back to the young wheat aglow in the golden light of the sun as it began its descent into the hazy Edinburgh skyline in the far distance.

'Why is everybody acting weird? What's the bubbly in aid of? They're not engaged are they?' He nodded his head towards the bar.

Sitting down beside him, Kelsey turned her face to meet his.

'No, it's not that… um… It's for me, actually. I've got something to tell you, and I'm so sorry, I know I should have told you sooner.' His glowering perplexity dampened her spirits, but she was determined to get her news out. 'You know how I've always loved Shakespeare?'

'Obviously, yeah.' He took a long drink of champagne, maintaining eye contact cautiously.

'Well, I've got a job. A good one actually. Tour guiding. Talking about Shakespeare and theatre and that sort of thing.' Fran was listening and nodding, so she persevered. 'It's in Stratford-upon-Avon. Just temporary, like. I only just found a flat there this morning – well, it's more of a bedsit really, but anyway... I'm leaving on Wednesday.' Rewarding herself with a big gulp of bubbly, she let Fran take it all in.

'You're moving to England? On Wednesday?' Fran's slow monotone confirmed her worst fear. He wasn't going to like this. 'How long for?'

'Just the summer. I'll be back in September.' Seeing Fran's face fall she quickly held her glass out, more in desperation than in hope. 'So... cheers?'

Absent-mindedly, he chinked his glass against hers but he didn't speak and he didn't drink. This was going even worse than she'd feared. She gazed at the wildflowers in the field margin – towering red spikes of valerian mingled with pale peach hollyhocks – giving him processing time. After a few minutes, she was getting anxious.

'Please say *something*, Fran.'

He nodded as though deep in thought, so, buoyed by the bubbly, she persevered. 'If you think about it, it's sort of a dream job, isn't it? I get to talk about poetry and plays and history all day long, and they're going to pay me for it. And I get to go to the theatre and see all those plays I've read, like, a hundred times.' A buzz of excitement ran through her body just talking about it. 'I might even get free tickets from work.'

Realising that Fran hadn't offered her any congratulations yet, she pressed on with an increasingly imploring voice. 'There's *Othello* and *Antony and Cleopatra*, and this visiting American company doing *A Midsummer Night's Dream*: all my favourites. I'll never get this opportunity again.'

She was drawn up short as she spotted what looked like a sneer appearing on Fran's top lip, but he was trying to hide it. He laughed instead, but it wasn't warm or amused. At last, he spoke.

'So… what? You're running off to find yourself, are you?'

'Come on, Fran, it's just one summer. I'll be back before you've had a chance to miss me, and you can come and stay any time. Anyway, you'll be busy, you've got that school leadership conference.'

But Fran wasn't hearing her.

'This is so like you, you're always off in Kelsey's dream world. Well, I'll let you into a secret. Life isn't all *Romeo and Juliet* and "I wandered lonely as a cloud", or whatever.'

That's Wordsworth, you div. Eyes fixed on the ground, Kelsey didn't correct him. Now he'd hit his stride, she couldn't get a word in anyway.

'You do know none of that's real, right? Life isn't like a play with a happy ever after. It isn't perfect, and it isn't easy; you just have to work at it, but that's what being a grown up is about, Kelsey. Running off isn't going to help us, is it? You'll be back in September and jobless again.'

Kelsey chewed her bottom lip, another of her habits Fran didn't like.

He was still talking. 'What are you expecting to happen to you? None of Shakespeare's heroines ever ran off to do a one-woman Andean trekking adventure, or open a little fudge shop by the sea, or… whatever… And some of them met pretty sticky endings!'

'You're making fun of me?' she said in a sad, quiet voice. 'I've had a rubbish time since uni, since Dad died, even.' Getting tearful now, she tried to fight it back. 'I've had all this drama and tragedy in my life and… and you're making fun of me for wanting to find a little bit of poetry?'

'Kelse, I haven't a clue what you're on about. One minute we're buying a flat together, the next you're running off to spend the summer with a bunch of luvvies doing God knows what a thousand miles away from me. When you figure out what you want, you'd better hope I'm still hanging around waiting for you.'

'*I'm* the one who doesn't know what they want? Me?' Looking around, she realised she had the attention of everyone in the pub garden, so she lowered her voice. 'You're the one who blew our flat deposit on a car. And I'll be three hundred miles away, not a thousand.'

'All right! Don't get hysterical.' Fran shook his head, holding his hands up defensively and doing innocent puppy-dog eyes. 'The thing that hurts most is that you didn't even ask me what I thought about all this. You just took the job.'

'I know. I'm sorry. I should have told you about it. I just couldn't face having this argument and maybe never getting the chance to go.'

'That's you all over, Kelsey, isn't it? You never think about anybody but yourself.'

The world lurched as though it had spun momentarily off its axis. The tiny, long-suppressed spark of resentment within her suddenly seemed to be burning out of control sending firecrackers exploding in her brain. Before she even realised what was happening, she was standing up and there was a voice she barely recognised growing louder in her ears.

'Well, you know what, Fran? I think Shakespeare had it pretty spot on, actually. Maybe if Juliet had concentrated on enjoying being a teenager instead of giving up her future for some Flash Harry she'd have had a chance at life! Or if Cleopatra had stopped trying to juggle a whole bunch of dumb blokes and just got on with her PhD… or, or… if Lady Macbeth had ignored her power-crazy dick of a husband and just focused her ambition on going to night school or, I don't know, building herself a house with her bare hands or… *anything* else… these tragic, sad women might have been a whole lot flaming happier! Maybe that's what he's been trying to tell us.'

Gasping, she held her fingertips to her mouth in amazement, her body shaking with adrenalin and elation. *Where did all that come from?*

Fran watched her tirade through wide, incredulous eyes as if she were crazy.

She let her shoulders fall, releasing the tension in her body. 'Fran, maybe we should use this summer to figure out what we want because this doesn't feel good. None of this feels good. And what were you doing buying a car with our money if you want us to move in together? Is that really what you want any more?' Her voice broke with emotion.

That's when she felt her knees grow weak. Just as she thought she might be in danger of crumpling, exhausted, to the ground in front of Fran and grovelling an apology, Mirren and Preston appeared at either side of her. Saying nothing, they each slipped an arm around her waist and led her out through the busy pub to Mirren's car.

Fran watched them leave without a protest. Slumping down off the wall onto the grass he stared out over the fields until long after the sun had set, the champagne turning flat in his glass.

Chapter Eight

'You that way, we this way'
(Love's Labour's Lost)

Lining up the bulging suitcase and her camera bag — freshly stocked with new film — by the bedroom door, Kelsey stood back to look at them, tiny flutterings of excitement mixed with trepidation in her stomach.

This is really, actually going to happen.

The past few days had raced by in a strange blur. At first it had felt as though she were making the arrangements for someone else as she booked train tickets and dragged the suitcase down from the loft.

Fran's reaction had put a real dampener on her high spirits since Norma Arden's job offer. He still hadn't called but then again she didn't expect him to. Whenever they argued he'd ignore her calls for a few days and Kelsey knew it was best to leave him to mope. He'd always make the first move towards reconciliation when he was ready. But this felt different. She was leaving for the summer. She'd tried to reach him that morning, but had been greeted by the crackling emptiness of his voicemail. Unsure what to do, she'd hung up without speaking.

Thankfully, there hadn't been too much time to fret over the uncertain state of their relationship. Norma, as good as her word, had sent the tour information booklets along with a short, simple contract which Kelsey had signed and hurriedly posted back. Flicking through the booklets, she'd winced at the pages upon pages packed with dates, facts, and anecdotes she was expected to memorise.

'I'll read them on the train on Wednesday,' she'd told her mum. Right now, her head was spinning and she couldn't take it in. There were so many other more pressing things to be sorted out before then anyway.

'Just how do you pack for a whole summer living and working miles from home?'

That was all Mirren had needed to hear before she was at Kelsey's door, notebook in hand.

'Show me your summer capsule wardrobe, Kelse,' she'd demanded.

Pulling the closet door open, afraid to ask what exactly a capsule wardrobe was, Kelsey lifted out her only summer sundress; a knee-length midnight blue floaty affair with dark yellow sunflowers printed all over the crinkly fabric. It was years old but she loved it.

'And?' Mirren wrinkled her nose.

'And what? That's it, really. Apart from some jeans and there's these, I guess?' Kelsey shrugged, holding out for inspection a pair of tight-fitting cherry-red capri pants that she'd bought on impulse and never dared wear. 'At least I don't have to worry about work clothes; the contract says I get a uniform.'

After an appraisal of the entire contents of Kelsey's modest wardrobe, which didn't take long, Mirren had picked out a few outfits that would see her through her days off, ticking each item off her list of essentials. Mirren loved a list.

'OK, let's see… Sunglasses, swimsuit, raincoat, brolly – because you just never know – flat black pumps, check. Black leggings, check. Jeans, I guess. Is there any point in asking where you keep your date outfits?'

'I doubt Fran will be coming to Stratford, Mirren.'

'It wasn't Fran I was thinking of. There'll be thousands of brooding intellectual arty types milling around those theatre bars, Kelsey. And where there's life, there's hope.'

'I'm going to be working most of the time, Mirr, and even *if* Stratford turns out to be a haven for hot blokes, *I* won't be looking. Not with things like this between Fran and me.' Kelsey was packing her hair straighteners.

Mirren sighed, shifting on the bed. 'What do you want to do about Fran?'

'There's not much I can do if he won't talk to me. Him and his sulks! It's been like this for a while, Mirr. Some weeks we barely speak. I always seem to be doing something that irks him, whether it's because I'm not earning enough, or I'm not being ambitious enough. And let's not forget it was him who pushed me to learn to drive but when I actually passed my test, he wanted me to put my savings in the joint account so I couldn't afford a car of my own anyway. It's all right for him with his salary and his grand plans. He can't have it both ways, can he? Telling me to aim high then curtailing me when I try?'

'Don't you think he'll come to see you in Stratford, have a romantic reunion?'

Kelsey shrugged doubtfully. Every time she pictured herself there, she couldn't quite see herself with Fran, or with anyone, for that matter. The future looked strangely blank, and Kelsey couldn't deny that the opportunity to colour in that blankness was exciting.

'Maybe Fran's right. I do live in my own little dream world, reading my sonnets and plays, wishing I was living them. I've never been very practical or go-getting.'

'That's not entirely fair, Kelsey. You've had a hard time of things, of course you've wanted to retreat into yourself.'

'It's a bit pathetic, though. I mean, do *you* spend half your life fantasising you're somewhere else?'

Kelsey didn't notice Mirren swallowing hard as she inwardly answered the question before shaking the thought from her mind. Mirren worked at the evening newspaper office in Edinburgh as one of two reporters covering all the news from the city's Magistrates' Courts. She liked her job and knew there were thousands of people who'd kill to take her place. It paid well enough and was interesting, but the hours were long and she couldn't see any opportunities for promotion on the horizon. She really wanted to be a features editor on the paper's weekend editions, but for now she was biding her time. Just like she was biding her time with Preston, hoping she'd at last conquered her roving eye, trying to settle down and be contented.

Mirren steered Kelsey back to the task at hand.

'At least pack some decent lingerie, Kelse. This is the underwear of a woman who's given up on life.' Mirren gingerly picked a voluminous pair of grey cotton knickers from the suitcase. Kelsey grasped at them, stuffing them back into her luggage.

'They're comfy, all right!'

Mirren, cross-legged on the bed, shook her beautifully poised head with the air of a wise – if slightly oversexed – Buddha. 'Well at least take these.' She reached into her dress pocket before throwing a pack of condoms onto the bed.

'You've got to be joking! I haven't had so much as a snog for weeks with Fran and you think I'll end up being pity-shagged by some sleazy thespian.'

'I heard Eddie Redmayne was in Stratford last summer, and Keanu Reeves the year before that,' Mirren replied knowingly. Those particular men were Kelsey's kryptonite.

'Fair point.' Kelsey threw Mirren's parting gift into the bag alongside the factor thirty, her mascara, and lip gloss.

'Good girl.'

'You will come and visit me, won't you, Mirr?'

'Course I will. Here, I got you a proper present.'

Inside the pretty gift bag Kelsey found an orange leather photo album, a matching notebook, and a shiny rose-gold fountain pen. There was a tiny card inside too, printed with spikes of lavender and inscribed in Mirren's neat slanted handwriting, 'Go girl, seek happy nights to happy days.'

'Aww, that's beautiful, Mirr. Thank you.' Kelsey grinned broadly, holding the card to her chest. It was a line from *Romeo and Juliet*. 'I'm going to miss you so much.'

They hugged and said their goodbyes before Mirren reluctantly left her to finish packing. Kelsey slipped a few treasured photographs into her new album and put all the presents in her satchel beside her purse and train tickets. Her *Sonnets* were already in there along with a map and directions from the station to the Norma Arden Historic Tours Agency.

There, I'm ready. I think.

★

There's bright and early and then there's ludicrously early. Kelsey, her grandad, Mari and Calum looked up at the train departure boards. Apart from a man emptying the bins and a young woman unlocking a coffee kiosk, they were the only people on the Waverley station concourse. The old station clock told them it was ten to five. Mari held Kelsey's hand, asking anxiously if she'd remembered tissues and hand sanitiser and a bottle of water.

'It's OK, I've definitely got everything I need, Mum. Don't worry. I'll ring you once I'm in my flat.'

Calum was chattering excitedly about the big screen actors who were in Stratford that summer, people he'd seen in sci-fi movies who were now in *Hamlet* and *King Lear*, showing they've still got what it takes to 'do Shakespeare.' Kelsey promised to get him an autograph if she saw anyone remotely famous, enjoying an unrestrained thrill at the thought of being in a town where actual movie stars hung out.

Kelsey's grandad cast his eyes over his granddaughter with a look of pride so unmistakeable she could barely return his gaze for fear of crying. Stepping towards her, he held out a white paper bag.

'I'm sorry it's not wrapped. It's from all of us, but there's a wee something in there that's just from me.'

She hugged him close, taking the bag from his hands. Inside was a beautiful hardback edition of *A Midsummer Night's Dream* with cream canvas covers.

'Oh wow! Thank you. A comedy for a change. Are you telling me to lighten up?' Kelsey joked to cover her emotions which were threatening to bubble over.

'Open it,' he prompted with a fond smile.

There, inside the cover, was a braided plaid ribbon cleverly tied in a flat love knot.

'That's the Anderson tartan. Now, you know what the Anderson clan motto is, don't you?'

Turning the ribbon over in her hands, she shook her head.

'It's "Stand Sure". Now remember that. Wherever you are, you're an Anderson, steady and sure and brave. And you're my wee lassie.'

There was a sparkle in his eyes that wasn't just pride as he reached for his handkerchief. Kelsey buried her head in his shoulder and thanked him with a whisper; she couldn't manage anything louder.

And then the rush began: the train's arrival, a flurry of kisses and hugs, the search for Kelsey's compartment, and her luggage being stuffed into the overhead rack. Within minutes she was sitting behind glass grinning at her family on the platform. But they weren't looking at her, they were looking along the platform at the figure running towards them shouting her name.

Kelsey staggered towards the open train door in time to see Fran, unshaven and panting, waving an envelope in the air. Kelsey, stared at him, open-mouthed.

'I thought I'd missed you,' he gasped. 'Here, take this. It's everything you paid into the deposit. I've closed the account. Just go and do whatever you need to do.'

The train guard stepped out of the driver's carriage, getting ready to blow his whistle.

Soft bleeping sounds came from the speakers above the doors as the train's engine whirred louder. Fran looked desperate. 'I'll see you in September, OK?' The doors closed between them.

Kelsey's heart was still pounding in her chest with the sudden rush and panic of her departure. Unsure what to do, she smiled apologetically as the train eased away. She watched her grandad walk over to Fran, shake his hand gently, and put an arm around him. Calum and Mari ran alongside the train waving frantically, her mum blowing kisses, and trying not to let her see that she was really sobbing. Kelsey pressed her hands against the glass and mouthed, 'Love you, Mum,' as the train disappeared into the station's dark maze of tunnels.

Forcing herself to breathe deeply she flopped down onto her seat, just as the train re-emerged into the June morning light. The conductor was making his announcements, saying, 'Welcome aboard this service to Birmingham New Street,' as the train rolled out of Edinburgh.

Making a small rip in the corner of Fran's envelope Kelsey gaped at the sight of the thick bundle of notes, all fifties, two thousand pounds at least. She stuffed the money into her satchel, being careful to buckle it up properly again. This would certainly help pay her rent this summer, something she'd been worrying about. Kelsey had been too shocked to ask Norma about the rate of pay during their hurried phone call and her contract had merely mentioned she'd be paid minimum wage. She could have cried with gratitude for poor Fran. *Imagine rushing to the station at this time of the morning!* He'd looked so sad and imploring it gave Kelsey a sharp twinge in her chest.

Taking one last look at the Castle Rock looming up over the tracks, she clasped her grandad's tartan ribbon tightly in her shaking hands. Stand Sure? Kelsey had never felt so unsure of herself in her entire life.

Chapter Nine

'This royal throne of kings, this sceptred isle [...]
This blessed plot, this earth, this realm, this England'
(Richard II)

The sign by the roadside blazoned, 'Welcome to Stratford–upon–Avon, Birthplace of the Nation's Bard, William Shakespeare.'

OK, I'm here, just being cool. Just walking along. Nothing to panic about. Oh shit! Oh shiiiiit!

Nothing looked as Kelsey remembered as she followed the crowds from the packed train, decidedly creased and hot after the long journey. Tourists trundling wheelie cases, business women in clicking heels, and noisy teenagers stuffing themselves with after-school sweets were barging past in all directions. Looking down at the map in her hands she noticed it was trembling.

Well, this might as well be upside down and written in Russian. Where am I?

It was now almost five in the afternoon. She'd have just enough time to catch Norma before she went home if she hurried. But where was she hurrying to? Spotting a sign pointing towards Shakespeare's House, she thought this seemed like a good option, knowing that it was in the dead centre of town and Norma's office was somewhere near it.

Wow, it's hot.

Dust rose in the air with each unsteady footstep, giving the impression it hadn't rained for weeks. Walking past a pretty thatch-roofed pub she stopped to read aloud the sign by its door. 'Do you think because thou art virtuous, that there shall be no more cakes and ale?' A quick thrill of nervousness ran up her spine, making her light-headed. *It must be a Shakespeare quote, but I've no idea which play it's from.*

She had spent the entire journey trying to memorise Norma's information packs, her concentration shot through with the image of Fran's desperate, mournful expression at the station. None of the dates and facts about outbreaks of the plague and destructive town fires had sunk in.

What kind of tour guide am I going to be if I don't have all of that stuff on the tip of my tongue? What am I even doing here? Norma's going to take one look at me and know for sure she's made a terrible mistake.

The panic in her chest spiked. A cold sweat sent her from being a hot mess into sudden shivers as she realised she was still frozen to the spot, staring at the mystery quote on the sign.

Everybody must think I look crazy.

But glancing around, she realised no one was looking at her at all. She was nowhere near home and utterly invisible, all alone in a strange town where nobody knew her. There were no landmarks she recognised, not even familiar chain stores or restaurants that could help ground her.

The thought of Norma waiting for her at the agency spurred her feet to move and she joined the thronging crowds heading into town.

★

'Come in, darling. Yes, yes, yes… come on in. Oh dear, look at you. You've had quite the expedition today, haven't you? Kettle's on, chop chop!'

Kelsey had only managed a surprised 'hello' when Norma Arden appeared suddenly to greet her on the stairs just seconds after she'd buzzed her into the building. Dressed in a deep purple, expensive-looking skirt suit (*vintage Chanel?* Kelsey wondered) and hot-pink pumps in a quilted-leather effect with little gold tassels over the toes, Norma Arden was a shock to Kelsey's already shocked system. Her bluntly cropped bob was an outrageous bottle red. Kelsey had relaxed the instant she found the door to the agency and rang the buzzer, but following the friendly whirlwind of energy that was Norma Arden as she ascended the stairs, she suddenly felt even calmer.

'Sit, dear, sit,' jostled Norma, putting Kelsey in mind of a dog handler at Crufts. Norma was already stooped over the tea things, pushing her thick purple-rimmed spectacles up onto the bridge of her nose only for them to slip back down again, settling precariously on the tip.

'Biccies? Yes, of course. Yes, of course. We do like our biccies!' she shrilled at lightning speed.

Already exhausted, Kelsey barely had the energy to follow Norma's abrupt movements. Her new boss thrust a delicate lilac sprigged teacup filled to the brim with milky tea and wobbling on its saucer into Kelsey's hands and at last came to a stop on a swivel chair behind her desk.

'Down the hatch.' Norma raised her teacup, flashing lipstick-smudged teeth at her new employee. Kelsey already liked her immensely. Far from being the battleaxe she'd feared, Norma seemed unthreatening and charming with it, if a bit batty and unintentionally brusque. She'd have to be batty to hire someone she'd never even met before.

'Norma, thank you so much for this opportunity. I can't quite believe I'm here, it's like a dream really. This morning I was at Waverley station, now I'm in Stratford. It's surreal.'

Kelsey tried to stop herself wittering by taking a sip of tea, spilling some in the saucer.

'My pleasure. I'm glad reinforcements have arrived. We've been struggling to maintain the front lines. With the addition of you, my dear, we've got enough guides to manage the summer bookings, as long as we don't get any unexpected ones coming in at short notice.'

Norma took a huge slurp of tea, almost emptying her cup in one go. Kelsey took the brief respite from the machine gun chatter to study Norma's heavy make-up and a jawline that suggested more than a hint of Botox. At a loss to guess her age, Kelsey would have put her at anywhere between fifty and seventy.

'Do you need me to start right away? I've tried to memorise all the information you sent me, but I can't promise it will all come out in the right order.' Kelsey offered a smile and a modest shrug with this honesty. Best to tell the truth right from the start.

'Oh, no, no, no, no! You won't have a group of your own for a few days. I've assigned you to another guide who'll show you the ropes. You'll watch him do his tours, take some notes, get the gist, and *then* we'll set you loose on sightseers of your own.'

'That's good to know.' Kelsey exhaled with relief and downed the last of her tea.

'Your rota has you shadowing William Greville tomorrow and Friday. He's one of our longest-serving guides and one of the very best – he certainly gets the biggest tips. Been with us for donkey's years! He'll watch you taking your first group on Saturday too, see how you do, and all being well, you'll be off on your own as of Sunday. Oh, and there might be a few extra shifts available here and there, and once you're in the swing of things you can do the backstage theatre tours as well. Sound all right? Good!'

Norma hadn't given her the chance to respond, so Kelsey smiled in assent. She liked the sound of William Greville. Posh name, bit aristocratic maybe? Definitely a hundred and eighty years old.

'Sounds great,' she replied with real enthusiasm despite the creeping feeling of dread at the very idea of addressing a large group of tourists. The thought of the tips helped quell some of the uneasiness.

'I'll take as many extra shifts as possible, please, Norma.'

There was still rent to pay and it was going to be pretty steep. She'd been stunned at the price of some of the larger lets in town and plumped for the smallest one available, and even that sounded pricey to Kelsey.

'So, um…we haven't properly talked about the hourly rate. Can you… tell me what it is, please?'

'Oh, didn't I mention that? Why didn't you ask before? Well, I'm afraid its minimum wage, dearie. You'll bring in about two hundred and fifty pounds a week before tax.'

Kelsey swallowed hard. That would only just cover her rent. Kelsey thought of the cash-stuffed envelope in her satchel. What would she have done were it not for Fran and his sudden change of heart about the deposit? Sitting there in Norma's office, so tired and so far from home, Kelsey couldn't bear to think about what it meant for their future together. If he'd cleared her savings from the account, the account that represented their shared future, what did it mean for all of Fran's plans? Was she included in them any more? Did she really want to be?

Norma's swift appraisal of her new protégé's features told her something was wrong.

'Try not to worry, little one. There are always plenty of extra bits and bobs up for grabs in the summer. I know a director who's looking for a few end-of-season helpers, and the backstage tours pay extra, so we won't let you starve! Don't want you popping your clogs like young Chatterton, eh?'

Kelsey nodded, slightly uneasy at the thought of this poor Chatterton, wondering if he'd been one of her predecessors and suddenly worried about what kind of a racket she'd got herself involved in. Norma saw through her bluff like a purple Miss Marple.

'Darling, Thomas Chatterton, the tragic poet? Haven't you seen the painting? *The Death of Chatterton*? Henry Wallis? Dear, dear! What *do* they teach you young ones at university these days?' Norma cast her eyes heavenward.

Thrown, the colour rose in Kelsey's cheeks. *Oh great. I can add that to all the other stuff Norma expects me to know that I just don't. I am a total imposter. A bloody fraud.*

'I'm teasing, sweetheart,' smiled Norma, sensing the change in mood. 'Right, dearie, let's get you on your way to your lodgings, eh? You've had a long day and tomorrow's going to be busy. You'll be needing these.' She handed Kelsey what she assumed must be her uniform wrapped in clear plastic bags.

Kelsey smiled weakly to hide her look of horror. *Oh no. Not a fleecy gilet! And in burgundy too? Please tell me it's not.* Whatever it was, it did not look appealing. Norma thrust a shift rota into her other hand. The entire company of guides' names were listed in the first column beneath her own: William, Myrtle, Valeria, Gianfranco, and Lukas.

'What lovely names.'

'They're all lovely people, and great tour guides, the best in the business. Between you all, you speak eleven languages.' Norma beamed proudly.

And I only speak English. She must think I'm useless. Kelsey took a deep breath, trying to silence the perpetually critical voice in her head. *Did it ever take a day off?* With an uncomfortable jolt, she realised how much the voice sounded like Fran.

Norma, jangling a bunch of keys, walked Kelsey downstairs and out into the street where she took the crumpled map from Kelsey's hand.

'This is the way to your lodgings, along here, then down there.' She ran her red painted fingertip along the page. It looked like an easy enough walk. 'Come back here for nine a.m., Will Greville will be waiting for you. Any worries, ring me at the office. OK? OK, good.'

Kelsey nodded, giving up hope of getting a word in between Norma's rounds of heavy artillery speech. Norma looped the handles of a fancy tote bag over Kelsey's arm and walked away in the opposite direction, before stopping suddenly and turning on her heel with the look of a person who'd forgotten to say something very important.

'Oh, and, Kelsey, dear? Beware of the midsummer madness.' Looking Kelsey up and down with a faint smile at the corners of her mouth, she added, 'Something tells me you'll be particularly susceptible to it. Be wise, dearie. Be wise.' With that, Norma blew two sharp air kisses towards her and bustled away, leaving Kelsey convinced she could hear her new boss's cackling laughter ringing in the still, airless afternoon.

'What the…? She's as mad as a brush,' Kelsey muttered under her breath, smiling in astonishment at her first new acquaintance in Stratford.

She remembered with curiosity the bag Norma had pushed over her wrist and took a peek inside. It was full of treats: Darjeeling tea, a thick slab of fudge with a picture of Shakespeare on the wrapper, a jar of cloudy Warwickshire honey, and a huge diamond-shaped loaf in brown paper wrapping – obviously fancy artisan bread, nothing like the plain loaf her mum usually bought – and a pint of milk in an actual glass bottle, gold top, of course. Kelsey got the feeling Norma was used to the finer things in life – either that or she was insanely generous. The smell of the bread hit her and made her tummy rumble immediately. Reaching into the bag she broke off a hunk, munching it greedily.

Mmm, divine. This isn't going to last long. Cheers, Norma!

The ancient broad street had all but emptied by now. Kelsey presumed the pubs and restaurants were packed with the pre-theatre crowds and the nine-to-five workers had all gone home. The afternoon sun lit up the enormous floral displays attached to each of the old-fashioned street lamps lining her route. There was a coat of arms on every lamp post, just visible beneath the drooping begonia heads. Each coat of arms was shaped like a shield with a yellow background and a golden spear lying diagonally across a black stripe. Kelsey felt a triumphant bolt of recognition.

It's the Shakespeare family coat of arms, if I'm not very much mistaken!

She'd remembered something. Maybe she'd be a better tour guide than she'd feared. With a few days shadowing old Mr Greville and a bit of practice, she might well become a proper tour guide, a good one even. She walked on, now with a little swagger. The excitement was returning at last.

And suddenly there it was, appearing in front of her as she rounded the corner of yet another ancient twisting street: the house where Shakespeare was born. Without a second's hesitation, she reached for her father's camera, releasing it from its padded case, raising it to her eye, and framing the ramshackle old cottage. She was finally back in the birthplace of all the poetry, drama and romance that she'd dedicated her daydreams to since she was a teenager.

'I'm home, Dad,' she whispered.

Chapter Ten

'I like this place, and willingly could waste my time in
   it'
(As You Like It)

It sounded nice, Saint Ninian's Close. Kelsey imagined
it as cloistered and sacred. She was hoping for a tree-
lined avenue, rambling roses and steep steps leading up
to a romantic garret where shafts of light from old leaded
windows would illuminate the dancing dust, a timeworn
desk under a beamed ceiling maybe, where she could
write long letters home. As she trundled the suitcase
behind her, she imagined herself, white feather quill in
hand, dipping its elegant silver nib into blackest ink. Very
Shakespeare in Love.

*How can I be lost? Where's a friendly local guide when you
need one?*

After much searching, a few dead-ends and a wrong
turn along an overgrown canal towpath, Kelsey found
herself in the shadow of Number One, St. Ninian's Close,
a tall Victorian red-brick with a blood-red door set within
a smart porch. Looking again at the map, she realised that
she'd completely missed the turning Norma had pointed
her towards and in fact she was now only a few hundred

yards down a back street from the beautiful gardens of Shakespeare's Birthplace. Too tired to beat herself up for her pathetic map-reading skills, she searched for the key. She just wanted to unpack, have a bath, and fall into the sumptuous white sheets of the antique four-poster bed she'd been dreaming of.

Mavis Thornton, her new landlady, had told her she'd find the keys under the windowsill to the right of the door, and sure enough, there they were, hanging on a small silver nail obscured by the spiderwebs and the freshly unfurled foliage of the tangled Virginia creeper that covered most of the building. At first she'd thought it strange that the key would be left out for her where any passing tourist could spy it. Of course, nobody felt the need to lock themselves inside their homes back in the village, and her mum often left the door unlocked even when she nipped out to the corner shop, but Stratford was an altogether busier place, wasn't it? And yet out here, just a few hundred yards from the main drag, in the shadows of the smart pre-war houses and beneath the canopies of tall oaks and chestnut trees the streets were quiet and still. The road was lined with parked cars but there was something contained and calm about this affluent residential area that reminded her of village life. So she unlocked the door with a familiar sense of homecoming that surprised her.

Having come this far in the blazing June sunshine, struggling over the threshold with her suitcase, camera bag, satchel, and Norma's groceries took a Herculean effort. She was immediately struck by the sudden change in temperature as the heavy door closed behind her.

The hallway was cool and spacious and smelled strongly of lavender and beeswax. Two doors led off to the downstairs flats and a wide oak staircase stood before her with a big-eyed owl carved into the balustrade. The handsome old tiles from the porch continued all the way inside, bright and gleaming under her feet.

Someone must really look after this place.

The walls were papered in an elegant deep-green leafy wallpaper that looked about a century old. The overall effect was very grand and welcoming. Glancing back towards the door, she noticed a tall table with a bulbous flowerpot on top that was spilling over with the frothy fronds of a huge fern, and beside it hung the mail rack. Kelsey peeped hopefully into her own little compartment, flat 2B, wondering if anyone she knew had thought ahead and sent her a housewarming card.

Nope, empty. Hardly surprising really, this has all happened so fast.

She made a mental note to send a postcard to everyone back home in the hope of getting some mail of her own soon. And she'd have to contact Fran too, just to let him know she had arrived safely. Sensing another drop in temperature at the sudden memory of Fran and their argument at the pub, goosebumps prickled on her arms. If he'd simply congratulated her and wished her well, she'd have felt certain she was going home to him at the end of the summer, but the way they'd left things… Kelsey shook her head abruptly, trying to clear her mind. Somehow, it felt as though their rushed parting at the station had taken place weeks ago, in some other world. Had it only been this morning? With a shudder, she turned back to look at the stairs. It hurt to think about him, and she didn't want to start wallowing in guilt or self-pity, not tonight.

Onwards and upwards, Kelse.

The stairs looked positively mountainous in that moment as a heavy fatigue caught up with her. Beginning the climb, she noticed there were fewer and fewer of the original Victorian features that had graced the ground floor. The first floor landing was far less spacious and modern fire doors led off to its three apartments. *No more lovely leafy wallpaper up here then.* Kelsey looked in dismay at the 1980s puffy vinyl that had been painted over many times in thick white gloss as she gripped the curving banister and climbed up and around again.

Flat 2B was immediately in front of her on the landing and there were three other flats off to its sides. The stairs continued upwards behind her, but they were narrower and steeper, presumably leading up to the attics. She slipped the smaller of her two keys into the lock and walked inside.

'OK, this room's teensy. What the hell?'

Kelsey glanced around her bedsit. There was a single bed with white cotton covers, one long kitchen unit with a cupboard underneath, a sink and a portable two-ring electric hob – not that she planned on taking it anywhere. The only pops of colour in the room came from the mint green toaster with matching kettle and microwave; everything else was white, including the carpet, which looked brand new.

In front of her was yet another door, leading to the world's tiniest toilet cubicle. It was going to be a squeeze getting in there without actually having to stand on the loo to swing the door closed. She walked back into the tiny bedroom to search for her mobile.

'Mum? I'm here. I've just got into my room. It's so wee! It's cosy though, in fact it's boiling. The heat must get trapped up here at the top of the house… Yeah, it's spotless, immaculately white in fact. Oh my God, get this. There's a shower cubicle right up against the end of the bed. How am I even meant to get in there?' Laughing incredulously, she tried pulling open the flimsy Perspex door. 'Riiight, I can't. It only opens about eight inches before it hits the bed. Well, this is going to be interesting.'

They laughed and chatted for a few moments more before Kelsey blew her mum a goodnight kiss down the phone. She needed to get some sleep before her first day in her new job.

Not bothering to unpack, she took out the photo album Mirren had given her. There was a picture of her and Fran back at uni. Both of them were laughing and holding each other tightly. He looked so handsome and clearly in love. She worried her bottom lip with her teeth. If she didn't send him a message now, she might never do it, she thought. So reaching again for her mobile, she typed the words.

I'm here. Hope you're OK. Thank you for coming to see me off this morning. I know I should have talked to you about the job offer before I took it. I'm sorry. I'll miss you.

As the message flew through the ether to Fran, Kelsey turned the page on the photo album, standing it on the shelf by her bed so that two pictures were displayed. One side showed her mum, dad, Calum, and grandad standing in front of Shakespeare's house all those years ago, and the other was of Mirren and Kelsey roaring with laughter on a picnic blanket at the beach back home. She placed her grandad's tartan ribbon between the open pages as her eyes drooped in the warmth of the little white room.

After a long swig of milk, she opened the window wide and lay down on top of the covers, still dressed. Within a minute she was in a still, dreamless slumber.

As she slept, distant church bells rang out, their music carried on the wings of the dipping and soaring house martins who flitted between the hazy lawn below and the eaves above her where tiny fledglings chirped softly in the warmth of their safe nests.

Chapter Eleven

'But yet thou shalt have freedom'
(The Tempest)

The morning dawned cool and quiet as Kelsey, bundled in her white cotton sheets, came round then dozed away again. The morning air from the window with its gently flapping lace curtains smelled of hot dust and sweet, distant summer rain. Slowly, the memories came back to her: the long journey, the shock of arriving in her new town, the fact that she would be diving headlong into a new job today. The world outside was still asleep and there were no sounds at all from the neighbouring rooms.

Reaching for her phone, she hoped Fran had seen last night's message. Nothing. *He's probably busy getting ready for work. Or, he's heartbroken and inconsolable round at his parents' place?* No matter how sad and alone that thought made her feel, she knew she had to face the day. Standing, straightening her spine with a long stretch, she tried to breathe away thoughts of Fran.

Making the three short steps from her bedside to the tiny nook that constituted her kitchen she cut two wonky slices of bread, popping them into the toaster. The mouth-watering scent of walnuts and sunflower seeds turning deep brown and starting to sizzle and crack made her ravenous. Holding the honey jar close to her nose as she popped the lid, her senses were assaulted with the deep fragrance of sweet clover and dark molasses. There was nothing to distract her from the slow pleasure of watching two dripping spoonfuls pour onto the hot toast.

Gathering up her breakfast, a mug of milky tea and her camera, she tiptoed out the door, taking her keys with her. She was about to head downstairs for a barefoot stroll around the dewy lawn, but decided to have a quick peek upstairs first.

There can't possibly be more flats up there under the eaves, surely? We're squeezed in like battery hens up here as it is.

The stairs leading upwards from her own small landing were straight and steep and made of black cast iron. At the top there were two small hatches. One had a laminated sign pinned to it.

'Cleaner's Store. Oh well, that solves that mystery then.' Kelsey was getting used to talking to herself already. 'This is how all mad women in attics start out,' she told herself as she pushed the other door, its round wooden handle turning easily in her hand.

Kelsey inhaled sharply as she opened it, slowly at first before letting it swing open with a bang on the wall behind. She was met by the rush of fresh air and the bright glare of the June morning sunshine. Grabbing the handrail she pulled herself up the last few steps out onto a tiny terrace sunk between two sloping slate roofs; one obviously belonging to the original building, the other newer and part of the extension that housed her own apartment.

On sun-baked terracotta tiles there stood a chair and a small mosaic table. Squeezing past them, Kelsey looked out over the low railings that enclosed the little suntrap, but a vertiginous dizziness forced her back from the edge. The view was beautiful in the morning light beneath a cloudless sky and there was heat in the sun already.

The spire of the big church by the river was just visible over the tree tops and red roofs. Far off to her right she could just make out a strange monument, a towering stone obelisk standing alone on a range of low rambling hills that she didn't even know the name of. There were no signs that anyone had been on the terrace recently; no plants growing in pots or cigarette ends in ashtrays. It was as immaculately tidy as the rest of the building.

Settling down with her breakfast, Kelsey didn't mind the astronomical rent on her tiny bedsit quite so much in that moment, not if she had the use of this perfect little space high above her new town.

There's plenty time to shower and dress before work. My new commute's going to take no more than ten minutes on foot. Kelsey stretched her body in leisurely comfort. For now, she was going to enjoy her amazing find in perfect solitude.

Chapter Twelve

'There is flattery in friendship'
(Henry V)

*No, no, no, no, I'm so late! Mr Greville's going to be furious.
And what will Norma think?*

Kelsey's feet pounded the pavement as fast as they could
carry her. It had been the uniform's fault.

She'd been so sleepy the night before she hadn't
thought to look at it, but after breakfast as she'd stood
by the bed in her pristine white room – now very
steamy from her morning shower – wrapped in her towel,
hair dripping over her shoulders, she'd unwrapped the
uniform, examining it in dismay. Sure enough, inside
the bag there were not one, but two, thin fleece zip-
up gilets, both a very murky burgundy. She was relieved
to see the label read 'small.' There were also two white
short-sleeved shirts, possibly designed for a skinny man,
definitely not cut for a woman. She almost screamed as
she discovered the final item: a bottle green and burgundy
striped neckerchief, like the ones cabin crew wear, except
this one wasn't cute and sexy like the Virgin Atlantic girls';
this was like something you'd wear over your perm at a
Balmoral grouse shoot. And that was it.

No trousers? I thought 'uniform provided' meant an actual complete outfit.

There followed a frantic half hour of flinging clothes from her suitcase and realising she had no choice but to wear the capri pants, hoping that the cherry-red colour wouldn't clash too much with the burgundy gilet.

She'd done her best to create what Mirren would call 'a look'. She swept nude-pink gloss across her lips, attempted a bit of mascara, and *a lot* of powder – the clammy heat in her room had left her skin shiny and flushed.

As she ran, she caught sight of her reflection in the glass of the bus shelter. This was not her best look. She was so glad she'd packed her new black pumps. They were comfy and fairly smart, and together with the cropped capris they had a cute 1950s feel. At least her bottom half looked all right. She'd tucked the shapeless shirt in, trying to create a sense of a waist and left the top buttons undone, tying the neckerchief of doom in as small a knot as possible to complement the gamine Audrey Hepburn sunglasses-on-head style she was trying to channel.

It was after nine when she arrived at the Agency door, breathless and hot. *Right, where's this old Mr Greville then? Perhaps he's wandered off, disgusted at the tardiness of the younger generation. He's probably gone upstairs to tell Norma.*

Just as she was reaching for the office buzzer, ready to face the music, she spotted a man in a burgundy gilet just like her own coming out of the coffee shop on the other side of the road. He was carrying two frappuccinos and had an umbrella tucked under one arm. Except this was no decrepit old historian as Norma had suggested. He looked only a few years older than her and even in that uniform it was obvious that he was gorgeous. He casually crossed the street avoiding the traffic, grinning at Kelsey, or maybe he was laughing. Kelsey smiled as he stopped in front of her on the broad pavement.

'*You're* the man I've been looking for?' She regretted her choice of words immediately.

Amused, he flashed perfect straight teeth. 'You're the tenth pretty girl to say that to me this morning.'

They both laughed, Kelsey a little nervously.

'Pleased to meet you, I'm Will Greville,' he said, with a sudden air of formality.

'Norma said you'd worked here for donkey's years. I thought you were going to be ancient.'

'Glad I'm not?' His eyes sparkled with good humour. Kelsey looked at the ground, abashed. He deftly offered her one of the plastic cups. 'Iced coffee?'

'Thank you. Your voice is so posh, like Prince William! I didn't think real people actually talked like that.'

Will gleefully cocked an eyebrow, his lips quirking wickedly as Kelsey inwardly flinched with shame. *Why did I say that? Stop talking, Kelsey!* She was going to have to force herself to be sensible. 'What I mean is, thank you very much for the coffee, William. I'm Kelsey, by the way. I'm sorry I'm so late. First day glitches and all that.'

She offered him her hand and he clasped it firmly, his touch pleasantly cold from carrying the coffees.

'Honestly, I have no idea what you just said. I'm going to have a hard time deciphering your accent. It's very nice to meet you all the same. It's just Will, by the way. Only Norma and my grandmother call me William.'

Kelsey stiffened her neck in confused response. *Is he being kind and pretending not to have heard me gushing nonsense at him, or is he just bloody rude?*

Will was leaning back on one foot shamelessly surveying Kelsey with an appreciative look from the ground up. 'Well, I must say, *that* is one way to rock this uniform.'

His eyes, she noticed, were mossy green. These, combined with his auburn hair – which he kept pushing backwards only for it to flop endearingly onto his forehead again – made a striking first impression. Suddenly aware she was staring at his face, Kelsey stumbled for words, any words.

'Yes, well, I didn't have time to shop for trousers or anything. I like yours much better. Your uniform I mean; not your trousers.' She pressed her lips tightly together with a mortified squeak. *Jesus Christ, Kelsey. What is wrong with you?* She had to attempt to save herself. 'At least you don't have to wear this weird monstrosity around your neck,' she offered.

Will, she'd noticed, was wearing a smart tie in the same striped colours as her budget-airline bandana.

Raking his fingers through his hair he leaned towards her, intoning in a low conspiratorial voice, 'I think it looks *very* sexy on you.'

Kelsey attempted a casual shrug as though she were accustomed to compliments from hot strangers. He let out a throaty laugh. She had never met anyone as disarming as this before.

'Come on, let's walk and talk. We've got a group arriving in thirty minutes.' He motioned in the direction of the church.

Kelsey trailed alongside Will, a little too distracted by him to appreciate the beautiful sights they were passing. They made small talk about her journey the day before and the unusually hot weather, all the while Kelsey was taking quick sidelong glances at her new mentor.

He was clean-shaven and fresh-looking, and had his shirt tucked into black jeans with a brown leather belt. In fact, Kelsey noticed, he had a whole brown leather thing going on; from his watch strap to the leather bands on his other wrist down to his shining boots. Even the gilet looked good on him and the whole effect, along with his short sleeves showing off the muscles in his tanned and freckled forearms, was rather delicious – sort of sexy woodsman in the city. Kelsey suspected Will knew that women appreciated it.

'I almost forgot, these are for you. Your brolly and your ID badge.'

He handed her the badge – it simply had her name on it – and the burgundy golf umbrella he'd had tucked under his arm.

'It isn't forecast to rain, is it?'

'I doubt it. No, this is for holding up so your group can find you in among the crowds. Sometimes there are three or four guides working on the same street, it can get pretty jumbled.'

'Right-o,' she replied meekly, turning her attention to the flimsy, plastic badge.

'This is hardly an ID badge, is it? I could make this myself on a computer.'

'Question is, *Ms* Kelsey Anderson, why would you want to?' That grin again, he was enjoying her discomfort. 'Wait there a sec. Just nipping in here.'

With that, Will handed her his coffee cup and disappeared through the doors of a smart pub with a carved bird of prey above the door and a sign that read 'The Osprey

Hotel'. Kelsey took a moment to catch her breath. Will's easy confidence, charm and, let's face it, his looks, had thrown her. So much for the octogenarian Shakespeare boffin she'd expected. Instead she'd got this young, flirty, fit Englishman.

He's worked for Norma for donkey's years? How old is he then? He looks about my age, bit older maybe? And that accent! He's all suave and posh, like Hugh Grant before he went off the boil. And just where the hell has he disappeared to?

Will reappeared a few seconds later, catching her trying to peer through the frosted glass of the bar-room window.

'Missing me?' He was attaching his name badge to his shirt pocket with a wry smile. Trying not to squirm with shame, Kelsey felt her cheeks flush, not helped by the sight of Will resplendent in his shirt sleeves – he'd ditched the gilet – with a long peacock feather tucked under his arm and a large backpack over his broad shoulders. 'It's going to be hot today. Do you want to leave your fleece here too? My room's just upstairs.'

'Your room? You live here?'

'Actually, my parents own it. They let me move in over the summer when I'm working the tours. I'm usually away during the winter: skiing, snowboarding, surfing, that kind of thing. And then there's the occasional acting tour.'

'Hold on. You're a surfer-tour-guide-actor?' Kelsey laughed, and he smiled back, his eyes sparkling.

'That's me. Will Greville, Renaissance man and poly-math.' He slipped on dark sunglasses from his shirt pocket. Kelsey had no idea what a polymath might be, so she quickly steered the conversation back to safer ground.

'Your parents live here too then?'

'Not in the hotel, obviously, but yes, they're from Stratford. Mum lives in the Cotswolds now though, and Dad lives across the river with his girlfriend. They kept the hotel going through the divorce. They're pretty good friends, actually.'

In warm and genuine tones he filled her in about his close-knit family. He obviously admired his parents a lot. Listening and nodding, she almost had to run to keep up with his long strides. As they dodged the clusters of tourists smiling up at cameras on selfie sticks, the conversation shifted to surfing. He was heading off to Taghazout to catch some waves in October. Kelsey admitted she had never even heard of the place. She finally felt herself loosening up as she told Will about her love of photography.

'Do you reckon Norma will mind me bringing my camera to work some days? I'd love to take some pictures during my breaks.'

'Sure, as long as you're doing your job Norma's pretty easy to please, especially now she's decided to close the agency.'

'What? Hasn't it been open for years? Seems a shame to close it now when business is obviously booming.'

'I think she's wanted to stop for a while. This is its twentieth summer, so she's going out on a high, big anniversary and all that. She's off to Italy in September. Retiring. And if you believe the gossip, she'll be taking Gianfranco with her. He's one of the other guides, you'll meet him at the pub tomorrow night.'

'So you're taking me to the pub, are you?' Kelsey attempted a flirtatious smile.

'Yes. All the guides meet there before the Bard Crawl. You know, the weekly pub tour? We join forces and take the day's groups around the bars. Well, some of them; some go to the theatre. Isn't it on your rota?'

'Uh… I don't think I noticed that,' she recoiled with embarrassment. *What are you doing? You've just had a huge break-up with Fran, or whatever that was, and now you're flirting, really badly I might add, with the first fit bloke you meet. Get a grip, Kelsey.*

As they approached the church, Will sharpened his pace, striding ahead to welcome his group: twenty Canadian undergraduates. Kelsey watched him from the pavement as he counted each one off their minibus, taking names and affably shaking hands.

The town was getting busier as the first of the coaches rumbled by, heading for the big coach parks in the centre, and the hotels emptied of guests ahead of a long day of sightseeing, sunshine, and Shakespeare. Kelsey was intrigued to see Will at work. *If he's an actor, I bet he'll be a natural. And he's so cocky, I bet he's got nerves of steel.* She didn't feel quite so excited at the prospect of having a group of her own on Saturday. How could she possibly hope to match up? But for now she was simply going to enjoy the sights. *And that does not include your new colleague,* she told herself sternly.

'All right. Gather round, my friends,' Will called out in a jovial voice, holding the peacock feather high above his auburn head.

The students stopped talking immediately and shuffled into a semi-circle around him.

'Our tour begins here, in front of Stratford-upon-Avon's beautiful Holy Trinity Church.'

One of the students, a pretty girl in her late teens, raised her phone to take a quick snap of Will as he motioned towards the churchyard behind him. Without stopping, he flashed a grin at her. She looked at the image on her screen, smiled coyly then made a show of devoting her entire attention to him, nodding fascinatedly as he spoke.

Kelsey rolled her eyes. *Now I get it. He's the big man about town. The girls, and quite a few of the boys by the looks of things, go crazy for him. Look at him. He's in his element.*

Will was powering on. 'Baby William Shakespeare was baptised here in 1564, and this was also his last resting place in 1616. Follow me please as we make our way inside.'

Joining the back of the group, Kelsey started scribbling notes with the rose-gold pen and jotter that Mirren had given her. They all filed respectfully past Shakespeare's grave in the cool chancel. Gathering the group closely around him, Will continued in hushed tones, his voice husky and low.

'Here you can read the inscription on Shakespeare's tomb. He was terrified his body would be exhumed by treasure hunters, so he put a curse upon his grave.'

Will was really good at this. The students leaned in, open-mouthed in fascination as Will, thoroughly enjoying himself but with a face as serious as the grave itself, dramatically recited the four-hundred-year-old spell.

'*Good friend, for Jesus' sake forebear to dig the dust enclosed here. Blessed be the man that spares these stones, and cursed be he that moves my bones.*'

Kelsey shivered to think of the cold skeleton beneath their feet. The students had brought a wreath of rosemary and bay leaves and as one of the boys placed it reverently beside the grave Will caught Kelsey's eye, shamelessly winking at her over the solemnly bowed heads. Flickering candles illuminated the students' faces as they stood in silence before trooping out past the pews and into the sunshine again.

Will strode confidently ahead, reciting facts and dates, making sure everyone got the same amount of attention, answering questions and making everyone laugh. They wound their way down to the river which was softly lapping against the reedy banks. The branches of tall weeping willows dipped into the water while baby moorhens darted in and out of the dappled shade. They passed a group of fluffy grey cygnets making ripples across the surface of the broad river. Couples visiting the town on romantic minibreaks were holding hands as they climbed into white rowing boats at a shaded wooden jetty, looking forward to an hour or two of idle rowing down river.

Kelsey watched as two young women, clearly deeply in love, gripped each other tightly and clambered into a little boat with the name 'Viola' painted on its helm in curled black letters. They screamed and laughed as the boat rocked and dipped. Settling down side by side they kissed briefly, smiling into each other's eyes. The young lad in charge of the boats passed them two white oars and loaded a picnic basket into the prow by their feet. Pushing their boat out onto the river he waved them off but they were oblivious to him, so enraptured were they with each other.

Kelsey sighed, with a sharp stab of sadness. Here she was in the most romantic spot in England and she was alone. It was beginning to sink in that she might never see Fran again. It had all happened so quickly; the argument, Fran closing their bank account, her hasty retreat down south. She'd hardly had time to process it. Wrapping her arms tightly around herself, she stared after the lovers on the river.

'OK, everyone, we'll stop here briefly.'

Awakened from her reverie by Will's velvet voice further along the riverbank, she rushed to catch up with the group. Will was spreading woollen picnic blankets on the grass beside a rose bed that was spilling over with huge blowsy pink blooms. He took a stack of plastic cups out of his backpack and handed them around before reaching in again for two large bottles of sparkling elderflower pressé and a bowl with a clear lid through which Kelsey could see the glisten of luscious red berries.

'Let's cool off for a moment or two,' Will was saying. 'Sorry I don't have any ice. The roses in this bed are called William Shakespeare, by the way. Aren't they beautiful? But a rose by any other name would smell as sweet, right?' He pulled a daft face at his rubbish joke as the group groaned and laughed jovially, settling down to fill their cups. Will motioned to Kelsey to sit beside him with a gentle pat on a stripy blanket. 'I also have some strawberries, raspberries, and blackberries for you; all grown here in sunny Warwickshire.'

The students' eyes lit up. Kelsey helped herself to a large strawberry, keeping her eyes on Will who was kneeling propped up on his heels, slightly elevated above the crowd. He reached into the back pocket of his jeans, making an announcement in a commanding voice.

'As you enjoy a little taste of the English summertime, I'm going to read to you.'

Kelsey gasped audibly as she saw Will reveal the exact same book of *Sonnets* as her own treasured copy. He noticed the look of awe on her face and, smiling, held her gaze as he spoke.

'This is my favourite sonnet by William Shakespeare. He wrote it for his wife, Anne. It's about how a poet's praise can immortalise their beloved, keeping their love alive forever.'

Will Greville certainly knew how to weave a romantic spell. Kelsey broke her long gaze into his smiling eyes to glance around the group. Some of them, obviously couples, were holding hands, engrossed. Without once looking down at the open pages of his book, Will's clear English accent rang sonorously in the still summer air.

'*Shall I compare thee to a summer's day? Thou art more lovely and more temperate,*' he began.

Kelsey watched his suntanned cheekbones and full pale lips moving as he sounded out each word with relish.

'*Rough winds do shake the darling buds of May, and summer's lease hath all too short a date.*'

She couldn't help but let her eyes wander across his moving throat and bobbing Adam's apple and down across his chest which was rising and falling with the passion of his performance. She drifted off into a daydream of what it would be like to be held against that chest. Realising she was no longer hearing him, she tried to focus on the poetry. He was speaking softly now, with a honeyed warmth in his voice.

'*But thy eternal summer shall not fade, nor lose possession of that fair thou owest, nor shall death brag thou wanderest in his shade, when in eternal lines to Time thou growest.*'

She let the awakening pull of attraction to Will take over her thoughts as he took a long, slow breath before sighing out the poem's final lines, looking directly into Kelsey's transfixed eyes.

'*So long as men can breathe or eyes can see, so long lives this, and this gives life to thee.*'

The students burst into applause. Will made a small bow of his head, his auburn hair flopping over his temples.

'So you see,' he continued, 'Shakespeare experienced a love so strong, so overwhelming, he was moved to write this sonnet in the hope that his lover could cheat death and live on forever. How could he possibly have imagined that we'd be here, gathered from all over the globe, four hundred years later, on the banks of the River Avon, celebrating the strength of his enduring love? Now *that* is romance.'

Will was still enjoying the compliments and pats on the back as everyone cleared away their little picnic and folded up blankets ready to continue the tour. He edged over to Kelsey as the students chatted happily and took selfies on their phones, posting them to social media with messages for their friends back home.

'So, what do you think? Enjoying the tour?'

'It's lovely,' she replied, shaking her head slowly in admiration. 'You really know how to draw them in, don't you? Poetry and roses? It's like a performance really, isn't it? And the elderflower juice and local berries. That was a nice touch.'

'They're from Waitrose, but don't tell them that.' He laughed in low tones close to her ear. 'But the poetry recital's straight from the heart,' he added mirthfully, placing his hand on his chest and raising his eyes to the heavens in mock earnestness.

She couldn't help but laugh at his clowning. He didn't take himself seriously and that was very attractive. He seemed to swing between being very flash and authoritative, then very silly and fun, but always supremely confident.

'There's no way I'll be able to do what you do,' she confided, remembering what was expected of her on Saturday with a horrid anxiety.

'Well don't. You've got to find your own style and just enjoy it. I'll let you in on my secret, shall I? I remind myself that I'm the only person in the group being paid to be here, then I don't feel so nervous.'

'You? Nervous? I'll never believe that,' Kelsey exclaimed.

'You'd be surprised, Kelsey Anderson.' He screwed his lips up to one side into a shy pout, casting his eyes downwards. It looked kind of cute and a bit camp and Kelsey laughed again as Will's face broke into a broad grin.

The pair walked on to meet the rest of the group, enjoying their easy rapport, which Will clearly had with everybody he encountered. The rest of the day was just as pleasant as they visited ancient timber-beamed buildings with wonky floors and wandered in Elizabethan knot gardens with low box hedges forming intricate topiary patterns. They stopped for lunch in a café by the river where everyone sat outside in the sun and ate jacket potatoes with melting Red Leicester cheese. Afterwards, they all relaxed on a canal boat ride, the students chatting about their studies back home.

Kelsey filled pages of her notebook with ideas about how to get her own tour groups invested in the history of this beautiful town, knowing that not all of them were going to be as interested in Shakespeare as these English majors. Will knew how to get people emotionally engaged and she wondered if she could do the same thing. It was going to take a bit of practice, she realised, and a lot of self-assurance. She really needed a confidence boost if she was going to replicate Will's relaxed delivery.

At five o'clock she said goodbye to her new Canadian friends, promising to meet them on Facebook. On her way back to her bedsit, she stopped by the convenience store in the town centre loading her basket with microwaveable meals and a bottle of cheap white wine. Walking back to her new home at a slow pace in the late afternoon sunshine she thought over her day out in the fresh air surrounded by vibrant young people and historic wonders. She found she was already enjoying the excitement and novelty of her new way of life and realising that she wasn't wishing herself back in Mr McLennan's camera shop any more. It struck her how lonely she'd been there. A change had been needed, and this sudden, drastic move now felt very right indeed.

Eating by herself on her sunny little roof terrace that evening, she allowed herself a smile for her new friend, the funny and charming Will Greville.

Because that's what we are: friends. God knows, I need a friend here. The last thing I want to do is get involved with a colleague. Nope, from now on it's just me. And that's fine. Even if he is all hot and posh and clever… Kelsey, no! Just because I'm on my own doesn't mean I'm all alone. I can do this. This is the all new Kelsey Anderson. Independent, confident, self-sufficient…

As she poured herself another glass of wine and settled down to read the opening acts of *A Midsummer Night's*

Dream, she felt convinced this was true. It wasn't until she climbed into bed that night that she checked her phone to find three missed calls, all from the same familiar number, and a text.

Kelsey-boo, I miss you. F x

She shuddered at the cold jolt of sadness as she switched the phone off. Hiding her head under the covers, she tried not to think about Fran all by himself in his flat, his dreams and plans shattered. She suddenly felt very alone.

Chapter Thirteen

'Self-love, my liege, is not so vile a sin, as self-
    neglecting'
(Henry V)

Determined to arrive at work early that morning, Kelsey had wolfed her breakfast and thrown on her uniform, but with jeans this time, leaving her blow-dried hair wild and loose and remembering to open the window wide to stop her bedsit turning into a sauna after her shower.

Thinking of how frazzled her skin had been yesterday she slathered on sun cream, loving its scent. Even in the depths of winter on rainy days at home she'd been known to smear on her summer sun lotion. You simply can't have the January blues when you smell like banana daiquiris and coconut.

Passing the rainbow-striped strap of her camera over her head and across her body she felt instantly complete, her mind abuzz with thoughts of the beautiful photographs she might capture today.

There on the floor beside the camera bag was Fran's envelope brimming with cash. Crouching down to lift it, thoughts of Fran flooded back, and she felt the wind leave her sails again. She hadn't called him yet and even though she didn't really know what she'd say to him if she did, she knew she'd have to, and soon. Yes, she missed her family and Mirren, but there just wasn't that same tug of homesickness when she thought about Fran. Instead there was overwhelming guilt and another, more subtle feeling, still too new for her to recognise fully: the growing glow of self-reliance. Shoving the money into the zip compartment of her camera case, Kelsey rushed for the door. There were errands to run before meeting Will.

First, she made her way to the bank on the high street and hurriedly paid in the money, relieved to get rid of it. It simply wasn't safe having that kind of cash just lying around, but it certainly made the prospect of a summer away from home a lot more enjoyable. It meant she needn't worry too much about paying her way and it was going to make her second errand a lot more fun.

Kelsey made a beeline towards the smart shopping arcade near the river, scanning the rows of shops for a clothes store. She passed the florists, art galleries, hair salons, jewellers, patisseries, and coffee shops before spotting the little cluster of quirky independent clothes shops with cutesy names like 'Flora and Frieda', 'Watermelon', and 'Boo and Blue.'

I've got to come back here on my days off, it's gorgeous.

Her heart was beating faster. She couldn't remember the last time she'd shopped for herself. Fran always noticed on the rare occasions she wore something new and he'd sulk about it, asking how much it had cost. Well, today she was going to shop, or rather, speed-shop.

The boutique was smart if rather tiny and sparse inside. Kelsey was the only customer and the girl behind the till looked surprised to see someone in the shop so early. She closed her magazine quickly and greeted Kelsey politely. 'Come on in. Are you looking for anything in particular?'

Kelsey eyed the rails of expensive-looking clothes. 'I *was* looking for boring work trousers, but now I'm here…'

Twenty-five minutes later Kelsey was running as fast as she could towards Will, two large bags bumping up and down on her hips. And she was laughing like a maenad. Her working summer holiday in this shopper's paradise had got off to the perfect start.

'*Ciao, bella,*' Will called out. He was leaning on the lamp post opposite the agency doors.

'Eh? Oh, *ciao*, I guess. You're very chipper this morning.'

'You're looking pretty happy yourself. And, I must say rather sexy too, except…' He was eying her new cropped dark grey pants. 'Perhaps ditch the price tag?' Reaching a swift hand down towards Kelsey's hip Will yanked the label from her trouser pocket.

'Oh my God. Thank you, I think.' *Blushing again?* She cursed inwardly, exasperated at Will's ability to fluster her. Trying to collect herself, she pressed on. 'Can I drop these bags at your hotel this morning?'

'Of course, let's go.'

Will slipped on his sunglasses, his hair falling messily around their dark frames. He looked just as good as she remembered but she couldn't help fulminating over how this posh-boy stranger could make her feel so attractive and so young and silly at the same time. What frustrated her even more was her suspicion that he knew exactly what he was doing, in fact, he seemed to delight in it.

'Doing a bit of swanky shopping then? Good for you. You're a beautiful girl; you deserve nice clothes, especially if they make up for having to wear this godawful uniform.'

Walking on, chatting about the day ahead, Will told her they were hosting an Italian group all day and they wanted the exact same tour the students had yesterday. Kelsey waited on the busy pavement as Will ran up to his room in the Osprey Hotel.

Unexpectedly, she felt a gentle hand on her shoulder as she was greeted with an enquiring 'hello?' Startled, she spun around to be met with the bright smiling eyes of two women, both wearing the Norma Arden Agency uniform.

'Hello! More tour guides? I'm Kelsey. Lovely to meet you.'

Trying to read her new colleagues' name badges, she made out only one, 'Valeria', belonging to the petite, glamorous woman with the long glossy brown hair who was already hugging her.

'Welcome to Stratford,' she was saying in a soft accent that Kelsey couldn't place. 'I'm Valeria, and this is Myrtle.' She placed a hand on Myrtle's back and pulled her into the conversation. Myrtle, a little older and broader than Valeria, with cropped pixie-cut dyed white hair, leaned forward to shake Kelsey's outstretched hand.

'Glad to meetcha, Kelsey. Is that an Irish name?' she said in a slow American drawl that reminded Kelsey of Jerry Hall.

'It's Scottish, I think. Do you know, I'm not sure? But *I'm* Scottish.'

'What we really want to know is why you're hanging out outside Will's rooms.' Valeria's voice crackled wickedly. 'Shall we all set off and leave him wondering where you are?'

'Depends where you're going,' Kelsey replied.

'Same place as you, honey. We're all doing the Italian tours today,' Myrtle drawled.

I really bloody must memorise that rota! 'Fabulous!' Kelsey compensated for her embarrassment with enthusiasm. 'We'd better wait for Will, though. He's stashing my shopping in his room.'

Her fellow guides glanced at one another with a flash of amusement and slightly raised eyebrows. The look lasted a millisecond, but Kelsey knew what it meant. They were thinking that Will had his hooks into the new girl already. A tiny pang of offense pulsed through her and she felt her cheeks redden. She wanted to have them know she was newly single – well, possibly, sort of single – and not about to fall for just any old Flash Harry, but instead she looked down at the street, lost for words. Myrtle had her arm around Kelsey's shoulders in an instant..

'Yep, let's wait. He's a sweetie, all right. Showing you how it's done, is he?' Myrtle's voice was kind but Kelsey still felt stung and flustered.

'Kind of. I hope *I* can do it. He's pretty good, isn't he?'

'Honey, you ain't seen *us* at work yet,' Myrtle said with a laugh, just as Will stepped through the hotel doors and out into the sun. He was carrying four bottles of mineral water.

He kissed Myrtle and Valeria twice – a friendly smacker on each cheek – and handed out the bottles.

'Just one of the perks of having your own bar.' He flashed that Cheshire cat grin again. 'We'll need them this morning; it's set to be the hottest day of the year so far.

Right, let's do this. I'll take the church first. Myrtle and Valeria, start by the river? Then we'll swap, yeah?'

They walked down the wide curving road to the church where three large coaches were lined up. Tourists were pouring out onto the street. Kelsey had no idea what they were saying. Will casually took her hand and pulled her towards the front coach.

'This is us, Kelsey Anderson. Watch and learn, kid.'

Will produced a clipboard from his backpack and started rhyming off names in a thick Italian accent, calling the group to order with nothing but charm and an obvious love of being the centre of attention. Soon they were under his spell, listening intently to their guide's perfect Italian as he led them through the shady churchyard.

Valeria winked at Kelsey as she walked briskly past, her group rushing to keep up with her as they made their way down to the riverside. In the distance Myrtle was trying to herd her group off the bus and onto the safety of the pavement, her voice raised to a loud shout over her gabbling crowd. 'This way, folks.'

She seemed to have less command over her lot than Will and Valeria, but Kelsey was still in awe of her courage and that loud voice. Soon she'd be trying out her own voice in front of the crowds. The quick dread flooded her body, suspending her breathing and quickening her pulse.

Chapter Fourteen

'What's to do? Shall we go see the relics of this town?'
(Twelfth Night)

After visiting Shakespeare's grave again, the group wound their way down to the shaded riverside where Will expertly recited the same sonnet as yesterday, this time, of course, in luscious Italian. Kelsey had to look away to stop her mouth falling open. Who knew it was possible to make Shakespeare sound even more romantic? Kelsey looked at the notebook open on her lap; today's page was blank. Excluded by the language barrier, she certainly wasn't learning anything new, other than how flirtatious Will could be.

It wasn't easy catching his attention as he stood in the middle of a circle of unbelievably glamorous women of all ages who crowded around him on the steps of the main theatre, but by eleven she'd had enough.

'Will? Excuse me, *Will.*'

His momentary look of confusion told Kelsey he had completely forgotten she was tagging along, and that smarted a bit, though she wasn't entirely sure why her pride would be stung. Will was just doing his job.

'I haven't a clue what you're all saying. Do you mind if I sneak off the tour? I think I'd get more out of today if I just found a quiet spot and read through Norma's information booklets again.'

'Yeah, sure, no worries. Just meet us at the pub later. You know, for the Bard Crawl? We've got a few Yanks, and some Brits booked in. Five o'clock? Do you know where the starting point is?'

Shaking her head, she shrugged. 'It's a pub called the Yorick, isn't it? But I've no idea where it is, Will.'

He made his way over to her, leaving the women to cluck crossly at his sudden neglect. Seeing the scowls, Kelsey felt inwardly rewarded. He smiled as he held her firmly by the arms and spun her round, pointing to the lovely old cottage pub she'd been standing in front of all along.

'Seriously, look at your map, woman. It's right there.'

Spinning her around again, he leaned in and kissed her on both cheeks as casually as though he'd known her all her life. Kelsey stood frozen to the spot, dazed and aware that she was grinning stupidly, wishing he wasn't walking away from her. She watched as he disappeared, devoured by the ring of women already bombarding him with questions, each one jostling for his attention.

'See you later,' she offered, in a higher pitched voice than she expected, but Will was oblivious.

Turning with a deep breath to face the crowded riverside she was struck by a sudden giddy sense of freedom. The summer was in full swing, the sun was blazing down and she had the rest of the day to explore her new town. She knew exactly what she wanted to do.

With her camera cradled in her hands, she passed the theatres, heading down into the theatre gardens – a broad expanse of closely cropped grass criss-crossed with wide canals and bridges.

There in the canal basin, which had the air of a smart little marina, were narrow boats painted in every colour and moored in rows, some with little walkways jutting out into the water alongside them. A few boats had signs by them inviting visitors in. They were shops. Kelsey peeped inside the first one she came to, the brightest of them all. Its rooftop sign read 'Roses and Castles.'

Inside Kelsey discovered a little gallery selling miniature paintings on tiny wood-framed easels, and red flowerpots, yellow milk urns and black metal jugs all boldly painted with flowers in green, white, and gold. Spotting a painted heart hanging on a ribbon she immediately thought of her mum at home and reached for her purse.

'The colours are so vivid. Is it OK if I take some photographs in here?' Kelsey asked, as the smiling lady behind the counter in the stern busily wrapped the gift in tissue paper. She didn't mind one bit, even offering to pose for a shot in front of her workbench where she was painting a large box with a sloping lid that lifted up on hinges.

'It's a writing desk,' she let Kelsey know, pointing out the sunken glass pot for the ink.

After taking a few carefully lit shots using her flash to warm up the boat's dark interior, Kelsey thanked her before climbing out onto the gangplank that led back to the path. The next boat was even more tempting. It was an ice-cream barge.

Soon, Kelsey was sitting on the grass enjoying her mint choc-chip and watching the tourists bustling around the canal basin, feeling only a little guilty she wasn't yet brushing up on Norma's information booklets. She'd settle down to work soon. At times like this, only a selfie on a camera phone will do, so she did something she rarely attempted. Holding her phone up high, licking the melting ice cream and winking cheekily at herself on the screen, she tried to capture her best angle.

Eat your heart out Mirr! 32 degrees here and I found a boat full of ice cream. When are you getting here? Kelse xx

Shielding the screen from the sun's glare she could just make out Mirren's reply – a picture of her friend hunched over her desk in the newspaper office wearing a thick cardigan and miserably holding up a healthy muesli bar.

Sucks to be me right now. See you mid-July, got a whole weekend off. Also got a night in late August. Want a visitor then too?

Kelsey smiled broadly to herself as she finished her ice cream and sent back just one word: 'YES!'

Kelsey's eye was suddenly caught by the familiar thick black font on a sign that read, 'Historic Walking Tours: Tickets Sold Here.' The sign stood on a narrow jetty jutting out into the water alongside a broad boat that seemed taller than all the rest. Its shutters were opened wide and inside she could make out a man sitting by a cash register. Making her way over to him, she guessed he was possibly in his late forties, though his dark skin, chiselled features, and bulging muscles made him appear far younger at first glance. He was squeezed into the familiar burgundy agency uniform. From his name badge she knew that this was the renowned Gianfranco, the one Will had told her about, Norma's squeeze. Just as she was about to introduce herself, Kelsey recognised a voice from further inside the boat.

'All right, Gi-Gi, you keep pushing those tickets for the Bard Crawl, and I'll see you tonight.'

Norma had just finished counting money from the till into a bank deposit bag, and was leaning down to kiss Gianfranco's handsome, placid face, when she spotted Kelsey.

'Kelsey, dear! How lovely to see you. Settling in all right, are we? Good, good.' As usual there was no time to reply. Norma ploughed on. 'Have you met Gianfranco? He's our best ticket seller. Doesn't say much, but the tourists love him.'

Norma's eyes sparkled as she looked down at him, and he returned the unmistakeable look of a man deeply in lust.

'Nice to meet you,' said Kelsey with delight, reaching into the hatch to shake hands. *Good for you, Norma.*

Gianfranco smiled coyly, revealing a little gap between his front teeth, putting Kelsey in mind of Arnie Schwarzenegger.

'Hello,' he said in a lilting voice that didn't seem to belong to this big beefy bloke. He had started tidying the already very tidy leaflets on the window ledge in front of him. Kelsey instantly understood why Norma liked this big shy hunk of muscles. He barely spoke. He just listened. Perfect for Norma.

'Kelsey, dear, aren't you with the Italians today? Little break, eh? Jolly good. Can't stand here chatting all day. Off to the bank. Count out those pennies, eh?'

Norma gave the money bag a sharp shake before kissing Gianfranco on his silent upturned face, first on the lips and then leaving a gentle kiss on the tip of his nose. The pair smiled sweetly at each other, as Kelsey watched on, feeling every bit the gooseberry. He whispered something inaudible that seemed to make Norma blush as she clambered out the low door and down the gangway, rushing as usual, and a little flustered too.

'Norma?' Kelsey cried out after her. 'Thank you so much for the lovely welcome gifts.'

'My pleasure, darling,' she called back as she marched off into the crowds.

Kelsey smiled at the blushing Gianfranco who was looking down at his broad thighs, trying not to meet her eye. *I'm guessing Norma didn't hire this big softie for his tour guiding skills.*

'So are you mainly ticket sales, then?' She grasped for something to say in the awkward silence.

Gianfranco nodded, keeping his eyes cast down. 'Yes. You will be with me soon, no? Selling tickets. On Tuesdays?' He was practically whispering in his soft accent somewhere between Spanish and Italian.

Selling tickets on the barge? I forgot about that. That's it, I am stapling that rota to my forehead. She manged a sensible, 'Right, great. Well I'll see you then.' *Looking forward to the great chats.*

Gianfranco went back to shuffling the leaflets about with a silent, affable nod.

It was getting on for lunchtime and Kelsey's stomach was starting to growl. One ice cream cone just wasn't going to cut it, and she could smell the food cooking in the town's restaurants and pubs that were by now in full-on lunch service mode. Calling out her goodbyes to Gianfranco she wandered on, not relishing the idea of a sunburned picnic on the riverside in the blazing heat.

Chapter Fifteen

'Who ever loved that loved not at first sight?'
(As You Like It)

Spotting the café hadn't been difficult. Even from the other side of the marina and over the busy crossroads its candy-pink and white stripy awning was strikingly bright. Trying to run without looking like she was running, Kelsey zigzagged through the thronging crowds, her eye firmly on the prize, that single empty chair, and what might be the only available lunch spot in town.

Nearly there. Still free, it's still free. Yes, winner!

At the exact moment she threw herself down onto the seat under a Barbie pink parasol, making a celebratory fist-pump, her hip clashed painfully with a tall, firm body travelling from the opposite direction. They had both been aiming for the same spot in the shade.

Kelsey gasped, regretting the fist-pump and springing to her feet again. 'I'm so sorry! Please, you take it.' She looked up into the man's discomfited face. He too had leapt from the seat at the first touch of their bodies.

'No, *I'm* sorry. Are you OK? Did I hurt you?' His strong American accent told Kelsey he was another sight-seer.

'I'm fine, honestly,' she replied, rubbing her achy hip and finding the pain melting away under the tall stranger's concerned scrutiny. 'I wasn't looking where I was going, too busy thinking about my rumbling tummy.' Smiling apologetically, she hoped he would laugh.

His serious expression appeared to be relaxing, when a woman wearing a pink gingham headscarf dashed over to them and parked a folding chair behind the man's knees.

'Here we are,' she flustered. 'Sorry about that. Ketchup spillage. It needed a good wash down out the back. Menu's on the table. I'll be back to take your order in a second.'

With that, she bustled off, leaving Kelsey unsure what to say. They looked at each other, mouthing exasperated half-words until the tall American broke out into actual speech.

'Uh, hi… I'm Jonathan. Are you, uh, meeting someone or…?' Still embarrassed from the crash, he gesticulated as though he were ready to leave should Kelsey say the word, but his feet seemed rooted to the spot and he looked pretty reluctant to go.

With a casual wave of her hand, Kelsey dismissed the idea. 'No, I'm alone. Sit down. Please?'

As she spoke she found her accent coming out strongly in response to his kind, open face and deep, dreamy voice. She drew in the contested chair and settled down again, all the while looking up at the poor guy.

'I didn't catch your name. Did I say I was Jonathan?'

Kelsey laughed gently. 'Yes, you did, and I'm Kelsey. Are you on holiday, I mean, vacation?'

He looked calmer as he settled himself in the chair, his long body relaxing at last. Kelsey was suddenly struck by the pale blue, almost grey, eyes that frankly met her own.

Surrounded by the overblown pink of the café décor, they shone out. His mouth twitched into a small smile at the corners.

'Actually I'm here to work. I'm in a play, *A Midsummer Night's Dream*?' He said it like a question which momentarily confused her.

Does he think I might not have heard of A Midsummer Night's Dream?

With a jolt of recognition, Kelsey realised he was with the touring company she'd read about back home.

'You're with that American theatre group? You're here for the summer, right? For the festival of plays? I was reading about it online. I was going to try to get tickets to see it.'

At that he broke into an incredible American smile, the tips of his pearl-white teeth just showing under his curling pale lips and setting off his healthy tanned skin. She'd never seen a face so transformed by a smile and was taken aback by how arresting it was. Did that surprise show on her face? Hastily, she pressed on to cover it up.

'So, what role are you playing?'

'I'm Oberon, King of the Fairy Kingdom?'

It was beginning to dawn on Kelsey that this guy finished his sentences with an upward inflection that sounded like a question, but wasn't. That, combined with his deep voice and *that* accent, drew Kelsey's gaze towards his enticing mouth. He was slow-burn handsome and she was beginning to feel it.

'Anyway, Kelsey, what about you? Are you a local?'

'I wish. Though, I suppose I am, just for the summer. I'm a tour guide, hence the… whatever this thing is.' Pulling sharply at the burgundy and green neckerchief she made a face and his ready laughter surprised her. She watched as his bright eyes moved down to her throat and lingered there for a second before flashing back up to hold her gaze.

'So, you're having a summer adventure too. Sounds nice. But you're *not* English? I'm detecting an accent?'

He leaned in closer, placing an elbow on the table and absent-mindedly rubbing his fingertips on the nape of his neck and through his short, mussed-up, brown hair. She was enjoying his slow, sonorous voice and the intense way he was looking at her. He seemed genuinely interested in what she had to say.

'I'm from a little seaside village near Edinburgh. What about you?' She threw his question back, unconsciously mirroring his movements by leaning one elbow on the table, resting her jaw on a soft fist.

'Edinburgh? We toured there last summer. It's an amazing place.' He stopped talking briefly, seemingly just to smile again, before he continued. 'Oh... I'm from Tulsa, Oklahoma. Haven't been home in a *long* time! Man! I love your accent, it's so beautiful.'

Leaning back as he spoke, he stretched out his broad shoulders, his long frame obviously getting uncomfortable on the flimsy café chair. For a second Kelsey just watched him. She liked the way he moved his body, it was like nobody she'd ever seen before. Of course, he was an actor; he'd probably taken movement classes and workshopped all his lovely, loose gestures, and by the looks of things he worked out a little bit too. His pale blue plaid shirt looked as though it had been washed a thousand times, its soft, thin fabric lightly cladding his rangy musculature. His collar buttons were undone and Kelsey found herself glimpsing time and again at his throat and the slightest stubble on his jaw which jutted forward just a little bit. Realising in the silence that she had to say something and quick, she searched her mind for words, only half aware that her new acquaintance was simply studying her face too, watching the summer breeze shifting the soft wisps of her wild hair.

The words formed slowly in Kelsey's mouth. 'So… I'm starting to think that hardly anybody was actually born in this town. It's like it's full of arty nomads, just drifting in for the season.'

Jonathan nodded his head towards the camera she'd just placed on the table between them.

'You might be right. It looks to me as though you're actually a photographer.'

Before Kelsey could answer, the waitress was back again holding her order pad, her pen poised. They hadn't even looked at their menus and they both smiled in acknowledgement of how distracted they'd been in one another's company. They quickly scanned the salads, both choosing the same dressed baby leaves, stilton, walnut, and apple with sparkling orange juice.

Over their unhurried meal Kelsey, told Jonathan all about the camera shop and how her precious Canon AE-1 had belonged to her late father and how, years ago, when she was a student she'd had her photos exhibited in a gallery. Jonathan listened closely with genuine sympathy in his eyes, mixed with deep admiration for her passion.

'You know, if you're looking for a commission, I could really use some new head shots? I haven't had any taken in years.'

Kelsey felt her heart swelling. *He thinks I'm a photographer. An actual professional.* 'I could, I mean, I'd love to. I just don't have any reflectors or anything. We'd have to improvise a bit.'

'Sounds good to me. We could use some of the theatre lighting? When are you free? I've got rehearsals and tech all weekend and next week through Friday. How about next Saturday morning?'

What the hell, say yes. Kelsey couldn't resist the idea of spending more time with this sweet guy and she'd be doing her favourite thing. 'Week on Saturday? That's my first proper day off… so, yes. I'll look forward to it.'

She handed him her phone and watched him type his number carefully. He smiled as he passed it back and asked her to check that it worked, trying to sound casual.

Thinking of all the times she'd watched Mirren give over-enthusiastic blokes in nightclubs the wrong phone number trying to shake them off after an ill-advised snog, Kelsey clicked 'call' and heard the phone in his shirt pocket ringing.

'There, now I've got your number.' He grinned, looking a little flushed. 'Meet me at the Willow Studio, that's where the play is. It's just over there by the Yorick?'

'OK, great. Ten o'clock?'

Jonathan didn't get a chance to answer. A tall, willowy woman with long flowing brown hair appeared suddenly over Jonathan's shoulder. She was stunningly beautiful even though she was scowling.

'Jonny, I've been hollering up and down the riverside for you. Did you get my Smartwater? And my vitamins? Come on, the first tech starts in two minutes.'

She ignored Kelsey, focussing all her energy on the startled Jonathan, who looked at his watch then back to Kelsey apologetically, running a hand through his hair, but his voice was calm and kind when he replied.

'I totally lost track of time. Peony, this is Kelsey. She's a photographer.'

Kelsey felt herself blushing at this. She attempted a smile and was about to confess she was nothing of the sort but the pretty, angry woman wasn't interested in pleasantries. She was tapping her foot, her arms folded. 'That's nice,' she said hurriedly, keeping her eyes on him. 'Let's go, hon. We need to run through the first half.'

Jonathan looked reluctant to move from the shady seat in the pink café. He was still set on making polite introductions, seemingly unfazed by Peony's brusqueness.

'Peony is my... Titania,' he offered.

Kelsey could really see this Peony as the Queen of the Fairies. She was the perfect match for Jonathan's King Oberon. She was tall and lithe with long elegant limbs. They both had the same healthy tan and super-white teeth. Kelsey was aware of an uneasy sinking feeling in her stomach, the unwilling acceptance that she'd really liked this gorgeous man and hadn't read his signals correctly. Jonathan was slipping a twenty-pound note under his plate and standing up to leave.

'It was great to meet you, Kelsey. See you real soon for those head shots?' He looked intently into her eyes, the same grave attentiveness on his face that he'd had in the moments after they'd crashed into each other.

Kelsey watched them go, unsure of what had just happened. Had she come between two lovers? He'd been chatting to her with so much interest and charm. Was that just his friendly Oklahoma ways? Why was Peony so angry? Whatever it was, he was sweet and gentle and she had liked the feel of his eyes on her, and now she had a photography commission.

Kelsey didn't budge from her shady spot for the rest of the afternoon. She'd spotted homemade lemon meringue pie on the menu and it was so good she'd stayed for two slices with iced coffee. After a couple of hours spent memorising facts from Norma's information booklets, she realised she was no longer absorbing the information as well as she could, so she settled into reading *A Midsummer Night's Dream*, all the more interested in the strange, magical romance now that she had a picture of Oberon in her mind; tall, slim, and handsome with a smile that made you melt. She pictured Jonathan's lovely curling lips and square jaw moving, delivering the lines in his dreamy low voice. After a while, she admitted to herself that she had outstayed her welcome at the busy little café in the hope that Jonathan might rush back for a coffee mid-rehearsal.

Just as she was leaving, she felt a sudden impulse to look back. Raising the camera to her eye, she focused her viewfinder on the two empty chairs by the little pink table in the shade and let the shutter snap. Walking away, she didn't quite know why she'd done it.

Chapter Sixteen

'You have witchcraft in your lips'
(Henry V)

It had gone five o'clock as Kelsey stuffed the newly acquired postcards and stamps into her satchel and bounded up the stone steps of the Yorick. The guides were already assembled inside the olde worlde pub. Will stood by the bar with Norma and Gianfranco, and Valeria and Myrtle were ensconced with another uniformed guide – Kelsey guessed he must be Lukas – inside the biggest fireplace Kelsey had ever seen. They were perched on stone seats cut deep into the huge chimneybreast like a cosy cavern. There obviously hadn't been a lit fire in there for years and all the brickwork had been painted a gleaming white. Kelsey stooped her head underneath the high oak beam garlanded with dried hop flowers that served as a mantelpiece and lowered herself onto the empty spot beside Lukas. Valeria poured her out a large class of cider from a brown earthenware jug.

Lukas was only twenty-one and very easy to talk with. She discovered he was a student and spoke his native Russian, as well as German, French and, of course, perfect English. He told her he was now studying Latin.

'I guess when you're fluent in all the living languages, you have to move onto the dead ones, right?' Kelsey joked, making Lukas chuckle.

The tourists had arrived and were checking in with Will for the pub crawl. He was putting everyone at ease as he chatted among the group, taking care to memorise their names – another one of his clever tour-guide techniques. Kelsey was struggling to remember the names of the other guides, let alone the group of thirty tourists who were now filling the bar ready for the long evening tour ahead.

'So, what do I need to do tonight?' Kelsey asked Lukas as she sipped the warm cider.

'Just follow Will and Myrtle. They'll do most of the talking. You must help Valeria and I to herd the drunk tourists, making sure we do not lose anyone,' he said in his wonderful thick accent.

'I can do that. How many pubs do we visit?'

'Only six. One drink in each. Will and Myrtle recite some poetry at each one and tell a little history. Norma likes all her guides to work on the Crawl. Safe in the numbers, yes? We are allowed to enjoy a drink or two as well, so long as we don't go overboard.'

'I can imagine it gets a bit messy. There'll be a few drunk stragglers, I guess?'

Across the crowded bar, a brassy chime rang out. A space cleared revealing Will holding a bell. He was preparing to make a speech, his chest swelling.

'My friends, welcome aboard the Norma Arden Historic Tour Agency Bard Crawl.'

The whole gathering broke out into restrained applause.

'My name is Will Greville. There will be much merry-making and ale-drinking tonight. You all have your route maps, but please keep me and my colleague, the wonderful Myrtle Hardcastle, in sight. I'll be taking a headcount in and out of each pub, so fear not, we won't let you lose yourselves. We're all meeting as strangers this evening, but let us end the night as friends. My namesake, the great Will Shakespeare said that good company, good wine, and good welcome can make good people. So, without further ado, let's put that theory to the test. Here's to a very good night indeed with exceptionally good people.'

Will raised his glass in toast to the crowd who were very much enjoying his speech. Kelsey shook her head at Valeria and rolled her eyes.

'He's a bit hammy isn't he?'

'Will doesn't do subtle,' Valeria said with a chuckle as they all began to shuffle their way out into the warm summer evening, Will Greville's peacock feather bobbing above his head at the front of the merry group.

By nine o'clock Kelsey had enjoyed two glasses of cider and switched to cola two pubs back, but she was still feeling giddy as she mingled with the red-cheeked tourists. Some of them asked her questions about Shakespeare and the town which, to her surprise, she found she could answer, and if she was unclear on any of the finer points, Lukas and Valeria were on hand to help her out.

Will was entertaining two very beautiful young women out in the beer garden at the back of the pub that had long ago, Kelsey was horrified to learn, been used for bear fighting. Kelsey could just make out the back of Will's head through the garden doors. He was talking very loudly and acting out comic scenes from the plays, deeply enjoying his starring role in his one-man show. Kelsey didn't mind; she'd enjoyed getting to know the other guides a little better, except for Gianfranco who had disappeared with Norma a couple of hours ago.

'Aren't we off the clock now, guys? The tour's overrun a bit. When can we head home, I'm exhausted?' Kelsey said, hopping off the bar stool.

'You can't leave yet. You haven't seen Will's grand finale,' Valeria exclaimed.

Kelsey pulled a puzzled face, intrigued.

Valeria laughed. 'You'll see.'

Will was on the move again, like a posh Pied Piper, the peacock feather bending under the doorframe of the pub as he strode outside. The trail of tourists was now very long and slow, some of them having a little difficulty keeping up. Kelsey joined Will at the front of the group.

'Are you enjoying the tour, Kelsey?' he asked. She nodded in assent, gazing up into the cloudless sapphire sky. The stars were twinkling overhead, and the town was falling quiet as Will led the group to a spot on its very edges.

'Where on earth are you taking us?' Kelsey wondered aloud, as they came to the end of a very tall neatly clipped hedgerow.

He stopped suddenly, indicating an arched wooden door interrupting the hedge. Will swung the door open dramatically, allowing Kelsey to lead the way into a dark garden surrounded by high yew trees and the ivy-clad grey stone of a gothic-looking house. In the gloaming light, Kelsey could just make out long meandering flower beds all around and a shimmering pond in the middle distance. There were a few lanterns hanging on hooks here and there lighting their path across the neat lawn towards some trestle tables with two big plastic boxes filled with ice on top, the slender necks of green bottles just visible above the ice.

Smiling slyly and without saying anything, Will popped the corks one after another. Kelsey filled the tall flutes and handed them out. The group gathered around exclaiming in wonder and surprise at the moonlit garden and the golden liquid sparkling in the glasses – such an unexpected end to their evening.

Will announced dramatically, 'There's just enough time for one last toast, my friends. Please take a glass of Warwickshire pear perry, in my opinion more delicious than even the finest champagne. Here's to new friends and to safe travels and to very brief hangovers. Cheers!'

The crowd were still clinking glasses and sipping the light amber nectar as Will took Kelsey by the elbow. 'Come this way, I have something to show you.'

She let him lead her into the shadows of an orchard of strange gnarled trees at the darkest end of the garden. Suddenly Will's teasing voice was very near Kelsey's ear.

'Right, close your eyes, Kelsey Anderson.'

'What?' she laughed in alarm.

'Just trust me. Have you got them closed?' he said from a little further off.

Kelsey stood in the near darkness, her eyes tightly shut and her arms hanging by her sides, listening for Will's return. *What the hell is he doing?*

'I'm here,' he said softly, taking her hand in his. 'OK? Now open your mouth.'

'Will, what are you up to? This is a bit weird.' Nervy laughter rippled her voice.

'Just open up,' he instructed suggestively. Kelsey felt Will's fingertips at her parting lips as he gently pushed a soft ripe berry into her mouth. It was perfumed and bursting with juice that tasted sweet and musty at the same time. It was delicious. 'It's a mulberry. This garden is full of four-hundred-year-old mulberry trees. They were planted when Shakespeare was alive for silkworms to live on. Well, that was the idea anyway, it didn't quite work. Wrong kind of mulberries.' He was murmuring deeply, close enough for Kelsey to feel his breath raising goose-bumps on her neck.

She gasped, shocked at the strange spiced taste of the fruit and a sudden chill in the air that made her shiver. As she opened her eyes, Will's handsome face was just inches from her own. He slowly placed a berry into his mouth, its purple juice running down his fingers. He was dazzling in the blue starlight and he was looking at her hungrily, tracing his fingertips from her wrist up towards her shoulder, making her skin tingle. It would be so easy to tip her head upwards to meet his mouth, letting the sweet potion in the berries take hold of them both. For a second, she almost allowed herself to take the step forward into his arms, and she would have done if she hadn't heard a voice from deep within herself whispering, *be careful*.

She drew back sharply with a startled sense of sudden awakening. 'I should go.'

Will, catching her around the waist with a strong arm, spoke again, a note of impatience in his voice. 'Wait! Please. Do you have a boyfriend back home or some-thing?'

'Hah! I have *literally* no idea,' she replied with a faraway bemusement.

Will freed her and watched her walk back up the lawn towards the opening in the hedge where they had all spilled into the green world of the secret mulberry-scented garden.

Kelsey walked all the way home with her head raised to the silver constellations, feeling more sober with every step. *Not Will, not now. You only just got here and you're thinking about messing around with the guy who's supposed to be mentoring you? What about poor Fran? Just get it together, Kelsey.*

Unlocking the door of Number One, St Ninian's Close, and without switching on the hall lights, she tiptoed quietly upstairs to her little sanctuary. As she climbed, she caught sight of herself in the landing mirror. Stopping, she steadied herself in front of it, peering closely at her reflection. She could just make out her wide, piercing eyes framed by the wild waves of her hair and a dark mulberry juice stain spreading across her lips like a bruise.

Before Kelsey fell asleep that night, she hurriedly wrote her postcards, telling her mum and grandad what a great time she was having, how hot the weather had been, and how tomorrow she'd guide her very first tour group under Will's supervision, making no mention of the strange, strained feelings she now had about her colleague. He intrigued and overwhelmed her with his acerbic aristo-cratic manner, his beautiful face, his sudden flashes of disarming humour, and the way he obviously revelled in the challenge of seducing the new girl.

She saved Fran's postcard until last. What would she write? Suddenly, feeling all the heightened emotions of the intoxicating evening coming to a head, sobs shook her as she rehearsed aloud, 'I'm sorry we weren't happier. I really did love you. I *do* love you. I think we just grew apart.'

But the pen would not move in her hand. Instead, she let it fall onto the bed and she glanced around for her phone. She was ashamed to admit to herself that relief flooded her body as she found no new messages. *Maybe Fran's given up trying to contact me? Maybe he'll never message again? Or maybe he's still coming to terms with the shock of finding himself abandoned by his so-called girlfriend for an entire summer and he'll be in touch in his own good time? He did say at the station he'd see me in September, didn't he? Maybe he's taking some time out and hoping we'll reconnect in the autumn?*

'What a mess,' she sniffed with a hopeless shrug, but nothing could persuade her fingers to scroll for Fran's name and ring him.

She couldn't shake the lonely realisation that she'd lost him somewhere long before she'd even heard of the Norma Arden Tour Agency. The dark feelings crowded in, stifling her in the warm, airless bedsit; the heaviness of her solitude and friendlessness so far from all that was familiar, the sadness of having no one special of her own to confide in, to share in all of life's mountainous challenges and little victories. Had she ever done that with Fran? Maybe in the beginning.

Something had needed to change, she knew. But Fran was right, running off to Stratford was just forestalling the inevitable: her return to Scotland, jobless and broke with no plans for her future, and maybe now she wouldn't even have a boyfriend waiting for her.

What am I doing? I could have stayed at home and let Fran support me like he wanted to until I found a proper job. Or I could have gone to college and trained to do something else? Bugger it, I should have taken that internship! Talk about looking a gift horse in the mouth. Some lucky girl's got that job now and in a few months she'll be trained up for the job market and I'll be nowhere at all.

Fran's postcard lay unwritten on the bed as Kelsey lay awake until the sun rose again, glad she had no neighbours to waken with her sobbing.

Chapter Seventeen

'Live a little; comfort a little; cheer thyself a little'
(As You Like It)

Will was waiting for her in their usual spot. Kelsey grimaced as she made her approach, hoping he couldn't see how exhausted and pale she was after her sleepless night, but mostly just embarrassed about how the pub crawl had ended. He'd really gone out on a limb last night and he probably wasn't used to girls rejecting him. *Thank God I didn't snog him. If I'd had more to drink I probably would've. Imagine getting caught kissing a colleague at work. What if Valeria or Myrtle had seen us? Is this the midsummer madness Norma warned me about?*

She had no idea what to expect from Will this morning, but she needn't have worried. Greeting her with his usual winning smile he held out two very virtuous-looking smoothies, one pink and one green.

'Morning, Sleeping Beauty, what time do you call this? OK, pick one!'

Kelsey glanced at the clock on her phone. 'I'm exactly on time, cheeky! I'll have the pink one please. *What* is that?'

'Avocado, green apple, and kale, I think. I should have got two strawberry and banana, huh?'

And, with that, they were back to how it had been before all the cider, mulberries, and moonlight, as though nothing had happened.

Thank God! He doesn't remember. Maybe he was drunk? Though I didn't see him touch a drop all night. Maybe he's just saving face? Fine by me. I've got enough to think about today.

And so they got on with their morning tour, Will taking a step back, letting Kelsey introduce herself and check everyone's names off the list before guiding them through the church and into the centre of the old town, her weariness of the long sleepless night before falling away as the adrenalin kicked in.

Kelsey discovered today's group were Texans and mainly retired couples or parents with adult children taking the trip of a lifetime around Europe at a baffling pace. They'd 'done' Scandinavia and Germany and had just flown in from Paris to London, spending the previous evening seeing a show in the West End, before piling onto their coach for a morning in Stratford. By bedtime they'd be in the Cotswolds, exhausted and bewildered, unsure of what they'd seen or where they'd seen it.

Kelsey felt a little sorry for them as they listened politely to her wavering voice. She was sure they could see her hands shaking as she gesticulated wildly to cover up her nerves. Will kept a close eye on her from the back of the crowd, smiling encouragingly behind dark sunglasses, arms folded, nodding his approval.

'And… and…' *You can do this, come on, Kelse.* 'And over here is the home of Stratford-upon-Avon's *second* most famous writer.' *Am I turning blue? I can't breathe.* 'In the late Victorian era she was as famous as, say, Charles Dickens, but today she is unfairly forgotten. I'm referring to Miss Marie Corelli. She penned over twenty sensational, romantic novels and was known as not only a great teller of tales, but rather eccentric.' *They're actually listening to me. I'm really doing this!*

Hearing her own voice settling down into its normal rhythms as she relaxed into her first ever tour, Kelsey pressed on.

'Corelli imported her very own Venetian gondola to Stratford and, punted by her gondolier Ernest, caused quite a stir on the River Avon. Let's step inside her home and take a look around.' *They're really doing what I tell them. Oh my God, this is actually fun.*

Three hours later, exhausted and elated, Kelsey waved the tourists off on their coach. Will placed a friendly arm around her shoulders – or perhaps she just chose to interpret it as friendly – and let her know how she'd done.

'You had them in the palm of your hands. You don't need me at all now, Kelsey Anderson. Good for you. I think they all loved your sexy accent too. Come on, let's grab some lunch with the others.'

She was met with a cheer as they stepped aboard the ticket barge. Gianfranco, Lukas, Myrtle, and Valeria were waiting with a hamper of sandwiches and flasks of scalding tea.

With that, Kelsey was a *bona fide* tour guide for the Norma Arden Historic Tours Agency. Her summer in Stratford was finally truly underway.

★

Over the coming days Kelsey fell into her new routine of waking early and heading straight up to the roof terrace with coffee and her duvet to keep out the morning cool. She'd head into town and swim a few lengths at the indoor pool before dressing for work, stopping to feed the swans on her way. She had the uniform cracked too, wearing a vest top under the shirt which she wore untucked and tied in a knot at her waist and, everyone agreed, it was just too hot for the gilet. She improvised each day with the scarf, sometimes knotting it around a high ponytail *a la* Sandy Dee in *Grease* or bundling her hair up into it like a wartime land girl or Rosie the Riveter, or occasionally going the full air hostess by tying it in a knot at her throat.

As she led her tour groups all over town, she felt herself becoming more confident when describing its landmarks. Will was now off with his own groups but she still managed to meet one or two of the guides in various combinations each day for lunch. She'd even had a stint selling tickets on the barge with Gianfranco who, she learned, was very sweet and interesting once he got over his initial shyness, if only she could tune into his whispered conversation.

The daily workings of the town, she discovered, formed a sharp contrast with the picture-postcard place of her teenage romanticising. She nurtured an increasing awareness of the everyday routines of the town's school kids, shop workers, and B&B owners, all bustling here and there alongside the hundreds of other people – invisible to the visitors passing through – who maintained the life of the theatres and playing houses. She was getting to know a few of them, too. Some recognised the agency uniform and would wave to her in passing, or stop to exchange small talk and theatre gossip, a pleasing confirmation that her new job rendered her a privileged insider in the town's theatrical life.

She was one of the people keeping the tourists entertained, alongside the costume designers, seamstresses, scene painters, lighting technicians, sound engineers, stage riggers, make-up artists, voice coaches, and the many, many actors observing their own rituals of rehearsals, matinees, and the brief afternoon respite before the evening performances, all working together to bring in the crowds, make them laugh and weep, making it all look so effortlessly easy. The vanilla 99s and cream teas for the visitors were just the icing on the cake – superficial, albeit sweet.

Kelsey was falling in love all over again with Stratford-upon-Avon, but this was something deeper – she really knew the place now, this was her home, and it was a romance she would never get over.

At night she'd buy fish and chips or something quick and easy for the microwave and eat up on the roof, tired of listening to her own loud authoritative tour-guide voice all day and content to be alone. Up there on her peaceful twilit terrace, she found she wasn't always thinking of Fran, or of Will, for that matter. For the first time in her life, she had no one to please but herself.

Will continued to be his usual dazzling, flirty self, of course, and Kelsey humoured him, reminding herself that although he *was* lovely to look at and dynamic to be around, he really did know it. She had a sneaking suspicion that the mulberry tree incident wasn't going to be his last attempt at seduction. He seemed to like a challenge.

She'd caught him eying her phone when Jonathan texted during their shared lunch break on Friday, a week after she had almost kissed Will in the garden. Kelsey was smiling to herself as she read.

It was great bumping into you last week ;) Hope you're still free Saturday for head shots. I reserved free tickets to 'Dream' for you and a friend, Jonathan Hathaway.

Glancing at Will beside her, Kelsey couldn't mistake the indignant look on his face but he didn't say anything, or if he did, she was too absorbed in her thoughts to hear it.

Jonathan Hathaway. So that's his name. It suits him. No kiss, I notice. Would that be weird: putting a kiss at the end of a text like that? I suppose we are only arranging a work thing.

She texted straight back, with Will observing over her shoulder, catching every word she typed.

Hi Jonathan, it was lovely to meet you too. See you tomorrow. Thanks so much for the tickets. Lucky me. Kelsey (Anderson btw).

Chapter Eighteen

'This bud of love by summer's ripening breath,
may prove a beauteous flower when next we meet'
(Romeo and Juliet)

Saturday came, Kelsey's tenth day in Stratford, and with
it the blazing sun and the close, humid suggestion of an
approaching storm. *Just my luck, rainclouds coming in on my
first proper day off.* Packing her umbrella just in case, and
double-checking she had plenty batteries for the camera's
flash unit, Kelsey nervously readied herself for the photo
shoot ahead. Today she took a little longer over drying
her hair so it hung in thick, silky waves down her back.
Running her hands over her hips in her sunflower print
dress, she enjoyed feeling feminine and cool after endless
days sweltering in work gear.

*This is it, my first ever photo shoot, and I'm going to enjoy
it.*

Arriving right on time at the Willow Studio, a modern
brick and smoked-glass building, slightly out of place on
the ancient street, Kelsey adjusted the camera bag across
her body and reached for the doorbell. All morning she'd
been trying to recall what the tall American looked like
but couldn't quite conjure him up, apart from the indelible

impression of a beautiful smile and his strong, calming presence.

The door pulled open no sooner than she had pressed the buzzer revealing Jonathan smiling with what looked like relief. He swept a low hand of welcome beckoning her inside with a, 'Hey there! Great to see you again.'

Squeezing past him, Kelsey caught his cool, clean scent, like washing powder and minty chewing gum.

'Where should I set up?' she enquired breezily, trying to sound calm and professional even though her mouth was dry with nerves.

'I asked the engineer to leave the stage lights up for us. Do you want to start there? It's a bit of a rabbit warren and you get to the stage through the dressing room.' He pointed her down the corridor, past the box-office hatch and the theatre bar. She passed through the dressing room door that he held open for her.

'Wow, this is just how I'd have imagined it.' She glanced around at the mirrors circled with white light bulbs and the organised chaos of assorted wigs and costumes hanging on rails. She took in the ass's head with its long ears that poor Bottom the Weaver would end up wearing under Titania's enchantment, and the pots of heavy stage make-up, sponges, brushes, and pins messily arranged on the dressing tables where Jonathan would sit each night preparing for the show. 'Except it doesn't say "star" on the back of your chair.'

'Not yet it doesn't. One day maybe,' Jonathan was laughing as he led her through the mess. 'Stage is this way.'

As she passed, she cast an eye over Jonathan's dressing table and the stacked dog-eared books, notepads, and stubby pencils. To their right were vases of long-stemmed red roses and the icy spikes of a tall silver crown on a dummy-head.

'It must be nice getting flowers sent to the stage door.'

Jonathan turned for a second. 'Those are Peony's, I never get flowers opening week, except from my mom, but Peony seems to pick up admirers wherever she goes.'

Kelsey cocked her head, scrutinising him for hints of jealousy, but he was simply smiling.

'Wait there a second, I'll clear some of this junk,' he told her, passing through a curtain with a sign above it marked 'Auditorium.'

Jonathan reappeared a few seconds later, his arms filled with bundled sheets and a tray of white paint and a roller brush. 'Nearly done.' He passed through the curtain again.

Kelsey glanced back at the dressing tables. Peony's mirror was surrounded with photographs of her with the rest of the cast, all grinning and playing up for the camera. Her heart stilled a little as she spotted the close-up picture of Jonathan planting a kiss on Peony's cheek, his eyes screwed tightly closed. The photo was crumpled and torn round the edges, obviously an old, treasured item that had adorned many a dressing room of Peony's. Kelsey's heart sank but she couldn't drag her eyes from it. They looked so happy, and that happiness somehow cancelled out a little of Kelsey's new-found contentment.

She heard the scrape of furniture behind the curtain and called out to ask if Jonathan needed any help.

'Just a second,' he reassured her.

The jutting edge of Kelsey's camera bag caught some cards on a low shelf, knocking them to the floor. She stooped to gather them up and looked at the images on the front, all wishing the actors luck and broken legs. One of

153

them however, sported a cartoon picture of two jars; one a grinning peanut butter, the other a bashful, blushing pink jelly. Kelsey flipped it open.

Here's to another triumphant season for PB and J.
Love you forever x

Kelsey shrugged. Some actors' in-joke, she guessed, and replaced the cards. At that moment Jonathan reached a hand through the curtain, followed by his grinning face. 'Ready?'

She nodded, taking his hand and ascending the steps into the cramped backstage area just beyond the curtain, cluttered with various bits of scenery and props. Her nose prickled with the smell of fresh paint and the dust burning on the spotlights. Just beyond the mess, she was greeted by a sight that took her breath away.

The house lights were down, the stalls in darkness, but the stage was glowing with coloured light in a dappled, leafy effect. A night-time woodland landscape painted on thin chiffon was draped across the back wall, and centre stage stood an old-fashioned garden swing seat, just big enough for two, swathed in billowing white material and forest flowers.

'Wow!' Kelsey exclaimed, lowering her camera bag to her side.

'Neat, isn't it? It's Titania's fairy bower where she seduces poor old Bottom the Weaver?' Kelsey remembered the lovely lilting lift at the end of his sentences and knew he wasn't asking her if she knew who Bottom was.

The auditorium was empty and silent except for Jonathan's deep drawling voice, even deeper than she remembered.

'Speaking of Titania, isn't Peony joining us?' Kelsey asked, hopeful he would say 'no'.

'Peony? No, she's doing her final costume fitting.'

Kelsey made her way across the stage and down the steps into the stalls. Turning round she gazed in wonder at the bright stage and Jonathan at its centre, resplendent in the light. She couldn't help thinking how handsome he was in his dark jeans over black baseball boots and the untucked white shirt that was crumpled where he'd pushed up the sleeves. His bed-head hair was mussed up but he was cleanly shaven, showing off his strong square jaw.

'This light is lovely,' she cooed, tearing her eyes from him, a little dazed. 'So, um… when's your opening night?'

'Monday,' he replied, sitting down on the bower seat, making it swing a little. 'I'm beginning to get the jitters.'

'Monday? That's Midsummer, isn't it? Was that intentional?'

Jonathan shrugged with a 'no idea' gesture.

Her eyes lit up as she remembered a tale she'd heard recently. 'I was reading somewhere that if you make a wish on Midsummer's night it's supposed to come true before the year's out.'

'You don't say? Then I'm going to make a wish just before I go on stage that I won't blank and forget my lines all season.'

Kelsey recognised the thrill of nervousness pass through his body in spite of his smile.

'You'll be perfect, I'm sure you will,' she said soothingly. 'The stage is set… do you feel ready for opening night?'

'I will, come Monday. Once I'm up here, actually doing it. I just suffer from first night nerves.'

'It shows you care about doing a good job, doesn't it?' Crouching down, Kelsey unpacked her camera. 'You know, I was nervous coming to meet you today? I really want to get some perfect shots for you.'

'Well, I'm ready when you are. What do you want me to do?'

Feeling instantly calmer as she raised the camera to her eye, she was back in her favourite place, behind the lens. 'Do you mind sitting on the edge of the stage for me?'

She watched as he lifted his long, agile body down onto the boards of the stage. 'That's it, just swing your legs over the side. OK, that's better.' Kelsey approached the stage coming to stand just a few inches from his spread knees.

Gazing through the lens gave her the luxury of really being able to drink him in: his skin, his parted lips, and his broad torso. He planted his palms flat on the stage behind him supporting his weight as he leaned back a little, relaxing his shoulders, lean and muscular under his shirt. Jonathan looked straight down the lens.

'OK. These are true head shots. They'll be very sharp and expressive. Oh, and this is a black and white film, so they'll be really classic-looking with lots of contrast between the light on your face and the darker stage behind you.'

To prepare for each shot, Kelsey turned the focussing ring on the long lens, bringing Jonathan's features into crystal clarity. Without a tripod to steady the camera she took a series of long slow breaths, letting the last breath out very slowly, bringing down her heart rate and stopping her hands shaking before she pressed the shutter button.

The flash fired brightly, illuminating Jonathan's face for a split second as the handsome vision in Kelsey's viewfinder seared itself in chemical reaction onto the exposed film.

'These will be beautiful,' she said, transfixed. Kelsey was getting absorbed in the camera work, thinking about the light and shutter speed, the aperture, and the intensity of the flash. Keeping her eye to the camera she made the most of Jonathan's intense, brooding expression. His pupils were dilated and his pale blue-grey irises shone, reflecting a billion light particles. Firing shot after shot, she didn't ever want to stop. This felt like bliss. Winding the film on, she felt the familiar stubborn pull of the end of the roll.

'Thirty-six shots already? That went fast. I need to change rolls, but I'm pretty sure we got it.'

Changing the film did nothing to break the strange, dreamy feeling of the shoot. Seemingly dazed too, Jonathan lowered his body off the stage, coming to a stop in front of her.

'That was incredible,' he said, running a hand through his hair, his eyes still fixed intensely on Kelsey as his pale lips curled into a hazy smile, revealing the tips of his perfect teeth.

'I know,' she said in wonder, looking up at his face.

'Thanks so much for doing this, it's so nice of you. How do I pay you?' His voice was slow and sleepy as he spoke.

'*Pay* me? Tickets to your play are more than enough payment, and it's not like this is my job or anything.' She laughed lightly, her own pupils dilating as she felt Jonathan's shirt sleeve brush her arm.

'Let me take you to dinner then?' He was smiling with genuine warmth, showing a tiny indentation on his chin which she hadn't noticed before, just a hint of a dimple which softened his defined bone structure. A strong impulse overcame her. Stepping forward onto her tiptoes she tentatively raised her hand to the tiny hollow spot.

'I love this little dimple.'

Jonathan was grinning now, raising his fingertips to join Kelsey's below his lips before reaching out and stroking her cheeks. 'You have some too you know, here and here.'

His butterfly light touch stirred her breath. She felt the tiny hairs on her skin lifting and had to strive hard to form words through the electricity connecting them.

He spoke on in a low drawl. 'Shakespeare said that dimples were a sign of where Cupid had placed a kiss on a newborn baby so he'd always have somewhere safe to curl up and sleep. I reckon it was Shakespeare, anyway. I've forgotten.'

Jonathan's eyes settled on her lips, his brow contracting, suddenly serious. Sweeping his fingertips under her chin he raised her mouth to his. Kelsey closed her eyes for the kiss.

But instead of the promised slow, languorous connection, she felt Jonathan jerk back as the lights in the auditorium suddenly flared up, drowning them in glaring white light, leaving them squinting and shading their eyes with their hands. Kelsey's heart sank as she heard the voice over the speakers.

'Jonny. You're wanted in the technician's booth.'

It was Peony. Jonathan chewed his lip in what looked like stern frustration. Kelsey strained her eyes against the dazzling lights coming from the back of the stalls. There was Jonathan's co-star, all dressed in her white gossamer stage costume and looking like an angel – well, a *livid* angel – standing behind glass in the booth, leaning over a microphone with her balled fists pressed into her hips.

'I guess I shouldn't keep her waiting.' He still had his fingertips extended out, resting on Kelsey's arm, but the harsh lights and annoyance in Peony's voice had short-circuited the connection between them. He took a lingering look across Kelsey's face and neck, shaking his head slowly in frustration.

'I'd better go… I'll see you at the show, I hope? Just let the box office know which performance you want to come to.'

Kelsey nodded, putting the film in its canister.

'I'll get these developed right away and send you the proofs. It might be a week or two.'

'Jon, I'm waiting,' Peony announced again.

Jonathan hastily showed Kelsey out into the street. The clouds must have closed in over Stratford while they'd been absorbed with one another in the studio. The sky was dark and the intense heat of the approaching storm hung in the air.

'I'm so sorry. She can be one serious prima donna, but I guess we *do* still have a lot of work to do before we open. I'll talk to you soon, yeah?' There was apologetic regret in his voice, and something else. Guilt? If so, was it guilt for cutting short the shoot, or for letting himself get wrapped up in it and almost kissing her?

'Sure. See you,' Kelsey said, bewildered, as he closed the door upon her.

Turning to walk away, her whole body sang with the thrill of the unsatisfied tension between them and the memory of his eyes fixed upon hers. As she walked home, searching through her contacts on her phone, she clicked 'call' and, getting no answer, left a desperate voicemail.

'OK, Mirren! You have *got* to get here soon. This place is enough to make a girl mad! Seriously, get your train tickets.'

As she turned the key in the lock at Number One, St Ninian's Close, the clouds let their heavy burden fall. Huge raindrops plashed onto the dusty tarmac, forming dark spots. They grew heavier and heavier until the earth heaved a slow sigh, cooling off after the raging heat of early summer.

Closing the door behind her, Kelsey took a last look at the pouring rain, listening to the thunder rumbling in the distance, making the earth shake as if it were about to be rent apart. An electric pulse of desire shook her body at the memory of Jonathan's fingertips on her skin. She had never experienced anything like it, not with Fran, not with anyone. But the feeling was tainted with restraint.

She had no intention of coming between Peony and Jonathan, just as she had no intention of sharing a man with anyone. Whatever was going on there, they had their own stuff to work through and it would be easier on Jonathan if Kelsey was out of the picture. She obviously got under Peony's skin, and no wonder; there was an undeniable magnetism between Kelsey and Jonathan, something chemical, something magical.

★

Back in the darkened theatre, Peony sat in the empty stalls. Jonathan was nowhere to be seen, and she was crying inconsolably, hugging her knees to her chest, her heart breaking.

The lightning storm fractured the skies above Stratford as life in the busy town paused momentarily for the downpour.

Chapter Nineteen

'The storm is up, and all is on the hazard'
(Julius Caesar)

The rain poured in torrents over the next few days. Tour groups were cancelling at the last minute leaving Kelsey at a loose end on dark, dreary days. Taking the opportunity to FaceTime her mum, catching her between appointments one morning, Kelsey's heart swelled to see her face.

'How have you been, sweetheart?' Mari asked.

'Great, thanks. There's so much going on. I'm getting the hang of the tours now, and I got my first pay packet which is always nice. And, I, um… I did a photo shoot at the weekend, for one of the actors.'

'Kelsey, that's wonderful! Good for you. Who's the actor? Anyone famous? Was it that Kenneth Branagh? I like him!'

'You won't know him, he's a theatre actor in an American touring company.'

'And is he still in town?'

Kelsey detected the change in tone, the hint of teasing in her mum's voice and the sparkle in her eye. 'Yup, they're here all summer for the big festival of plays.'

'That's nice. And have you, um… spoken to Francis at all?'

Kelsey swallowed. 'Not yet. He texted, but when I rang him back, he didn't pick up.' She knew this sounded feeble and that she could have tried much harder to get in contact.

'I'm sure you'll reach each other, eventually. It's been a fortnight since you left, love. The summer's flying in, isn't it?'

Kelsey let this pass with a silent nod and a twinge of burning anxiety. She knew what her mum was getting at. She owed Fran a call.

'So are you doing any more photo shoots? Or… meeting your actor friend again, what was his name?'

'Jonathan. I doubt it. He'll be busy.' *With his girlfriend.*

Kelsey thought it best to change the subject at that point. She didn't want her mum worrying that she was already mixed up with some new bloke when she didn't have the courage to even talk to Fran. It was easier to chat about the weather, and all the sci-fi conventions Calum was planning to drag Mari to over the summer.

'Make sure you take every opportunity to enjoy yourself, sweetheart, that's what I'd be doing if I were you,' Mari said before they ended the chat.

The familiarity of her mum's placid, cheerful face helped comfort her as the rain pounded down on the pavements outside, and she resolved not to waste these unexpected days off, no matter the weather. Mari was right; there were still adventures to be had.

Taking her umbrella and camera with her she followed the canals as far as she felt safe into the lush, overblown greenery of the surrounding countryside, and sat in cafés for hours at a time, working her way through overpriced cappuccinos. She'd finished reading *A Midsummer Night's Dream*, adoring its strange plot in which the fairy folk trick and confuse the hapless mortals in the wood. Finding herself hooked on Shakespeare's comedies, she'd spent hours in the antiquarian bookshop looking for her next play, at last picking *Love's Labour's Lost* from the shelves. To her delight, she found it was about a bunch of flashy, clever blokes who virtuously swear off women to concentrate on their studies, only to be thrown among some seriously tempting ladies. The plot made her laugh, the poetry made her sigh, and it helped pass the rainy hours.

Meeting up with the other guides for lunch or a drizzling stroll around the marina, Kelsey became aware of Will's conspicuous absence. The whispered gossip from Gianfranco was that he'd gone down to London for a big acting audition and he didn't want any of the other guides to know, which instantly piqued Kelsey's interest. *Just how important is this role exactly?* Gianfranco had grinned mischievously as he passed on the news and Kelsey wondered how long it would remain a secret. She hadn't had sweet, quiet Gianfranco down as a lover of gossip. *It's always the quiet ones*, she mused, taking a mental note not to tell Gianfranco anything about Will's flirting with her in case the details made their way around the agency.

Will's absence didn't bother Kelsey too much, but there was something dragging her down; a strange, unsettled feeling ever since the photo shoot. She reluctantly admitted to herself she was scanning the streets hoping for a glimpse of the tall, handsome American who'd made her feel so interesting and capable and talented. He was ensconced at the studio, of course, with Peony.

How can you miss someone you barely know? That's ridiculous, right?

There was nothing else for it but to order yet another muffin, swallow down the sad feelings, turn another page of her play, and try to distract herself.

Fran still hadn't been in touch and she found herself wondering where he was and what he was doing. Was he busy networking at the teachers' conference, finally getting recognition for being the ambitious, hardworking man that he was? She missed him, but mostly, she hoped he was happy and not missing her too much.

Making the most of her agency discount, she splashed out, buying tickets for all the plays running in the main houses, seeing the evening performances back to back over the course of the long, wet week, loving every second of them.

There was the jealous and brooding Othello taking poor, innocent Desdemona's life. Kelsey had inwardly raged at the stupidity of the man and the vindictiveness of Iago who'd told him Desdemona was a cheat. It had been nearly impossible to sit still. She'd wanted to shout out, 'Don't be a twat, Othello, she clearly loves you! That Iago's a spineless prick, don't listen to him.' But she sat there fidgeting and getting cross instead.

Then there'd been a smart and sassy Cleopatra, played by a megastar of 1970s TV, who still very much 'had it' in her late sixties. It was easy to believe she could seduce bluff, brazen Antony. Kelsey was held, transfixed, by the passion and the all-or-nothing commitment of Cleopatra's love. Then there had been an exhilarating *Hamlet* and a weird, other-worldly *King Lear,* and a sparklingly light *Twelfth Night.*

During these brief interludes in the theatre, Kelsey forgot herself – forgot Fran, Will, and Jonathan too – she was transported to other times in other worlds. But afterwards, as she stepped out of the glamourous playhouses into the drizzling darkness, real life closed in on her again, and it came back in waves – memories of Jonathan's gestures, or his scent or something he'd said.

She'd been tempted to text him, but what would she say? She'd done the shoot now, his pictures would be arriving soon. What else was there? Peony had very publicly staked her claim to him and they were obviously more than just fellow actors in the same company. She remembered with some pain the photograph of Jonathan kissing Peony that she'd seen in their intimate little dressing room. Her thoughts careered down and down in free fall.

They're obviously together. They must be. If not, she has quite some hold over him. Is she his ex, maybe? I can't very well ask him, can I? I'd look ridiculous. He hired me for my photographs, I took them, now he's disappeared into his cloistered little theatre world and I'm not part of it.

Torturing herself, she imagined the two of them up on stage in the pretty fairy bower on their opening night wrapped in each other's arms, reciting beautiful poetry, Peony looking stunning in *that* costume. *And they'll be doing this every day, two shows a day. Of course they're together. How could I be so stupid?*

And so, on a drizzling Midsummer's night, after that first rainy weekend spent struggling with herself, she resolved to begin the slow process of accepting that

Jonathan was just a friend – not even that, an acquaintance, if anything. Telling herself that she'd imagined their intense connection – it had been the build-up of the electrical storm in the air or her hormones and missing Fran at home, or Will and his damned mulberries – she buried her feelings deep.

Examining her features in the landing mirror on that rainy summer solstice, she gave herself a pep talk. 'Whatever was going on in that studio, you've got to get your head back in the game. This is supposed to be your summer of enlightenment. This is your *Eat, Pray, Love* summer – but without the effort of all the yoga and meditation stuff, or the dysentery risk.' She practised a breezy smile and watched her reflection as the forced grin fell. 'But how I wish, I *wish*, Jonathan Hathaway was mine.'

★

As the early July days progressed and the rain clouds rolled away from the Welcombe hills (she'd discovered that this was what the hills in the near distance were called), tour guide life resumed as before. Will had come back from London in a foul mood and was keeping a low profile. Sure enough, word had spread among the guides, but no one dared ask him how his audition had gone, it was all too obvious, and they weren't supposed to know, anyway. The sun shone again and Kelsey's rota seemed relentlessly busy.

It was getting on for a fortnight since the shoot that had ended so abruptly and awkwardly, when two things happened to disturb Kelsey's usually quiet and very early breakfast.

The first was a text from Mirren.

See you next Saturday. Train arrives in SUA just before 2pm. You've got me till Monday morning. M, xxx p.s. Can we top and tail? Can't get a room in town for love or money.

Just as Kelsey was coming up with ideas for things they might do together – get out of town into the Cotswolds, maybe – she heard the postie dropping the mail through the letter box. The heavy slap of a large parcel falling onto the doormat reverberated in the tiled hallway and up the stairs. She knew exactly what it was: the proofs from the shoot, along with other photographs she'd taken around Stratford, fresh from the developers. Abandoning her breakfast, she rushed downstairs.

The pictures were better than she had anticipated, even with her handsome subject. The light wasn't too harsh or too soft on Jonathan's perfect features, the contrast between dark and light wasn't too severe, and, apart from one dodgy one, they were all in perfect focus. The pride swelled in her chest as she pored over the photographs spread out over her bed. There was no denying it; looking at his face replicated over and over again in velvety monochrome and remembering the intensity of that hour in the studio theatre, she knew for sure she couldn't help falling for him, and hard.

If I hurry I can get these to him before work.

Forty minutes later she was at the door to the Willow Studio which was wide open. An A-frame sign stood by the steps with a poster pasted to it. It read, *A Midsummer Night's Dream by the Oklahoma Renaissance Players. Performances 2pm and 7pm. Box Office Open.* There was a picture of Bottom the Weaver beguiled and confused in his ass's ears reclining in Titania's arms. Peony was, of course, utterly gorgeous and ethereal in her white gossamer fairy costume and crown. Kelsey swallowed hard, trying to ignore the sudden guilt.

I'm not here to steal her man. I'm here to complete my assignment. Head shots delivered. Done and dusted. That's all. Oh, I hope he's here!

The lady at the box office shook her head. 'Sorry, love, he doesn't usually arrive until after lunch. Can I give him a message?'

'Tell him Kelsey, I mean the photographer, dropped by with his new head shots, please. Oh, and he left two tickets here for me, they're comps.'

Kelsey handed over the precious photographs. There was a code inside so Jonathan could log into the developer's website and order as many high-resolution copies of the digitised images as he liked. Kelsey had kept nothing but the negatives. As the photographer they belonged to her. They meant she would never lose this lovely man completely. He'd always be in her possession, in mirror reverse images on sleek transparent plastic where all that is dark appears bright.

Chapter Twenty

'The very instant that I saw you did my heart fly to
    your service'
(The Tempest)

'So, ladies and gentlemen, I hope you enjoyed your tour
today. Have a safe journey on to Heathrow and enjoy the
Netherlands.'

The elderly tourists were slowly clambering aboard
their coach looking forward to a long air-conditioned
snooze. Kelsey still held aloft the long-stemmed plastic
sunflower she had bought to replace the agency's standard-
issue golfing umbrella. It worked like a charm to keep her
groups together as they made their way between beauty
spots and historical wonders.

She had come to learn that the North American visitors enjoying their last day in the British Isles were the
most generous tippers, passing on unspent sterling to their
friendly, knowledgeable tour guides. Accepting the notes
with a gracious 'thank you', she'd slip them inside the
pages of her *Sonnets* – she'd taken to reciting poetry at
important sites in the town just as Will had shown her.
Later, at home, she'd gasp as she opened the book to reveal
crisp bundles of tens and twenties.

Just as today's last tour group were safely stowed on their bus, Kelsey's phone rang in her pocket.

'Hey, it's Jonathan Hathaway.'

As if he needs to tell me his full name. 'Hi, how are you?' *Be cool. Be cool.*

'I'm good. I just picked up your shots from the box office. Man, they are incredible!'

'Well, I had a pretty good subject.' *Nice one, Kelse.* 'Hey, how was opening night?' *That's good: friendly, not desperate... or besotted.*

'Awesome. But I was real nervous, I threw up before I went onstage. I... uh... don't know why I told you that,' he laughed. 'I was kinda hoping to see you in the audience. Did you get your tickets?'

'Uh-huh, picked them up yesterday, thanks. I'm bringing my friend Mirren on Saturday night. I can't wait.'

'I promise I'll try extra hard to be good on Saturday.'

She could tell he was smiling. He sounded as sweet and genuine as she remembered him being at the theatre.

'We never did get that dinner, you know? Come meet me Friday?' he urged gently. 'There's no evening performance this Friday. The director's doing an onstage Q and A schmoozing thing with the press instead that night.'

Kelsey's resolve to stay away from the Jonathan-Peony thing, whatever the hell it was, wavered as he drawled on with his sweet questioning inflection.

'Well... OK. But you know Friday's the Bard Crawl. I'll still be working, technically. Why don't you bring Peony along too?' *I'd better get my reward in heaven for this.* 'It would be nice to get to know her better.' *No it wouldn't, no it wouldn't, and NO it wouldn't.*

'Uh, I guess I could ask her?'

'Shall we say four? I'll be done with my second tour by then. Meet me at the Yorick? We could have a quick bite then go on the crawl?' *What am I doing? This is so stupid.*

'OK. The four o'clock early bird special at the Yorick it is! I'm already in love with their scampi and fries. OK, uh… OK. Bye, Kelsey.' And he was gone.

She hung up, sighing loudly and letting her shoulders fall. 'Bring Peony? Get to know her better? Ugh!' She sloped homewards, muttering under her breath, 'You are a sick, sick glutton for punishment, Kelsey Anderson. A cosy dinner for three with Peony and her evil-eye curse? You idiot!'

★

Friday rolled around slowly and Kelsey began to feel resigned to her friend-zone fate as she walked towards the pub. She'd done the decent thing and invited Jonathan for some platonic pub grub and extended the invitation to include Peony, just as she should. *She is, after all, Jonathan's girlfriend. Please don't let him kiss her in front of me.*

Making her way inside the cool airy pub and finding it almost empty, Kelsey ordered half a pint of the special guest ale, Drop of Mandragora, thinking how much she liked the name. She settled herself inside the cavernous inglenook fireplace, pulling one of the scatter cushions up across her tummy and sipping the amber-coloured ale. It tasted sweet, spiced, and autumnal.

I won't drink after this one, I don't want to make a fool of myself in front of Peony, or worse, make her feel any more threatened than she already does. Yup… this is fun; meeting two new friends for friendly drinks and then I'll go home alone and hurl myself off the roof terrace.

Before she could descend into further fits of anxiety, the bar door swung open and in walked Jonathan with the air of someone who'd been rushing but didn't want anyone to know. His cheeks looked flushed and he was a little out of breath. Kelsey looked past him, expecting Peony to follow behind, but there was no sign of her, or her thundercloud.

'Kelsey! Hi.' He strode across the bar room towards her, smiling broadly, making her heart thump hard in response. In one sweeping natural movement he stooped and pressed his lips against her cheek, sending her mind reeling. She told herself dismissively that this was just his bluff American friendliness, but it felt like so much more.

'I'd forgotten you were so tall. I mean… it's nice to see you again.' Kelsey fiddled with the beer mat. *And he smells so good. Is he blushing? Damnit! Stop being so flaming lovely, this is hard enough.*

He enquired how she was with an earnestness in his voice that she wasn't used to.

'Umm, I'm good,' she answered distractedly, looking past him again towards the door. 'Is Peony coming along later?'

'Uh, no. She's giving an interview to a newspaper then she's onstage for the director's Q and A thing. And anyway, I didn't invite her, sorry. I know you wanted to meet her, but I… I wanted it to be just the two of us.'

Kelsey took a long drink of her beer and watched him as he gesticulated towards the bar.

'Can I get you another drink? What is that?'

'Drop of Mandragora, it's the guest ale.'

Jonathan grimaced. 'I don't *love* English ale, but I'll drink it for the *Midsummer Night's Dream* reference.

Mandragora is in Titania's love potion,' he told her as he walked over to the bar.

Kelsey knew that, of course, but she simply smiled. Within moments he was back at the little cosy table under the towering chimneys and dried hop garlands. He placed another half-pint of the ruddy-golden ale in front of Kelsey, raising his own glass. 'Cheers?' His pale eyes gleamed in the afternoon light.

All that mental preparation for a cosy dinner à trois and here I am alone with this beautiful human being, and he is totally off the menu. What kind of sick joke are the gods playing?

Jonathan looked into her eyes. 'Kelsey, are you OK? You're very pale, if you don't mind me saying. Do you want me to take you home?'

With a splutter, Kelsey dribbled her ale down her chin and onto her shirt. She'd have to come clean, but what would she say? *Jonathan, I've thought of nothing else but you since we met and I'm having a hard time stopping myself crawling over this table and ripping your shirt off? Hmm… Maybe not.*

'Jonathan, the thing is,' she faltered, mopping up the beer with a tissue and keeping her eyes focused on that task. 'The thing is, I don't know if Peony would like us having drinks together, especially if you haven't told her you're here with me. She doesn't seem to like me very much, and um…' Her voice tailed off into silence and embarrassment.

'Peony wouldn't like us drinking together? What do you mean? Oh! Kelsey… I'm not *with* Peony. Is that what you've been thinking? Oh my God.' He pronounced it 'gawd'.

Tiny flutterings of hope flapped like butterfly wings in the pit of Kelsey's stomach. 'What?' Suddenly close to tears, she fought to rein in her feelings. 'But Peony...'

A furrow formed between Jonathan's light eyes. He reached over the table, making contact at last, his cool fingertips trailing over the back of her hand in slow circles. 'But Peony is always there?' he offered, helping her out, his eyes heavy-lidded and soft.

'Yes, and she's... you know, a bit cross,' added Kelsey, looking down at their touching hands, too abashed to look up and see that he was smiling.

'Kelsey... no. No, we're not together. We were once, but that was when we were kids at performing arts school. Oh man, I'm so sorry you thought that. It's just... we've known each other all our lives. Back in Tulsa we lived on the same street. I was twenty-two when I joined the company, Peony signed up too and we've been touring together ever since, but that's all.'

'Really? Does she know that?' Kelsey narrowed her eyes doubtfully, making him laugh.

'I guess she can be a *little* possessive and, you know, maybe she does harbour some... residual feelings for me, but mostly, I think she's just lonely. She doesn't have any family back home. The company's her family now. And you know, we're under so much pressure to add more and more performances and we're both exhausted. She's right that we don't really have time for long photo shoots or to put our feet up. She's worried we'll look like amateurs in the reviews. And she's under so much more scrutiny than me, being an actress and all. I don't get half the negative crap in the press that she does. Once you get to know her, you'll love her too.'

Kelsey was nodding, searching his face. 'Poor Peony, I didn't know. I'm sorry, Jonathan. Can we start this over again? I've been acting crazy.'

'No you haven't. I can totally see why you'd think what you thought. I'm just sorry because I really...' Pausing, he took a shallow breath and Kelsey felt his fingers spreading over her hand. 'Because I really like you. I should have told you sooner, huh?' He laughed and shook his head. 'I'm such a doofus when it comes to this kind of thing.'

'Whereas I'm totally down with this kind of thing. Look at me, cool as a cucumber.'

The tension was broken and for a moment a new atmosphere settled over the pair in their cosy nook, something fresh and simple.

'What about you?' Jonathan asked hesitantly, looking down at Kelsey's hand enclosed within his own. 'Are you seeing anyone? Anyone special, I mean?'

Oh no, here it is. Full disclosure. Feeling as though she'd been yanked by the heartstrings kicking and screaming back to a place she didn't want to go, her cheeks reddened at the sudden recollection of Fran. Reluctantly, she drew her hands away from Jonathan's and cradled her glass.

'There *was* someone until pretty recently, and it was quite serious. But... I don't know... it didn't end so much as it imploded. Anyway, I don't even know if he knows it's over, not properly over anyway. But it is.'

A little burning pang of guilt rose up at the thought of Fran's unanswered message still there on her phone. She heaved a deep sigh, knowing that she couldn't leave Jonathan with a half-truth, not when he was being so open with her.

'I mean… it *will* be over… I just have to face up to it and tell him once and for all, but he's being patient with me, you know? I think he's waiting for me to come round. We had something really special for a while there and it's been strange letting it go. It's not something you need to worry about though.'

She felt a sudden decisiveness hit her as she looked at the beautiful man listening to her so intently, the earnest look in his eyes making her feel grounded again after so long spent adrift. What had been 'Kelsey and Fran' had been hanging suspended, up in the air, waiting for resolution. Sitting here in Jonathan's solid, reassuring company she knew she was ready to let all that history fall to the ground now.

'Can you, um, give me a minute? I…' Kelsey stood to leave, taking her phone with her. 'I'll be back. Just wait there.'

Feeling drunk and light-headed and knowing it had nothing to do with those few sips of beer, Kelsey made her way to the ladies' room. Her hands were shaking with the strange insistent feeling compelling her to speak to Fran without losing one more second. How could she enjoy her feelings for Jonathan when they were cut through with the guilt of Fran pining for her in Scotland? *It's time to grow up and say goodbye,* she told herself as she scrolled up the screen. But she rang through to Fran's voicemail. The wry irony wasn't lost on Kelsey. It seemed fitting really; the last of many near-misses and failed connections with poor, striving Fran.

At the beep, the words poured out. She told him everything she wished she'd had the courage to say that night in the beer garden when she'd blindsided him with news of her sudden departure, that she loved him and always would, but it was time for her to find her feet on her own, to embrace new opportunities. She didn't mention Jonathan, that would be cruel and unnecessary, she thought, and besides, there was nothing to tell, yet. But she was sorry to say her last goodbye, and she wiped away tears as she left him with her hopes that he would find everything he was looking for in life.

Making her way back to the inglenook, for a split second Kelsey was struck with the irrational fear that Jonathan would be gone, that he was surely too good to be true, that he was somehow a fleeting summer's dream. But there he was, smiling and placid. She took her seat opposite him again, choosing to say nothing of the phone call she'd just made in case Jonathan thought it meant she expected something from him now.

Soon they had relaxed into each other's company again, enjoying the luxury of uninterrupted time together with no distractions and no misapprehensions. They didn't notice the pub slowly filling up as they ordered from the specials board and tucked into hot scampi and chunky chips with lemon wedges, minty peas, and fresh tartare sauce and they talked and laughed and sipped their ale. Kelsey could feel the cracks in her heart healing over.

Jonathan let her know again how much he loved her photographs and how he'd restocked his portfolio, ordering extra copies to send out to acting companies.

'Are you looking for a new company?' Kelsey asked.

'I'm not sure yet. Maybe.' He seemed reluctant to talk about the company and quickly veered away from the subject. 'So, tell me about the exhibition you mentioned.

Remember? The day we met?' he prompted her with an encouraging nod.

'You *remembered* that?' Kelsey was impressed. 'Well, OK. It was when I was an undergraduate, a million years ago, but I was really proud of it. My photography club rented a proper gallery space in Edinburgh and they displayed some of my landscape pictures. Some of them actually sold too, and not just to my grandad, though he did buy a couple.'

'That's very cool. I wish I'd seen that. So you're going back to photography at the end of the summer? I'm guessing you don't want to be a tour guide forever and you've got too much talent not to pursue it.'

She exhaled sharply, puffing her cheeks out. 'I haven't really thought about it. I have *no* idea. I know I don't really want to go home, not soon anyway.' A new light formed in Kelsey's widening eyes. 'Jonathan? Have you tried to imagine what Stratford might be like in the autumn? I have. I've been thinking about it a lot actually, wondering what the riverside will look like when the leaves fall and it's all dewy and fresh. Do you reckon the pubs light their fires?'

Jonathan joined in enthusiastically. 'I love the smell of wood smoke from the chimneys and bonfires when it's all mixed up with the fireworks and the mist. Fall's my favourite time of year.'

Kelsey sighed as her thoughts drifted to the colder months. 'What do you think it would be like at *Christmas*?' Her eyes grew wide as she imagined the ancient twisting streets, the thatched roofs, and the black and white beamed shops glimmering with silver frost and illuminated with twinkling lights.

Jonathan seemed to be thinking along similar lines. His deep, sonorous voice interrupted her thoughts. 'What must those old street lamps look like glowing in the depths of a winter's night, huh? And the river must be awesome when it's halfway to frozen.' He smiled dreamily.

'So… where will you be when winter comes?' Kelsey asked sheepishly, already afraid of the answer.

Jonathan's pinched brows and slow exhalation cast a sudden frost. 'The company moves on to Ontario for a Shakespeare festival in September, we're performing *Hamlet* from our repertoire. And, uh… in October I'll be jetting off on my own to California to take up my drama teaching residency for the winter.'

Falling into silence, he sat back, folding his arms. Kelsey couldn't bear to think of the summer's end any longer, so quickly tried to change the subject.

'That sounds… really special, a whole winter of drama. Tell me about how you first got into Shakespeare.' Leaning forward, she encouraged him to open up again.

The crinkle between his brows smoothed.. 'Shakespeare's in my blood – maybe literally. I *do* share a surname with Shakespeare's wife's side of the family.' He was smiling now, his lips curling at the sides in the most appealing way. 'My mother was an actress with the Royal Shakespeare Company in the eighties. She came out here from Oklahoma to try out for RADA and ended up onstage untrained and still pretty young. She was a real starlet for a while. But she gave up acting when she had me.' Kelsey noticed the tiny flicker of tension in his jaw. 'My father disappeared after he found out she was pregnant. He was… uh… someone in the company. She always said he didn't matter and that I was hers and hers alone. So we went back to Oklahoma. She worked in the 7-Eleven, did some drama teaching, ran classes at the Y, all kinds of stuff to provide for me. Eventually she married a guy called Art. I was still real little then and I grew up thinking of him as my *real* dad. Then they had my baby sisters, four of 'em.'

'Four sisters? You're so lucky, I'd love a sister.'

'Art always said that me and him were fated to be surrounded by beautiful women.' Jonathan smiled with a distant fondness. 'My folks gave me a great childhood. I'd love to try it one day, having kids I mean, a couple of little girls to run round after. Geez, they'd be so cute and I'd be such a sucker.' He said this with an unflinching gaze that left Kelsey utterly at a loss for words.

Feeling suddenly overwhelmed, she wanted to cool the intense connection that had re-established between them; it was all too much. Thankfully, Jonathan came to her rescue.

'Tell me about your family? You're close?'

'I can do better than that, I can *show* you them.' Kelsey reached for the album in her satchel. 'I started carrying this around a few days ago, I was getting a bit homesick.'

As she turned the first page, Jonathan effortlessly manoeuvred his long body around the table, coming to sit on the inglenook bench beside her. The heat from his closeness seared into Kelsey's flesh. Thankfully she had her photographs to concentrate on.

'I have lots of these at home. Sometimes I worry I'll wind up living alone, a mad old lady in a house full of photo albums and no room for actual furniture. That's the one problem with real pictures, they take up a lot of space.'

'Yeah, but who wants their life's memories stored digitally on a couple of memory sticks or backed up on an old hard drive that's gonna break one day, anyway? I like albums. You just walk over to the shelf and there it is, your life, it's all there.'

'That's exactly it!' Kelsey turned to face Jonathan, amazed. In response, he reached an arm around her shoulders, pulling himself a little closer, making her heart soar.

She turned the pages. All of her memories were there at her fingertips, sealed behind the clear plastic leaves. There was little Calum standing by the front door holding his brand new lunchbox on his first day of school; her mum's fiftieth birthday when they'd gone Segwaying in Fort William – Mari's idea; her grandparents' ruby wedding anniversary ceilidh when the extended 'clan' reunited from all over the world.

'That's my brother. He's fourteen now.'

'Looks like a cool kid.' Jonathan seemed to think nothing of the fact that he was clearly a gangly teenager dressed in a mask, cape, and tights.

'He is cool, and funny too. I guess being that much older than him and having to help look after him when Dad died meant we've never really had that typical big sister, annoying little brother relationship. He was so cute and tiny. He gave us all a reason to carry on when it happened. But there are hardly any pictures of Calum with Dad, they just didn't get enough time together.'

Jonathan hugged her closer to his side, his thumb rubbing gently over her forearm. She pressed on, turning pages.

'This is Mum and Dad.'

Jonathan smiled at the images of the woman with a huge belly, her eyes shining underneath a permed fringe. Kelsey's dad had his fingers spread out across Mari's baby bump. Then there was a close-up of Lewis taken seconds later, giving the bump a kiss. Then, a few grainy ones on the maternity ward of the little family huddled together, perched on the hospital bed.

'That's me,' Kelsey laughed. 'I was so moody at that age, but I can remember trying not to burst with joy holding Calum that day. Mum looks so young.' Kelsey's vision blurred as she held back the tears.

The picture showed her parents huddled on either side of her, all of them gazing down at Calum who looked like little more than a bundle of blankets. The image was faded with age but clear enough to show Mari smiling through her exhaustion and her husband's look of pride and relief with tears in his eyes and his heart in his mouth, the way good men feel when they see their family safely complete.

They pored over the next few snapshots of the family: Calum's christening and one of them all together on the pier at Blackpool with Calum wrapped up in his little grey buggy, only five months old. Everyone was smiling despite the rain and the wind whipping their hair up. Kelsey closed the book.

'And that's it. A few precious memories preserved forever, and none of them are Calum's.'

'What happened?' Jonathan said softly.

'A car accident. It was just after Hogmanay. Calum was eight months old. A burst tyre on the motorway. I remember the police at the door and then the funeral and all the tears.'

'God, I'm so sorry.'

'It's Calum I feel sorry for. He's only just old enough to process the enormity of having grown up without his dad. I was lucky, I had a few years with him and I can actually remember him, enough to dream about him.' Kelsey tried to smile, but a fat tear ran down her cheek. She didn't have the composure to tell him how every night she'd close her eyes and hope that tonight would be one of the nights she'd see her dad again as she slept.

Drawing his hands up to her face, Jonathan wiped away the tear with his thumb and pushed her hair back. 'Kelsey, that's so sad.'

'You know, it was Dad who brought me to Stratford when I was a kid? He wanted to encourage me to follow my interest in Shakespeare. That's what Mum told me, anyway. It was as though he could see I needed steering. I've always drifted a bit. Maybe he was worried about me, even then. I do feel as though I'm finding my way, now that I'm back here.'

Jonathan simply nodded, listening closely.

'We saw *Romeo and Juliet* when we were here. My first Shakespeare play.' Kelsey sniffed back the tears and smiled. 'Dad was holding Mum's hand all the way through it. I was cringing at the time, you know, I was just a kid. I remember him raising her hand to kiss it. They were so in love. They were teenage sweethearts, actually. I suppose I came back here looking for a bit of that happiness, but since I arrived I've been a bit lost, if I'm honest.'

'I've got you now,' said Jonathan.

They tipped their foreheads together. Kelsey relaxed into the comfort of his slim fingers running through her hair. Turning her head she let her lips graze the palm of his hand before pressing a slow kiss into the root of his thumb. He inhaled with a hiss through his teeth. The electric energy buzzed between them again just as it had at the photo shoot – an undercurrent, a promise of what the future could hold. Jonathan slowly drew his face across Kelsey's, circling the tip of his nose over hers but, tantalisingly, holding back from kissing her.

There was nothing Kelsey wanted to do more than take Jonathan's hand and walk him straight out of that pub. Her mind flitted to her little white room, her white bed, the wine in the fridge, the stars up on the terrace. All she had to do was ask. The desire written across Jonathan's serious, intent features told her he would follow.

Before she could speak, their cosy bubble was burst by a commotion at the pub door. Will Greville and the gang stumbled in with a loud flourish of hilarity and chatter.

'We're here! Let's get this show on the road,' Will called out in his familiar young Windsors way, clapping his hands together, as Valeria and Myrtle, howling with laughter, continued their conversation in the doorway behind him.

No one had yet noticed the intimate twosome secreted away in the inglenook. Kelsey wished with all her heart that it could stay that way as she discreetly removed herself from Jonathan's embrace.

Will was making his way through the crowd of assembled tourists, busily ticking their names off his list, readying everyone for the pub crawl. Tonight's guests were graduate students from all over the world in town for a big conference and obviously geared up for a wild night out after long studious days working in the theatre archives and listening to lectures. Spotting Kelsey in the inglenook, Will's eyes flitted quickly towards her handsome companion then back to Kelsey with a sudden flash of determination. He pushed his way politely through the crowd and kissed her on the cheek.

'Well, good evening, fair maiden. You look very lovely tonight. Are you going to introduce me to your friend?' His emphasis was on 'friend'.

What's gotten into him? Tipping her head, perplexed, Kelsey made the introductions.

'This is Jonathan Hathaway. He's an actor. You might have seen him in *A Midsummer Night's Dream* at the Willow Studios? Jonathan, this is Will Greville.'

The men clasped hands with what looked like warm accord, on Jonathan's part, anyway. Kelsey could see something in Will's eyes that troubled her.

'Glad to meet you, Will. Are you our guide tonight?' Jonathan was cordial and warm as always.

'Yes, sir. I have the very great pleasure of accompanying you this evening as we embark upon our Bard Crawl.' Will spoke loudly enough for half the bar to hear, gesticulating dramatically. 'It's always nice to meet a fellow actor,' Will added, sizing Jonathan up and still clasping his hand, not wanting to be the first one to let go.

Jonathan seemed oblivious, politely smiling at Will. 'You're an actor?' Jonathan asked with genuine interest. 'That's wonderful. You know, I was just about to tell Kelsey about the end of festival open-air gala. All the companies in town for the summer are putting on a night of drama and music. It happens at the end of every August apparently and it's the biggest night in the theatre calendar. Everybody's going to be there; all the actors and critics, and everyone who works on the plays. Oh, and lots of celebrities too. I heard Dame Judy will be making an appearance.'

Will dropped Jonathan's hand. 'Of course I know about it. I attend every year. Anybody who's anybody in theatre goes,' he said coolly.

Kelsey had never noticed this air of snobbery before, but there it was and it was *not* appealing. Seemingly undeterred, Jonathan carried on, turning towards Kelsey and smiling, occasionally looking up, careful not to exclude Will.

'This year they're calling the event Pretty Follies, and there are paying parts for amateur thespians up for grabs. I was going to try talking Kelsey into trying out for one of the fairies. Don't you think she'd be great? Are you interested in trying out for a role too, Will?'

Will's eyes glazed over with a strange darkness. 'Amateur? What makes you assume *I'm* an amateur?'

Will quickly tried to regain his composure, but it was too late. Jonathan was already apologising profusely and offering Will a ticket to his play but Kelsey knew Will had no intention of letting him off the hook. Losing out on that London audition had clearly left Will feeling sore, and seeing Kelsey with this gorgeous American who made his living from the stage must sting too, but, Kelsey thought, there was no need to be rude. She squirmed awkwardly in her seat.

'Will, I think it's time to get started, right?'

'Of course.' He was calm again. 'Can you gather the group and meet me out front?' He smiled, raking his hair back off his forehead, all politeness and poise. He didn't miss the opportunity to place a hand on the small of Kelsey's back as she stood up.

'I'll see you out there, Jonathan?' Kelsey tried to smile back towards her date, but stumbled over a chair leg as she made her way out. She recovered quickly, 'Right, friends and guests, the Bard Crawl has begun, please follow me. I'm Kelsey Anderson, one of your guides this evening.'

There were a few whoops from excited students as they filed out one by one into the warm summer's evening.

Jonathan gathered their empty plates from the table and carried them to the bar which was now littered with abandoned glasses from the dispersing rabble. Will was by his side in a flash.

'Jonathan, was it?' he smiled.

'That's me.'

'Jonathan, I don't know if Kelsey mentioned me at all, but she and I have had a pretty sweet thing going on for a while now.'

Jonathan looked taken aback, but said nothing.

'I don't know how they do things in Iowa…'

'Oklahoma,' Jonathan interrupted.

'Whatever,' Will shrugged dismissively. 'In England, it's not the done thing to swoop in on another chap's girl, especially when she's still undecided about that chap, you know?' Will was using his suavest voice. 'How do I put this, Jonathan? You need to *back off.*'

The furrow in Jonathan's brow set in again as Will confidently stared him down. There was nothing else for it but to simply nod in agreement and offer Will a polite handshake. He placed some money on the bar and walked abruptly outside.

Peering over the crowd, Jonathan caught sight of Kelsey at the far end of the street. She was laughing and whispering with Valeria. He looked his last before pulling up the collar of his light jacket and turning on his heel.

Walking in the opposite direction, he stopped once he was out of sight to type the message on his phone.

I'm guessing that poor schmuck was your sort-of ex-boyfriend, the one you hadn't properly ended things with? I'll get out of your way so you have a chance to talk and maybe then I'll be able to ask you out? Or is that too presumptuous? I don't want to put any pressure on you. Maybe you want to give him another chance?

Reading it over, he frowned and cursed out loud. Scratching the nape of his neck with his fingertips he deleted every word and stalked away.

Little did Jonathan know that Kelsey was walking on air because of him and their intimate, relaxed evening together. She was whispering to Valeria that she might well take Jonathan into the secret garden tonight and offer him a taste of a sweet, ripe mulberry under the light of the July moon.

A smiling Will sauntered down the steps of the Yorick towards his fellow tour guides, hurriedly catching up to Kelsey with a spring in his step. 'Ms Anderson, your beau had to go, I'm afraid. Something about being needed at the theatre?' he offered innocently.

Kelsey looked around as the crowd swept her along towards the next bar. Will was right, Jonathan was nowhere to be seen. Cold, creeping disappointment stole over her.

For a while she followed the visitors on their pub crawl, but her heart wasn't in it. Will bought her cocktails she had no appetite for and stayed by her side as the tour progressed, trying to make her laugh and, as usual, he was flirting wildly, but she barely took any notice. She slipped off home the very second her shift ended, her mind buzzing with the same thoughts.

I don't get it. Everything was so perfect and then… what happened? A phone call from Peony, no doubt. She really does have him at her beck and call. And he always goes running. How can I compete with that? But why did he just abandon me when we were getting on so well? And no phone call or message? Bloody cheek!

And so her mind whirled on and on, even as she climbed into her pristine white bed beneath the lacy-curtained window, still wearing her make-up, cold and confused, a woman on emotional autopilot.

Chapter Twenty-One

'Cupid is a knavish lad, thus to make females mad'
(A Midsummer Night's Dream)

The robotic voice from the tannoy announced the train's arrival, and there it was at the far end of the line, slowly rolling into town. Kelsey had slept fitfully after Jonathan's unexpected departure the evening before; but it was her day off, her best friend in all the world was on her way to see her and she was damned well determined to enjoy it, Jonathan or no Jonathan.

In her skirt pocket were their tickets for tonight's performance of *A Midsummer Night's Dream*, Jonathan's gift to her.

I can't tell Mirren about him. She can't come all this way to find me moping about with a stupid crush on a man whose glamazon ex-girlfriend manages to break up every single encounter we've ever had. And he just scuttles off to keep her happy. And why the hell hasn't he rung me since the Bard Crawl, for God's sake? Ghosted again. Nope, I'll keep that humiliation to myself, I think.

Kelsey paced the platform, deep in thought, as the train pulled up.

How can it be a month and a half since I arrived at this station? Six weeks since I last saw Mirren. And Fran. Straightforward Fran. He'll have listened to my message by now, surely? I hope he isn't too upset. He wasn't exactly a Romeo but at least he wanted me, and forever too.

She steeled herself against the sad grip around her heart that felt very much like loneliness, but glimpsing Mirren's grinning face at the grubby, dusty train window, she knew she would soon be brought back to life. The doors opened and Mirren rushed out, weaving her way across the busy platform, screaming so loudly that she startled a group of elderly Japanese tourists.

'Come here, Kelse! Oh my God, I've missed you! Give me some love,' she screeched as she pulled Kelsey towards her.

They hugged tightly. Kelsey's happiness bubbled over into relieved tears. 'I've missed you so much.' She hadn't realised quite how much she'd needed a girlfriend until now. 'I've got so much to tell you.'

'Lead the way. Take me to the nearest cream tea.'

'I just happen to know the hottest spot in town.'

Twenty minutes later Kelsey was hopping from foot to foot, her hands clasped under her chin, a secretive smile on her lips, as she encouraged the bemused Mirren to climb the steep stairs that led to the roof terrace of Number One, St Ninian's Close.

'I've been dying to show this to someone,' she said excitedly, as Mirren pushed open the hatch door and peered out into the cloudless sky.

'Bloody hell, Kelse!'

Kelsey had been hard at work all morning hanging strings of delicate fairy lights along the low iron railing that enclosed the terrace, and she'd dotted small pots of lavender and frilly white pansies that she'd picked up at the town farmers' market all around. There was just enough room for Mirren to tumble up the steps and out onto the warm terracotta tiles that Kelsey had covered over with a new hot-pink picnic blanket which was all set out with teacups and plates. Each cup held a slice of lime and a few blueberries inside. Mirren was too over-awed by the view to notice them.

'Beautiful, right?' Kelsey beamed, her head and shoulders just visible through the hatch. 'You stay there, I'll go get the tea things.'

Mirren sprawled out across the rug, gaping open-mouthed over the pretty town in the near distance. The sun was high in the sky and the air was still and dry. A perfect July day. Kelsey returned minutes later with a tray piled high with strawberries, huge lopsided scones from the town's old-fashioned bakery, clotted cream, and raspberry jam. She'd even bought a bright yellow teapot from the little Aladdin's cave of a homeware shop on the high street.

'Yummy.' Mirren smiled, inspecting the tray. 'Oh, you forgot the milk.'

'Nope, we don't need milk, Mirr,' Kelsey said as she deftly poured the icy gin, fruit juice, and tonic from the teapot into the already garnished cups.

'Kelsey, you wee legend!' Mirren leaned over to hug her friend who was already arranged comfortably on the rug beside her.

'OK, tell me everything. I've missed a whole month of gossip,' Kelsey prompted, as she sipped the cool clear liquid, the bitterness of the juniper and lime cutting through the icy freshness of the sweet berries and sugary tonic.

'Where to start? I saw your mum last week. She gave me a care package to bring with me. I only had a quick peek, but it looked as though it was mostly gossip mags, new pants from M&S, and a tin of shortbread.'

They were laughing already, relaxed and happy. There was nothing at stake emotionally, not like the past few weeks with Will, or with Jonathan. Kelsey was becoming aware of how exhausting it had all been. But here they were now, just two old friends picking up where they'd left off and feeling as if they'd only just seen each other the day before. It was funny how true best friends could do that for each other, Kelsey was thinking as the gin hit her bloodstream, and if it didn't happen, then they were probably not your best friend after all.

'Is Grandad all right? I've called him a couple of times but he's not great on the phone, he seems a bit more distracted than usual.'

'Erm...' Mirren wriggled slightly, enough for Kelsey to know that all wasn't well at home.

'He's fine... but... your mum's been worrying about him a bit. She's been trying to convince him to move into your old room. Not your *old* room, I mean, into *your* room.'

'Poor Grandad!' Kelsey exclaimed, feeling a wave of guilt for being so far away and not picking up on her mum's worries when they'd chatted.

Mirren was already busy telling her that her mum had kept it from Kelsey so as not to upset her, but Kelsey already understood. That was so like Mari.

'I hope he *does* move into my room,' said Kelsey, making a mental note to call her mum as soon as Mirren left on Monday. 'He won't like moving. That house is all he's known for sixty years and it's full of memories for him. I guess this is it from here on in. I must remember to send him some tourist toffee, the kind with the postcard stuck to the front of the box.'

'He's doing all right, please don't worry. Honestly. He's had lots of visitors and Preston's been calling in on his way to and from the recording studio most days.' Mirren cast her eyes down, looking rather solemn at the thought of her adorable, earnest boyfriend.

'What a sweetheart. How is Preston?' Kelsey chimed, remembering her lovely friend back home. He was the kind of person who was always doing nice things for everyone else but who often seemed to get overlooked. Kelsey was imagining her grandad and him listening to Preston's latest songs over a cuppa.

'He's good, same as always.'

Kelsey watched her friend's features shift – the change would be imperceptible to anyone else, but she had gotten to know it over the years; that same sad, remorseful look in Mirren's eyes. 'Things aren't getting any better, then?' She tried to sound casual as she worked her knife through the plump scones.

Mirren knew exactly what her friend meant and there was no use pretending. She sighed aloud, her shoulders drooping. 'He's the sweetest man in the universe, like, he's far too good for me. I don't know what's wrong with me. Why can't I just be happy? He works hard, and he brings home enough money to cover his share of the rent, and he's gorgeous and talented and kind… and… and everything, but…'

'But the magic just isn't there?' Kelsey offered.

'I do love him though. I am *in love* with him. I just feel so restless all the time. Sometimes I wish I could do what you've done, Kelse. Just move somewhere new and start again. With someone new, maybe? Or maybe not even *someone*, maybe I could just play the field a bit and see what's out there without all the guilt. Plenty of blokes are doing it, why should I feel bad about wanting the same thing?'

'You shouldn't,' Kelsey agreed, the gin warming her tummy and making her feel slightly anaesthetised. 'It's just that you can't do it while you're with Preston. That wouldn't be fair to him. Right?'

Mirren sighed hard and set to work slathering a scone thickly in clotted cream, trying to drown her sorrows in carbs. 'I'm not going to *do* anything, and it's ages since I… you know, cheated.' Mirren winced. 'I figure, in time, I'll feel more settled. He is literally the perfect man, and I'm trying to deserve him.'

Kelsey hated seeing her friend beat herself up about not feeling settled with Preston. God knows she'd tried. Kelsey had seen it all played out before, all the heartache and the sneaking around and the inevitable guilt.

'Don't be so hard on yourself, Mirr. No man is perfect. And even if he was, he might not be perfect for you. Maybe something's just off balance, you know, chemically.'

Kelsey's mind jumped straight to Jonathan and the day of the photo shoot and then again to the pub when her shatteringly primal attraction to him was activated as if from nowhere. It had made her believe in romance again, for the first time in a long time. And she was sure he'd felt it too: a true chemical, undeniable attraction. But then again, where was the good in that when he just wasn't available? The coldness of the realisation instantly shut down the warm memories.

Mirren watched Kelsey over the rim of her teacup, downing the last of her gin, squinting suspiciously. 'Oh yeah? What's been going on here then?' she teased, breaking out into a wicked grin, momentarily forgetting her own problems.

'I don't know what you mean,' Kelsey retorted, embarrassed that her friend could read her so well.

'Come on, spill it. Have you been seeing someone else?'

'Someone else?' Kelsey exhaled sharply. 'What do you mean someone else? I'm not seeing anyone, remember? You haven't spoken with Fran have you?' She thought of the hurried message she'd left for him the night before at the Yorick when she'd been stupid enough to think Jonathan was interested in her enough to actually stick around until the end of a date. The humiliation was replaced with a rush of guilt for poor Fran's trampled feelings. She really wasn't any better than Jonathan.

Alarmed at the sudden change in her friend, Mirren reached for Kelsey's hand.

'Kelse, I didn't mean anything. I know you and Fran are history. In fact, I should have told you this earlier.' Mirren filled her lungs deeply. 'He's been... he's been seeing someone he met at the teachers' conference. Kirsty somebody or other. They're pretty smitten with each other, apparently. He rang me last night, said he wanted me to break it to you. I'm sorry, I didn't quite know how to say it.' Mirren spoke with a confiding gentleness, adding a final apology and a conciliatory rub of Kelsey's arm.

'He's moved on? He's dating? That's great, I'm… *really* happy for him.' Kelsey blurted out the words, surprised at how heartfelt they were. Relief pervaded her dreamy gin-induced state. *So it's finally, definitely over.* Reaching for the teapot, she refilled their cups. 'Here's a toast. To Fran and Kirsty something or other. Good luck to them.'

They crushed their cups together and drank deeply, both realising at the same moment how intoxicating the 'tea' had been.

'We'd better stop soon, or we'll be too sozzled to drag ourselves to the theatre,' said Mirren, relieved to see Kelsey receive Fran's message without any obvious heartache. 'Well done you, scoring us some freebie tickets. That reminds me, I picked this up in Birmingham at the station news stand.' Mirren reached into her handbag and tossed a folded newspaper towards Kelsey. 'It's got a feature about the play we're seeing in it. Front page news.'

Kelsey unfolded the paper to be met with a picture of Jonathan and Peony from their production of *Hamlet*. Jonathan was beautiful, shrouded in black, a fencing sword at his side and Peony knelt at his feet, a weeping Ophelia all in white. The headline blazoned, **A STRATFORD LOVE STORY**. Kelsey cleared her throat, unsure what to do, as Mirren stood shakily in her heels and teetered downstairs to Kelsey's apartment.

'I'll pop the kettle on, make us a real brew. What do you say?' Mirren asked cheerily, utterly unaware of the million tiny explosions of rage, shock, and sadness going off in her friend's imagination at that moment. Kelsey barely noticed Mirren's departure. She read on, holding her breath.

Audiences are being treated to a spectacular summer love story this season as the Oklahoma Renaissance Players launch their run of A Midsummer Night's Dream at the town's Willow Studio Theatre. Stratford Examiner reporter, Adrian Armadale, caught up with stage stunner Peony Brown, 26 (appearing as Titania) between shows this week.

'I'm so fortunate to act alongside my real-life Romeo, my very own Hamlet and my Faerie King,' said the Oklahoma-born actress, confirming rumours that she and fellow actor Jonathan Hathaway, 30, are long-term lovers going back to college days when the teenage thesps set the stage alight in acting class. 'We fell in love playing iconic couples who transcend time. Touring together all over the world bonded us in ways few couples could ever hope to recreate. We're part of an amazing ensemble, a travelling theatre family.' Drama Queen Brown explained their nickname amongst fellow cast members. 'Jonathan and I have been called "PB and J" for as long as I can remember, and like peanut butter and jelly, we're a classic combination.' When asked if there were plans for the couple to wed, Miss Brown commented, 'Our careers come first, but I wouldn't rule out an engagement somewhere along the line.' Audiences can catch a glimpse of the all-American sweethearts before their run ends on 1st September.

Kelsey folded the paper away and reached for the teapot once more. Another slug of gin might numb the sickening wrenching at her heart. Jonathan Hathaway really was a good actor. He'd managed to deceive her into thinking he'd liked her and all this time he'd been playing poor Peony too. She swallowed down her feelings along with the sweet liquor and set a thin smile on her face. Mirren would never know the stupid, humiliating mess she'd narrowly avoided getting entangled in.

Chapter Twenty-Two

'I shall the effect of this good lesson keep as watchman
to my heart'
(Hamlet)

Later, with speech slurred and cheeks rosy-pink, after
they'd covered all the important topics like Mirren finally
getting in line for a chance at promotion in the newspaper office and Preston's band getting signed to an indie
label who were going to help them organise a mini-tour
across Scotland, Mirren wickedly found her way back to
her most pressing concern: Stratford's male population.
She had squeezed her fulsome body into the tiny shower
cubicle that stood at the foot of Kelsey's bed and was
washing the conditioner from her hair. Kelsey, on the
other hand, was already getting a headache from all the
sunshine and booze, not to mention the *Stratford Examiner's* sensational cover story. She slouched cross-legged at
the head of the bed with a cold, damp flannel pressed to
her eyes.

Mirren shouted over the sound of the water. 'Are you
expecting me to believe you haven't so much as bumped
into *anyone* you fancy in the entire town, Kelse? This
building might look like a nunnery with all the pris-

tine white and the lace, but really? There hasn't been the slightest hint of a snog? Tell your auntie Mirr.' She switched the shower off and squeezed her head around the door, reaching for a towel. 'Who installs a shower with a clear door right at the foot of a bed? A bloody pervert, that's who. Anyway, come on, you didn't answer me.' Mirren laughed, thoroughly enjoying teasing her friend and not ready to give up on the interrogation.

Kelsey groaned, knowing Mirren wouldn't stop until she'd had some details. 'All right, there was one guy, Will Greville. He's a tour guide – my mentor, as it happens – and I thought he was gorgeous at first. I mean, he *is* gorgeous. He's got dark reddish-brown hair and green eyes like you've never seen. You'd like him. And he's all posh and well-travelled… and rich, I'm guessing. His family are loaded, anyway. He makes me feel like I was raised in a cave by Neanderthals half the time.' Kelsey was laughing now. 'But he loves himself way more than he could love anybody else. It's a shame really, because he's always trying it on.'

Mirren had slipped a black strappy dress on over her head, and was now brushing out her wet hair. She stopped dead, looking straight at Kelsey.

'Are you telling me that a *certified hottie* is throwing himself at you and you aren't even slightly interested? Kelsey, you need to get straight back on the horse.'

Shaking her head dismissively, Kelsey lifted the flannel off her face long enough to roll her eyes at Mirren, before lowering it again.

'No, no, hear me out,' her friend persevered. 'You don't have to *keep* the horse. You don't even have to ride it every day. Just throw it a few sugar lumps and take it once or twice over the jumps.'

'Well, thanks for that great advice, Mirren,' Kelsey groaned, before throwing the flannel straight into the kitchen sink, just feet away. 'I'm just not… a very horsey person.'

'You do know I'm not talking about horses, right, Kelse? Anyway, you're leaving at the end of the summer. It's not like anyone's expecting a lifelong romance, is it? Have a summer fling then move on. You'll be back in Scotland before you know it.' Mirren nodded decisively as she spoke.

There it was again: that same urgent feeling Kelsey had experienced at the Yorick the night before when Jonathan had asked about her plans for the end of the summer. It was even stronger now.

'Actually, I *might* stay on after the summer,' said Kelsey, tentatively at first, as though she were testing out the idea. 'If I *were* to stay, I wouldn't want to make a fool of myself by burning any bridges here, and it wouldn't stay secret for long if I did do anything with Will.'

'Burn that bridge. Who cares? It's just a sex bridge, Kelse, just get on it and then get over it. Live a little.' Mirren was now waving her mascara wand across her thick black lashes.

'Bloody hell, Mirr! Sex bridges? Horses? You should write for *Cosmo*.'

They were still laughing when Kelsey, suddenly startled by a glimpse at the time on her phone, leapt up from the bed.

'We're going to be late. Can you do my make-up, Mirr? Ugh, and can you pass me some paracetamol, my head is killing me. Why did I think gin for lunch was a good idea?'

Mirren patted a spot at the end of the bed and Kelsey shuffled down ready for her makeover. As Mirren expertly set to work with the contents of her bulging make-up bag Kelsey mulled over her advice.

Maybe a fling wouldn't hurt, just this once. I am completely single now but if I did sleep with Will, I really would just be using him, not that I think he'd mind. It wouldn't have to be some great love affair and he is lovely to look at, and his body is definitely... intriguing. That tan and those muscles... and he'd probably know what he was doing...

Mirren sat back appraising her work and handed Kelsey her hand mirror to examine her shimmering silvery eyes, dewy cheeks, and fair sculpted brows. Kelsey snapped back to reality, banishing Will to her subconscious again.

'Ooh, it's very Midsummer Night's Dreamy. You really are very talented, Mirr. Thank you.'

'Just a little mascara and lip gloss and you're good to go.' Mirren slipped black strappy heels – never flats, not ever – onto perfectly pedicured feet.

Kelsey reached for a silvery maxi dress that hung on the bathroom door. Its thin cotton underskirt had a light chiffon layer over the top, giving the whole thing a diaphanous, barely-there look: another new purchase in the summer sales from the lovely shopping arcade in town.

I won't be able to speak to Jonathan up on stage tonight, but I can at least show him what he's missing out on. And if we happen to bump into Will Greville at the pub afterwards, I might just arrange to meet him one day after work. Why the hell not? Mirren's pep talk had left her feeling reckless and ready for some excitement.

As she slipped the stunning dress on over her glowing brown shoulders, Mirren gasped. Kelsey didn't know it, but her sunny summer, living alone and enjoying the freedom that her pretty little flat and her busy new job afforded her, had changed her. It wasn't just the new clothes, or the sun-bleached streaks in her wild hair, or the healthy shimmer on her skin: she was holding her head up higher and walking taller, in spite of all the offstage drama that had stolen so much of her sleep this summer.

Smiling in admiration, Mirren quickly held up her phone and took a picture of Kelsey who, grinning, raised one hand to her flowing hair, striking a pose. Mirren posted it to Instagram before Kelsey could even begin to protest:

#iftheycouldseemenow #Goddess.

Minutes later they were rushing out of Number One, St Ninian's Close, the heavy door slamming behind them, Kelsey clutching the tickets tightly in her fist.

They were almost late, tiptoeing into the packed auditorium of the Willow Studio and taking their seats just as the house lights dimmed and a tremulous, expectant hush fell over the audience.

Chapter Twenty-Three

'Speak low if you speak love'
(Much Ado About Nothing)

The goosebumps prickled on Kelsey's arms. It happened every time during those few seconds of anticipatory darkness before the action began on stage. All the familiar theatre aromas were there: tweedy old men, Brylcreem, mothballs, and everyone in their best clothes, all blending in the air with the dry ice, pre-theatre red wine, and a hundred different colognes and perfumes. But this time it felt even more intense and Kelsey knew the reason. She was going to see Jonathan again.

Why do I feel like this? He's Peony's man, not to mention a terrible, shameless flirt for making me imagine he liked me then ditching me without any apology or explanation. Her pulse beat loudly in her eardrums as she agitatedly arranged the slippery fabric of her flowing dress over her knees and tried to take some deep calming breaths. *'I've got you now,' he said last night at the pub, and like an idiot I felt all safe and wanted. How can he not be genuine?*

There, in the silent, dark auditorium, against all logic and common sense, her heart pounded with exhilaration. He was here. She was going to see him again. The beautiful American with the perfect pink curling smile and the deep drawling accent was at that exact moment waiting in the wings, ready to step onstage and bathe in the blinding spotlights as blue and piercing as his almond-lidded irises. Kelsey held her breath and tightly screwed up her eyes with anticipation. The auditorium seemed to swim and skirl around her as a flute and harp began to play offstage and the lights slowly started to creep up. A strange smile played across her lips in the darkness. Any moment now she was going to see him again.

Exhaling, Kelsey opened her eyes, but she wasn't greeted by the sight of Jonathan as Oberon. There on the stage in her swinging fairy bower was Peony, looking utterly resplendent and ravishing as the sleeping Titania, Oberon's cruel and contrary fairy queen. She was in the same flowing white dress that she'd worn the day she'd cut short the photo shoot, but now her temples, wrists, and plunging neckline were painted with black and white petals and the curling tendrils of pale green ivy leaves. Her hair was teased into a wild bundle on top of her head with long flowing strands falling down over her pale shoulders which glistened with a dewy silvery lustre that covered every inch of exposed flesh. Her tall, spiked, silver crown towered above her beautiful head and the spotlights reflected in its thousand twinkling, dancing diamonds.

As the music swelled, Titania awoke. She yawned and stretched her impossibly long, lithe body, letting her bare feet and slender ankles dip down to the floor. Slowly, she slipped out of her bower and onto the mossy green stage, revealing behind her a tiny changeling boy curled up asleep inside the fairy hideaway. The audience heaved a collective sigh at the sight of the beautiful child who was also covered from head to toe in shimmering silver.

Wordlessly, Titania scooped the little boy up into her arms and cautiously stole away with delicate steps as the forest scene fell dark again. The whole effect was utterly enchanting. The scene was now set for Oberon's entrance. He'd appear soon, maddened with envy that Titania was devoting herself to the tiny fairy child and neglecting him, her king.

When Mirren, smiling and amazed, turned her head to glance at her friend, she was shocked to see Kelsey's face wet with tears. 'What's the matter?' she whispered.

Kelsey shook her head dejectedly, taking the crumpled tissue Mirren offered. She spoke breathlessly, 'I'll tell you after.' More tears rolled down her blanched cheeks.

Mirren didn't have to wait until the interval to discover the reason for Kelsey's tears. Moments later, she'd observed her friend's expression change as Oberon stepped out of the gloomy wings and into the brilliant light of centre stage.

Illuminated in an ethereal halo, his muscular frame shone. He was clad in nothing but silver velvet breeches with a delicately glistening brocade down the seams. His skin was brushed over with glinting golden dust and his deep chestnut hair was slicked back with gleaming streaks of silver pomade and crowned with a delicate headdress of golden feathers. From the broad space in between his taut shoulder blades were fixed gossamer wings like an angel's. His brows, cheekbones, and jaw were lightly brushed with gold too, making him appear exotic and timeless. His eyes were lined thinly with smoky black kohl, reminiscent of a 1920s silent-film star in some sultry Saharan movie. His deeply bowed lips were bare save for the lightest touch of silver.

After drinking him in with her longing eyes, lost in wonder, Kelsey let her gaze fall down to her lap where Mirren's hand tightly gripped her own. Mirren knew the look of a broken heart. The friends didn't need to exchange another look or word throughout the long performance.

The audience laughed raucously at the action as the young couples in the forest, Lysander and Hermia, Demetrius and Helena, fell in and out of love, duped and dazed by spells and potions, magic and midsummer madness, but Kelsey was too overwhelmed by the shock of seeing Jonathan to take any of it in.

At the interval, Mirren leaned over, kissed her friend gently on the forehead, and slipped out to the foyer to get her some cool mineral water and a huge box of Maltesers. Kelsey sat in silence as the auditorium emptied and refilled again, barely hearing the happy vacationers' chatter. Had she looked up for one moment she might have spotted Jonathan in the shadows offstage, peering around a costume rail, trying to stay hidden from view of the audience but desperate to look at Kelsey, just for a few seconds.

'Psst! Kelsey… up here.'

But she couldn't hear him. She had no idea he was watching her, not caring a whit about appearing unprofessional.

Jonathan's shoulders dropped in resignation just as he felt Peony take his hand, yanking him back into the darkness of the wings. She shot him a steely look of warning before storming off, hurrying to make herself ready for their final scenes.

After the interval, when Oberon stalked back out onto the sylvan green set, spreading his magnificent wings and incanting the spell to awaken the poor lost and confused mortals on the stage, releasing them from their fairy curse, Kelsey felt sure he was looking directly at her with a strange wildness in his eyes as he delivered his lines in a perfect clear and crisp English accent.

'*Crush this herb into Lysander's eye – whose liquor hath this virtuous property, to take from thence all error with his might, and make his eyeballs roll with wanted sight. When they next wake, all this derision shall seem a dream and fruitless vision.*'

Kelsey looked on, her expression neutral, steeling herself not to betray the strong emotions bursting inside her chest. This was goodbye. She'd go home tonight with Mirren and tell her everything and cry her heart out and that would be an end to it. Only one scene left and all the dazed lovers would wake from their enchantments, pair up with their beloveds and leave the forest to prepare for marriage: a happy ending for everyone involved.

Kelsey however, hadn't anticipated the very last seconds of the drama as Titania and Oberon were reunited. She watched helplessly as Jonathan took Peony in his arms and kissed her softly on the lips. Kelsey wondered momentarily if the kiss was unusually brief for reconciled lovers, but mainly, she was just glad that the sudden clashing sounds in her ears and the stab in her chest as she watched them in each other's arms had been swift and sudden. It was all over.

She clapped mechanically in an exhausted daze as the cast took their bows. Some of the audience stood for an ovation. The play was clearly a great success, but Jonathan didn't smile, and his grave, intense eyes never once left Kelsey's face as he took two long, low bows. Peony, however, was grinning widely, bowing and curtseying, holding Jonathan's hand tightly, raising it up into the air in triumph over and over again.

I get it, Kelsey thought. *We mere mortals need to know when to give up. The fairies can have him. I'm done.*

Chapter Twenty-Four

'Summer's lease hath all too short a date'
(Sonnet 18)

Mirren let Kelsey sleep late the next morning. They'd talked for hours the night before, Kelsey fully resolved that she needed to move on from Jonathan. Mirren had helped a lot, asking the kind of questions that a friend who's sick of seeing men running hot and cold on their best mate should ask. As they'd ploughed through a huge bag of razor-sharp crisps sitting up on the terrace in the starlight, Mirren had wondered aloud, 'What do you really know about this guy, anyway? Or this Peony, for that matter? He tells you he loves her like a sister but he's kowtowing to her like a lover? And that cheesy newspaper article! PB and J? It's enough to make you spew.'

In the end they'd fallen asleep in Kelsey's bed as the sun was just peeking up over the Welcombe hills waking the raucous morning chorus in the gardens of St Ninian's Close.

★

Even though she'd have willingly shoved her own granny under a bus for a strong coffee, Mirren silently poured herself some milk, not wanting to wake Kelsey with the hiss and bubble of the kettle. She sat on the white carpet beside the bed sipping quietly, looking around her on the floor for a gossip magazine. There, under the bed, were two brightly coloured cardboard envelopes. She silently edged the envelopes out from underneath the piled up shoes and the slightly dusty editions of plays and photography magazines that had begun to clutter up Kelsey's bedside – a true sign her friend had made herself thoroughly at home in the toasty-warm little flat. Mirren noiselessly lifted out the gleaming colour prints.

She discovered lots of pictures of a beautiful old house and garden taken from over a low hedge in the evening sunlight. Mirren couldn't know as she flicked through shot after shot that the house was Shakespeare's Birthplace. Obviously taken some weeks ago, its flowers had all the blowsy freshness and vibrancy of early summer and were a stark reminder of how deeply they had already descended into the season. This descent was charted further in the photos taken more recently capturing the country lanes and hills around Stratford in all their overblown lushness and greenery, the thick hedgerows and chestnut trees casting dark black afternoon shadows upon the earth.

Then there were photographs of a smiling, jolly bunch of people Mirren had never met before. A big gap-toothed body-builder type, a young fair-haired boy – the slender studious type, a gorgeous red-headed guy in dark shades, and three grinning women, one dressed from head to foot in chic lilac and mauve. Judging by the others' uniforms she figured these must be some of Kelsey's colleagues. They looked so friendly and like a bonded little gang. 'Good for you. You're back to being the old Kelsey again,' Mirren murmured under her breath as she scanned the happy faces, recalling how her friend had once been part of a similarly cheerful group at uni when she'd been a member of the student photography society and busily planning their exhibition. All that had fallen by the wayside when Fran arrived on the scene with other priorities for Kelsey.

It was the buzz of a text alert that woke Kelsey at last. Mirren read the message out loud to her as she rubbed the sleep from tired, swollen eyes.

I hope you enjoyed the play last night. You looked kind of unhappy. Are things OK? Let me know when you're finally free. I'd love to buy you a coffee. Jonathan.

Mirren shrugged. 'What do you want me to reply?'

Kelsey thought for a moment. 'Tell him I'm unlikely to be free for the foreseeable future. Not for him anyway, the wanker.' Kelsey was too exhausted to re-tread old ground but her thoughts strayed to their date at the Yorick. *He is a wanker, a gorgeous, kissable, lying, cheating wish-he-was-mine wanker.*

'You're the boss. I'll put "Sorry. I'm not free. Kelsey". And send. Good riddance Mr Hathaway. Now, can we do something fun please, something that doesn't involve shady blokes?'

The rest of that day turned out to be one of those golden summer memories that live on like a hazy, half-recalled perfect dream, one of the most joyful, simple days of Kelsey and Mirren's friendship.

Even before mid-morning, Stratford was baking in the summer heat. Slathering themselves in sun cream and slipping on strappy dresses, dark shades, sandals and, in Mirren's case, an enormous black floppy hat, they wandered, hair loose and messy, arm-in-arm down to the bus station by the river where they were to collect their tickets for the Scenic Cotswolds Vintage Bus Tour. Kelsey had bought them online days ago, jumping at the chance to get out of town and explore the gently rolling hills and picturesque villages to the south that she'd heard so much about but never seen. They had half an hour and some errands to run before their little excursion started.

'Over here, we need to get provisions first.' Kelsey led her friend towards the deli barge in the canal basin and they stood in the shade of its blue stripy awning. After the queue cleared, they ordered their provisions: chicken, avocado, and bacon baguettes, a tomato salad with dill dressing, and two bottles of lemonade, one cloudy and one pink; the posh kind with the old-fashioned stoppers in the top, so you know it's going to be both delicious and expensive. Mirren insisted on paying, complaining that she hadn't been able to treat Kelsey to anything yet, and Kelsey packed all the provisions away in her satchel. All set, they walked down through the marina and across the theatre gardens.

'That's the main theatre over there, and you can just make out the statue of Shakespeare there, see? The bus station's just over this bridge and past my boss's ticket boat, not far now,' Kelsey said authoritatively.

'You really are quite the tour guide, Kelsey.'

As they passed the barge Gianfranco popped his head out the window and wordlessly, but with a gap-toothed smile, beckoned to Kelsey to come down the gangplank for a word. She introduced Mirren who, rather flirtatiously Kelsey thought, told him she'd heard all about him, and it had been 'all good things'.

Gianfranco managed to recover himself enough to whisper, 'Look what I have,' with a curiously excited smile.

Kelsey had never seen her big, quiet friend quite so animated as he reached into his pocket and produced the tiny purple velvet ring box.

'Tonight, I will ask,' he blushed, his voice barely audible as he opened the box revealing a gleaming amethyst set among tiny diamonds on a delicate white gold band.

'Oh Gianfranco! That's wonderful, congratulations. Where will you do it?'

'In the gardens here. I walk her beside the fountain and ask her to make me happier than any man deserves to be.'

Gianfranco's huge hands shook as he closed the box, replacing it in his pocket, his cheeks flushing pale then pink with emotion and nerves. Kelsey was almost jumping up and down with excitement when she heard the clip-clop of heels on the walkway behind them and Gianfranco's expression changed to sudden unconvincing nonchalance.

'Hello, darlings. What are you doing here on your weekend off, Kelsey, you naughty thing? Oh, do come and help me with this.'

Norma was dragging a large A-board sign with her. Gianfranco had already leapt out of the top hatch and was lifting it up onto the roof of the barge where he set it down as though it weighed nothing at all.

'To Let? You really are closing down then?' Kelsey asked, trying to get her words in between Norma's noisy directions to Gianfranco as he positioned the sign.

'Back a bit, left a bit more, darling.' Norma turned towards Kelsey. 'That's right, dearie. No time like the present. I'm not one to hang about, Kelsey, as you know, and it's high time I wound up the tours agency. Oh, hello dear, I'm Norma Arden.' She interrupted herself to shake a bewildered Mirren's hand before continuing without taking a breath. 'And so, it's all going. Goodbye tension, hello *pension*.' She pronounced this with a lavish Italian accent. Kelsey felt glad that she knew 'pension' was Italian for hotel. Norma barely paused.

'Just our little joke, you see, we're buying a little guest-house in Amalfi. Gianfranco's taking me home to meet his mother.' Norma laughed giddily.

Kelsey had never seen her boss so exultant. She thought of the surprise proposal coming Norma's way and her heart wanted to burst with happiness for the lovely, batty woman. Neither Kelsey nor Mirren had said one word before Norma was off again in full sail.

'Now, darling, I'm glad I've bumped into you. I have a little extra work for you in late August, if you're interested? Of course you are. The season always culminates with an open-air party, the Summer Gala they call it. Anyway, there's a few days' set-up work to be done; putting up lights, making little performance spaces, that sort of thing. It's easy money but it will make for very long days I'm afraid. Oh, and the director of the American company... oh, what *is* it called?'

'The Oklahoma Renaissance Players,' answered Kelsey in a grim, ominous voice, which Norma either didn't pick up on or chose to ignore.

'That's the one. Their director needs some extras for a *tableau vivant*. I said I'm sure you'd be keen. It pays proper Equity rates, you know?'

Kelsey was too thrown by the mention of Jonathan's company not to allow the confusion to show on her face. 'A *tableau*...?'

'*Vivant*, dear. A living picture? Goodness, the education system in this country; it's diabolical. The director needs some girls to be fairies. You don't move, you don't say a word, you just strike a pose, the curtain drops, everyone gasps at how lovely and enchanting you all look, the curtain goes up again, you get paid, and you go home. What do you say, sweetheart?'

Searching for the right words to let Norma down with, Kelsey became aware of Mirren chortling beside her, her head bowed beneath her huge hat to hide the laughter.

'Well, I... I haven't really done any acting since school, and I, eh...' She gave up, seeing the determined look on Norma's face, and, with a sudden wicked sense of revenge, blurted out, 'I'll do it if Mirren can do it.'

'What?' Mirren snapped her head upright, gaping in shock at Kelsey.

'Right, it's settled then. Thank you, ladies. I'll let the director know. And Mirren, is it? Cash in hand suit you too? I'm sure we can sort something out. Jolly good.'

Mirren was shaking her head and trying to protest, but to no avail. Arguing with Norma was like trying to stop a burst dam with a single dish cloth. Kelsey was slyly looking at Mirren out of the corner of her eyes and grinning widely when she remembered their bus trip. They excused themselves and, after winking conspiratorially at a blushing Gianfranco from behind Norma's back, Kelsey grabbed Mirren's hand and they ran as fast as they could for the bus station, dodging the slow-moving tourists who packed the pavements. All the while Kelsey was worrying about the clinking lemonade bottles, hoping their tops wouldn't pop in her satchel.

They screamed in delight as they rounded the corner catching sight of the lovely old bus that would be theirs for the day, all gleaming cream and pale green curves, dinky tyres, round chrome lamps, and windows that did up with brown leather straps. As they drew near it, their driver introduced himself with a finger-tap on the peak of his navy cap. His smart uniform and silver buttons set off the whole 'vintage escapade' scene perfectly. His name was Jim and, Kelsey thought, he looked as old as the bus itself. After he'd neatly clipped the corners of their tickets and offered them a polite, gloved hand up the narrow steps, he whipped out a chamois and gave the bonnet a quick and totally unnecessary once-over.

Kelsey and Mirren were the last passengers to arrive, and they greeted the others – smiling holiday makers from all four corners of the world – and made their way to the worn leather seats right at the back. Jim turned over the engine and they began their bumpy, spluttering exit from the bus station, across the busy bridge over the Avon and away from the hustle and bustle of Stratford and the summer season crowds.

'A *tableau vivant*, eh?' Mirren asked with a half-scowl, half-laugh.

'Well, you did say you fancied coming back to Stratford at the end of the season; this way you'll earn back your train fare while you're here,' Kelsey shrugged with a sparkle in her eyes. Mirren looked unconvinced, so she quickly added, 'and maybe you'll meet Benedict Cumber-batch.'

Mirren said nothing as she sat back in her seat, gazing out the window, a faint smile forming at the corner of her mouth as she contemplated that possibility.

The sun blazed down onto their noisy little coach as they made their way among the lush fields of grass, dazzling yellow sunflowers and, far in the distance, long, neat rows of blue Cotswold lavender. They passed solitary country pubs, millionaires' barn conversions, and farm shops boasting proudly of their freshly laid duck eggs and hothouse tomatoes. Everyone settled into the journey, gazing out at the cloudless skies opening up above them. Kelsey felt a quiet peace descend over her as her body surrendered to the roll and rock of the bumping wheels on tarmac as she and Mirren slumped together, shoulder to shoulder.

Soon they were approaching the first village. Each of its smart cottages was made of golden barley-coloured soft stone, and had its own immaculate front garden bursting with roses, all enclosed within neat, low, stone walls. Tall oaks, conifers, and monkey puzzle trees peeped over the roofs of the houses, hinting at the grand landscaped gardens hidden away behind them. And everywhere there were sudden flashes of bright red, from the phone and pillar boxes to the bold little robins in the hedgerows. As the bus bumped on, winding through the lanes and turning tight corners past bakeries and butcher shops and the one lone blacksmith's forge, Kelsey tried to imagine she was drifting back in time. It was easy enough if she ignored the heavy traffic on the open roads between the picturesque villages.

Jim spoke occasionally into a crackling microphone, pointing out important landmarks, like the church that had held onto the secret of its plague pit, sunken by mourners four hundred years ago just inside its lichen-speckled lychgate where the tragic bodies of mothers and husbands and adored children had been placed without ceremony and forgotten by the generations afterwards, only to be discovered recently by horrified workmen repairing a water main.

Jim revelled in the gothic horror of each tale he told and they grew increasingly far-fetched. Here, they were on a stretch of road frequented by a dashing seventeenth-century highwayman who always stole a kiss from the ladies in the rich carriages he stopped before tearing their shining jewels from heaving chests. Then there came a spot made famous in the civil war, but neither Kelsey nor Mirren could have told you precisely how it found its fame, they were only half-listening now, almost snoozing behind their sunglasses. Kelsey was so glad someone else was the tour guide for a change.

After an hour or so the little bus pulled into a larger village, constructed of a yellow stone as deep in shade and pitted and crumbling as a madeira cake. A wide, shallow river flowed right through its centre. There were day-trippers padding in the babbling water. Kelsey leaned across Mirren to peer out the window at the lovely shops lining their route on the far side of the river: cafés, bookstores, outdoorsy-type shops with waterproofs and sturdy boots, even a Christmas shop, its artificial fir trees in the window displays dripping with pale pink frosted-glass baubles, white feathers, and crystal angels, striking an incongruous note alongside the happy children in their brand new summer holiday shorts and T-shirts, gazing up at them, dreaming of December.

Jim found a spot in a busy coach park behind a pub and everyone stepped out into the sun to stretch their legs for a few moments. Kelsey had just enough time to take a few hurried pictures of the little footbridge that spanned the river while Mirren queued for ice lollies. As they boarded their bus again, Kelsey felt relieved to be leaving the crowds.

They headed out into wilder open countryside, passing a chandlery and the odd micro-brewery, farmhouse and parsonage. Jim pulled the bus into a large lay-by with a sign declaring it a 'beauty spot', as if that were in doubt. He stopped the engine and made his announcements into the microphone.

'We'll be making a stop here for lunch. If you walk a little further down the road, there's a very fine church of Norman origin, nice for a quick visit. Across the road and over this field you'll find the Wheatsheaf Inn, does a nice steak pie, it does. That's where I'll be. Or the river is a hundred yards in that direction.' He pointed a gloved finger across a wild-looking fallow field. 'Just hop over the stile and stick to the path.'

'River,' said Mirren decisively as they gathered their things, hoping no one else on the coach would follow them on their way, which, to their relief, no one did.

Away from the road and over the grassy field the traffic sounds faded away. As they followed the narrow path, made from hundreds of years of footfall, down towards the treeline, they set butterflies and moths fluttering up into the air from the bobble heads of flowering clovers.

'I'm so glad you're here, Mirr. I'd never have done this without you, and it *is* gorgeous out here.'

'Can't have you mooning about the gift shops of Stratford by yourself all day long, can we? How are you feeling anyway?' Mirren asked, as they strode along under the white sun.

'Let's not talk about it. I'm so tired of it all, and it's such a lovely day.' Kelsey craned her neck and shielded her eyes as she looked up at a buzzard hundreds of feet above them. It flew around and around in increasingly wide circles, its mate soaring around in a gyre even further above it, so free and breathtakingly high. In a few seconds they were nothing but indistinct black dots seemingly on the very edge of space.

They found the river running through a deep, narrow channel just on the edge of the field margin where it met the trees. Its waters provided a gentle shushing soundtrack to their lunch on the dry shady bank.

'Ah, I could get used to living down here,' Mirren said with a sigh. 'And it looks as though you have, Kelse.'

'It's true. I love Stratford. I love the job, the theatres, the buildings, everything. I'll really miss it.' Sitting by the bank, she unwrapped the sandwiches and took a big bite to punctuate her sentence, savouring the creamy avocado, before shovelling a forkful of tomato salad into her mouth. 'Mmm, and the food. I love the food too,' she mumbled.

Mirren smiled to see Kelsey so relaxed though she could also see the dark shadows under her friend's eyes from the evening before. After a few silent, appreciative bites of baguette, Mirren spoke tentatively.

'Kelse, I hope you don't mind, I found your photographs this morning… the ones of the town and your tour guide friends. They're really good. I mean, they're *really* good, your best yet. It was like there was something different about them. I can't put my finger on it, really.' Mirren tipped her head, squinting into the bright sky in thought. 'If they made me the newspaper's art critic… I'd write that there was a new freshness of composition and framing. No, more than that, more technical proficiency, too. You've managed to capture something special in them. They look like you've found a place for yourself here and I can see the excitement and the… fullness of your life here in the pictures.'

'Wow! Well thank you, here's your promotion,' Kelsey said with a laugh. 'If you think those pictures are good, you should see the headshots…' She stopped herself, not wanting to think about how carried away she'd let herself become with thoughts of gorgeous, unavailable Jonathan after the magic of that day in the studio.

Mirren quickly steered her away from danger. 'Hon, why don't you exhibit some of your landscapes, or the ones of the narrowboats? They were beautiful. Surely you could find a photography club in town, or you must know some nice restaurant owner by now who'd display them for you? I'll bet they'd fly off the walls. The tourists would love them. You could make some extra cash… and you'd be doing the thing you love again.'

'Naw, Fran was right when he said old school photographers were a dying breed. Who'd buy them anyway? Everybody's got a camera phone and they'll leave Stratford with a thousand pictures of the place. They don't need my ones too.'

'Nonsense. You're a *proper* photographer. Those are just crappy snaps that they'll never look at again or they'll

224

end up deleting or losing them. People still need treasured photos of special places and their special people.'

'OK, but how am I supposed to make any money, Mirr? Getting films developed is so expensive these days, and I'd need a digital camera and it would have to be a *really* good one.'

'Well then, invest in one, second hand if you need to. You'd soon make the money back. Anyway, didn't Fran give you your share of the deposit back? It's like life's telling you what to do. You can't be a tour guide for much longer, can you now?'

Kelsey thought about Norma and Gianfranco selling up and leaving town and the huge gap they'd leave in her little world. The agency had been her family and her home all summer. She sighed, wiping thin smears of mayonnaise from her fingers onto the dry grass beside her.

'I could do some teaching, I guess, retro photography, that sort of thing? Evening classes maybe? There's lots of retired folk looking for a hobby, and people our age who'll never even have seen a camera as old as this before, let alone know how it works.'

'Now you're talking.' Mirren nodded approvingly and popped the stopper on one of the bottles of lemonade before handing it to Kelsey who was deep in thought.

'But, how much do they pay to teach evening classes? Not enough to live off, not in Stratford anyway, I'll bet. I'd need two or three jobs to survive here forever,' said Kelsey pensively.

Mirren flinched inwardly at the word 'forever' and, not without some pain, let it dawn upon her that Kelsey would, more than likely, never be content to move back home to the village again, not after all this. Kelsey, who was staring down into the shimmering water of the river, lost in the effort of trying to imagine her future, kept talking.

'I suppose I could get work as a baby photographer, you know, on the wards at the hospitals? One of them used to come into Mr McLennan's shop to get her prints done. Gemma, her name was. She used to hang around the maternity wards and photograph all the babies on the day they were born and she'd get the mums' credit card details there and then. Made good money too.'

Kelsey remembered the times she'd sneakily looked through Gemma's prints after they arrived from the developer's. The babies looked lovely, of course, but Kelsey had felt sorry for the poor startled-looking mums at the edges of the pictures. They'd barely had time to brush their hair, let alone compose themselves for a high definition photo under a blinding flashlight. 'No, on second thoughts, it's not for me.'

'Just keep thinking of a way to make it work because you're the best photographer I know, and you'd be mad to throw away talent like yours.'

Kelsey smiled and sipped her drink, thinking how much Mirren sounded like Jonathan. He'd seen her as a professional too. He'd recognised her talent and accepted it. There wasn't a doubt in his mind that she wasn't the real deal. Anyway, *he* made a living from the arts, why couldn't she?

After lunch they'd walked around the margins of the field, Kelsey taking a few shots of Mirren spinning around dramatically in the long grass laughing and holding out the wide folds of her sundress, her hippy hat flopping over her face while the sun glinted into the camera lens, impressing exploding white sunbursts onto the film. Some days, the magic is there in the light, just waiting. All Kelsey had to do was find the right angle, hit the shutter button at the right moment and there it was, captured forever.

Their happy excursion was made up of the very best of the English summertime, but already high summer was far behind them and each day was drawing in a little shorter than the one before.

Back on-board Jim's bus, they threw themselves down onto the comfy leather seats and prepared for the long journey back to town. Kelsey reached into her satchel and rummaged for her copy of the *Sonnets*. 'Here he is. Right, which one are we having? You can choose,' Kelsey said, raising her eyebrows and holding the book up to cover her goofy grin. The peace of the countryside, the midday sun, and Mirren's uninhibited sense of fun had made her giddy and carefree.

'Which one? I don't even know how many there are?'

'There's one hundred and fifty-four in here. Pick one.'

'All right then. Twenty-nine,' said Mirren, yawning and covering her face with her huge hat before slouching down in the seat. 'Go on, I'm listening.'

'Ooh, you'll love this one,' Kelsey bubbled with excitement, opening the book at the so-familiar words. The pages were coming a little loose, she had turned them so often. 'It's about poor old Shaky. He's feeling as though he's lost everything but then he thinks of his old lover and just his memories of them are enough to make him glad to be alive. It's so gorgeous. Listen.' She began to read slowly and quietly, but with all the enthusiasm of a true poetry lover, close to Mirren's ear.

'When, in disgrace with fortune and men's eyes,

I all alone beweep my outcast state

And trouble deaf heaven with my bootless cries

And look upon myself and curse my fate,

Wishing me like to one more rich in hope,

Featured like him, like him with friends possessed,

Desiring this man's art and that man's scope,

With what I most enjoy contented least;

Yet in these thoughts myself almost despising,

Haply I think on thee, and then my state,

Like to the lark at break of day arising

From sullen earth, sings hymns at heaven's gate;

For thy sweet love remembered such wealth brings

That then I scorn to change my state with kings.

Closing the book, Kelsey smiled softly. 'I told you it was lovely. Do you think it's about his wife?'

Mirren made a sleepy, noncommittal groan beneath her hat so Kelsey pressed on undaunted. 'I love the idea that we still talk about Anne Hathaway four hundred years after she died because someone loved her enough to immortalise her.' Kelsey wrapped her arms around herself, hugging the book to her chest. She was getting carried away now. 'I want to be that woman; a woman so awesome and in control and remarkable that someone finds me fascinating or inspiring, or…'

Mirren lifted her hat off her face and interrupted her. 'Didn't Shakespeare have to marry her because she was knocked up, and then didn't he move to London to get away from her for, like, twenty years?'

'Ugh, spoilsport. Where's your sense of romance?'

All the way back to Stratford she thought about the poem Mirren had chosen. Could she be contented with just the memory of Jonathan and their few brief moments together? Could the fact of her simply having known him sustain her as she lived her life without him? Maybe one day she'd just feel glad to have met him, and it wouldn't hurt quite so much as it did now.

Chapter Twenty-Five

'Love is like a child that longs for everything it can
come by'
(Two Gentlemen of Verona)

Early the next day Kelsey dressed for work, kissed the
sleeping Mirren on the forehead, and silently closed the
door behind her. By the time her shift ended Mirren
would already be back in Scotland. She didn't have time
for a teary goodbye – or to fix her mascara afterwards
– there was a tour group waiting for her at the theatre
gardens, sixty of them if the rota was correct, and they
were booked in for the works: backstage tour, onstage
sword-fighting demo with one of the main company's
fight directors, the restaurant-barge river tour for lunch,
followed by a visit to the Shakespeare sites around town
in the afternoon. It was going to be a long day, perfect for
taking her mind off Mirren leaving, as well as the sorry
state she'd been in watching Jonathan and Peony up on
stage together on Saturday night.

Having gathered her tour group and ticked their names
off her list, Kelsey walked everyone towards the main
theatre, holding her tall plastic sunflower high into the
air so no one lost sight of their leader. Out the corner

of her eye, Kelsey threw a quick glance across the street towards the Willow Studio. Its doors were wide open and the sign outside with its picture of Peony as Titania pasted over with a banner that read, *Sold Out. Additional morning performances now available.*

Good for them. The show's a hit, and that's no more than they deserve – even Peony. She was amazing, actually. I should be glad for them. I should. And I suppose I am.

Kelsey worked late into the afternoon. The group were indeed sixty strong and made up of wealthy baby boomers from across the south of England on a mystery tour and, for once, she had trouble keeping them contained. Small gangs frequently broke off on their own or chattered and joked during her spiels. She had to add lots of exciting inflection and drama into her voice, modifying her usual script to get them engaged again, and as she succeeded in taming them all, captivating them one by one, she felt herself glowing again.

She'd told Mirren only yesterday how it had taken a few weeks but she was finally beginning to understand what it meant to be an actor. 'The show must go on, no matter how crappy you feel. You have to smile and bow and curtsey and give them what they're paying for.'

So that's what she did. By seven o'clock that evening, she was ready to collapse. The problem with pretending to be relentlessly bubbly and fascinating was the utter exhaustion that hit her afterwards when she was alone again. She trudged back to St Ninian's Close in the dying heat, watching the pavement slipping by underneath her feet as she went.

Her phone rang in her satchel just as she made her way into the cool of her hallway, closing the heavy door behind her, glad to be home again. Thinking it must be Mirren letting her know she was back in Scotland, she knew she didn't need to rush to answer, but there, on the screen was Jonathan's name.

What can he want? Is he phoning to apologise for running off the other night? He texted yesterday and didn't apologise. 'Let me know when you're free for a coffee,' indeed! Cheeky sod. Mirren sent him my reply, didn't she? Telling him to get knotted?

She answered with a curt hello.

He greeted her with what struck her as an unnecessarily exuberant 'Hey!' and asked her how she was.

'Um, I'm all right.' *So we're pretending everything's fine, that this is normal?* 'I see you're sold out. Not surprising really.' She rolled her eyes at herself and added begrudgingly, 'You were... you were really incredible on Saturday. Thanks for the tickets.'

'I'm just so glad you came.'

There was a long silence, neither knowing what to say next. Titania and Oberon's kiss replayed again in Kelsey's mind and the numbness struck her into silence.

'So, uh, anyway... I was calling about the gala night,' Jonathan said at last, waking Kelsey from her stupor.

'Oh yes, of course. The gala. I'm doing some living picture thing, aren't I? Am I onstage with the *Dream* cast? Am I... onstage with you?' Sudden panic flooded her body. She hadn't fully considered the ramifications of letting Norma strong-arm her into this.

'Only the girls are in the scene. You'll be one of Peony's fairy court,' he replied, dryly.

Perfect! Of course I will. She threw herself onto the bed, wanting to scream obscenities down the phone at the absurdity of the idea. *Can I pull out now? What would Norma say? I could do with the money, frankly.*

'But that's not what I'm calling about,' Jonathan continued, 'I hope you don't mind, but I showed your headshots to my director, and he showed them to the guy from the main theatre who's directing the gala night, and he wants you to photograph the whole thing for the website and social media. Are you interested? I said I'd ask you, and here I am, asking you. He wants to pay you, obviously; said you should name your price.'

'Name my price?' Kelsey had no idea how to respond. Here she was again, being mistaken for an actual photographer. 'I don't know, Jonathan. I'd need to buy some new equipment. I doubt they'd pay me enough to cover that?'

'I'll text you the director's number, you can talk it over with him. I just wanted to pass on the good news.'

Jonathan sounded so strained, Kelsey thought. *Maybe he's tired too. It's been a long summer.* 'Thanks for the heads up. I'll definitely call him.' *And say what? I have no idea.* Kelsey took a deep breath, feeling churlish at being so short with Jonathan when he'd passed on this amazing opportunity to her. She tried to recapture some of the enthusiasm she'd felt in front of her tour group that day. 'So, how's the run going? You looked like you were enjoying yourself on stage.'

After a split second of silence, Jonathan answered with a wry tone in his voice. 'We're already rehearsing *Hamlet* for the Canadian shows this fall, and that's in between all the extra performances of *Dream* they've added. Honestly, I'm kinda wiped out, Kelsey.'

His voice wrapping around her name sounded so inviting, she could have wept right there into the phone.

She shook herself. *He's got Peony to talk with about all that. They can console each other. Oh, come on, Kelsey, at least try to act like a normal, rational human being!* 'I'll see you at the gala set-up?' she said, steeling herself to hang up, but not really wanting to.

'Yup. Me and the other Oklahoma Players are setting up two performance spaces; one for your *tableau vivant* and one for some scenes from *Dream*. It's going to look awesome outdoors at night under the stars. I just hope the English rain stays away. I'll come find you at the set-up. I, uh… I guess Will's coming too?'

'No doubt. Try keeping him away,' she replied with a bluff dismissiveness.

'Right. Great. Of course. So, uh… OK. Bye, Kelsey. Take care.' His voice was deep and dry, fading away into a crackle as he hung up. Kelsey had managed a hesitant, 'Bye Jonathan… and thanks,' before she was cut off.

She sat for a long while looking at the phone in her hands wondering how it was possible that their electric connection could have cooled to this joyless, stilted acquaintance. Had she imagined it? Had she somehow mistaken his passing interest in her and his intense zeal for life in general as reciprocated attraction? It probably happened to him all the time. An extrovert like Jonathan could easily confuse and confound a naïve, homely woman like Kelsey with his sparkling enthusiasm, only for that enthusiasm to wane the second his attention drifted to something, or someone, else. She'd fallen for his charms, his confidence, his manners, and now she was paying for it, but that was hardly his fault, was it? Whatever she'd imagined between them, it was over now. All she had to do was survive the rest of the summer without getting into any more stupid scrapes, and with August approaching and summer's end just on the horizon, how hard could that be?

★

It had taken a few days to get her head around her next photography job. She'd had to build herself up to the phone call to the gala director by drinking half a bottle of wine up on the terrace beforehand, and it had been such a long, involved conversation about what he wanted, including photos of all the stars arriving, images of all the performers, and lots of atmospheric pictures of the partygoers taking in the spectacle. She'd made it clear that she too would be performing so she couldn't shoot the *tableau vivant* but he didn't seem to mind too much.

Then, she'd had to screw up all of her courage to give him her quote and, even after hours of deliberating how much he might have available to spend on a photographer she still had no idea if she was even in the right ballpark.

'I *think* it will be about five hours' work and with analogue *and* digital pictures, it'll be about two hundred pounds?' She said it as quickly as she could, trying to get it over and done with.

The director replied instantly with only one word, 'fine.'

After she ended the call, Kelsey spent a restless night wondering if she'd undersold herself.

He must have known I was a newbie with no idea what I was doing. Oh God, how embarrassing! How will two hundred quid cover everything? I'll need to buy a digital camera now, but which one, I have no idea. Film is one thing, but digital is just totally out of my comfort zone. And don't I need a super whizzy

235

tablet thingy to upload all the pictures? How do I even do that? And am I actually allowed to take his money? Don't I need to own some sort of company that pays taxes or something to do that? Oh shit, I have no clue.

The night passed with her tied up in panicked knots, the back of her neck sweating and goosebumped with feverish shivers. She knew one thing for certain: as soon as morning came, she was phoning her mum.

Chapter Twenty-Six

'We fail! But screw your courage to the sticking-place,
and we'll not fail'
(Macbeth)

'How's life in sunny Stratford? We've been watching the weather forecasts for England and it looks like you're baking down there.'

'We are, I've got an actual tan. Are you OK, Mum?'

'Smashing, doll. Run off my feet with work. And you know Grandad's moving in with me and Calum? Just for the short term, to see how he gets on with a bit more company.'

'I really hope he settles in. Just clear out my stuff, put it in the attic. I've got everything I need here.'

'To be honest, Kelse, I think he'll like things better the way they are, with all your pictures on the walls and your photo albums on the shelves. The doctor said it would be good for him to look through old pictures; good for his memory, I mean. Don't worry, you should be enjoying your adventure. I've got this, really I have.'

Kelsey knew when her mum was putting on a brave face, she'd been doing it for years, but there was an insistence and calmness in her voice that was reassuring.

'OK, well, he can have my room for as long as he wants it. I can crash with you when I get home in September.'

'We'll sort something out, don't worry. Tell me about Stratford. How are things going?'

'I could do with a bit of, um… business advice, actually.'

'Go on. Sounds intriguing.'

'I've been asked if I'll photograph this event that's coming up, some huge outdoor theatre thing to celebrate the end of the summer shows…'

Kelsey was stopped in her tracks by the ear-piercing scream from the other end of the line. 'That's brilliant! Well done.'

'Thanks,' she squirmed a little. 'It's not a big deal really, but the thing is, I said I'd do it before I thought about the implications. They're going to pay me. What am I supposed to do with the money? I mean, don't I need to have an actual business first?'

'Ah, right-o.' Mari was breezy and calm. 'You can take the money, you just need to tell the taxman. I'll help you do your tax return at the end of the year, if you like. If I can do it, you can. And it's all online these days.'

'Don't I have to do anything else? That sounds too easy.'

'If you want to do it properly, you could set up a business account, pay it all in there, if there's going to be other jobs, I mean.'

'But, I'm going to need to buy some bits; some film and maybe even a new camera.'

'Just keep all the receipts and the invoices for anything that you buy or anything that you earn. OK? Buy your film and pay your printing costs out of your new bank account, balance those outgoings with your incomings, and *voilà*, you're a business woman.'

Kelsey, feeling horribly out of her depth, bit her bottom lip but her mum's voice helped quieten her self-doubt, at least momentarily. She'd watched her mum do it. Mari had started with nothing and set herself up as a sole trader and eventually she had been able to provide for the whole family, all by herself: every pair of school shoes, every bite they'd eaten, every school trip they'd gone on, and endless rounds of pocket money and dinner money and bus fares. Suddenly, she was struck by the enormity of what her mum had done for her and Calum. Mari had pulled herself out of her grief to feed and clothe and house them. Kelsey only had herself to look after. How hard could it be?

'There's only one trick, love,' Mari was saying.

Kelsey sniffed away the tears that were forming in her eyes and making her nose run.

'What's that?'

'You have to have something people are willing to pay for and you have to value your time correctly. Don't undersell yourself. They expect the best, so you have to charge like the best of them.'

Kelsey was nodding but her mum's voice was being crowded out by a thousand anxious questions. *I only asked for two hundred quid. Why didn't I ask for more? And people will expect proper, professional invoices and receipts too, won't they? How do I make those without a computer? I don't have any of that stuff. Can I do it all from a tablet? How much do those cost? How am I to know which tablet and which apps are compatible with which digital camera? Oh, Jesus, I'll have to buy a camera, like, this week! And… what about a business name? And a logo? I don't want to look like an amateur.*

Mari was calling to her through the panicked cacophony. 'Kelsey! Kelsey, are you still there? Just breathe. You can do this. Start with this one job and you can conquer the rest of the world another day. Get your equipment together and go to that theatre shoot and enjoy it, OK? Now… can I send you any money, to get you started, I mean?'

Now Kelsey really wanted to cry. 'No thanks, Mum. I've got a little bit of what was the flat deposit left in the bank. Thank you… for everything. I'd best go get on with some research into digital cameras and stuff then. Give my love to everyone back home.'

'Don't worry, love, about anything, and good luck. Something tells me you're going to be fabulous.'

'I'm glad somebody thinks so,' Kelsey said to herself as she hung up the phone, and then remembered instantly that there was someone else who believed in her, enough to get her a second photography commission. How she wished she could ring Jonathan to thank him again, and this time she'd be kinder. Although, she told herself, once he'd done as he was asked and passed on the director's message he probably hadn't given her a second thought.

Chapter Twenty-Seven

'Lust's winter comes ere summer half be done'
(Venus and Adonis)

Where are you, Kelsey Anderson?

Kelsey swatted away the buzzing text alert, keeping her head hidden snugly under the pillow. The late afternoon sun beat down through the lace curtains casting its orange glow in filigree patterns over Kelsey's sleeping body.

Seriously, are you injured or dying? Do I need to break into your flat and perform CPR on you?

Another text. It was Will.
She made the Herculean effort to drag herself out of bed and type her reply.

I'm sleeping. What is it?

Rubbing her eyes, she watched the little rippling dots that said he was typing his reply. There on the floor by the bed among the bubble wrap – all now satisfactorily popped, of course – lay her new digital camera. Her busy morning was coming back to her through the dreamy haze.

Taking full advantage of her first day off since Mirren's visit a week ago, she'd trawled the internet on her phone looking for cameras in the summer sales, spotting a deal on a digital SLR with a decent wide-angle lens, as well as a tablet she could wirelessly upload photos to. That morning, she'd raced to the huge electronics store near the Bullring shopping centre where a really helpful and offensively young sales assistant had carefully explained some of the functions to her.

Spending so much money in one morning had left her slightly queasy, but she'd had the last of her share of the flat deposit just sitting in the bank and it felt good to redirect it towards her new enterprise. She fought back the nerves by holding on to Mirren's advice, the day they had picnicked by the river on their Cotswolds tour. This was an investment. An investment in a future she didn't really have mapped out clearly, but these felt like the first brave, and expensive, steps in the right direction. The whole shopping trip had taken so much out of her, she'd spent the afternoon sleeping.

Will's text pinged onto her screen.

We're all at the Yorick celebrating the upcoming wedding of the year. Get yourself down here, Kelsey Anderson, or I'm coming round to drag you out of your tartan nightie.

Certain by now there were no neighbours occupying the flats either side of her own, Kelsey screamed, jumping up on the bed, squeaking the springs. 'Norma's accepted Gianfranco's proposal!'

She could be there in ten minutes if she splashed some water on her face, brushed her teeth, threw on a simple grey dress over her white T-shirt, and hurriedly laced up her Converse. No need for make-up or anything else with her tour guide family. Within moments she was on the pavement, her new digital camera swinging on its black strap across her body.

Bursting through the doors of the pub and pushing her way to the inglenook where she knew they'd all be, Kelsey headed straight for Norma, throwing her arms around her neck. 'Congratulations!' she squealed excitedly.

Norma, for once, was quiet. Kissing Kelsey on the cheek she blushed. 'Thank you, dear.'

Gianfranco was by Norma's side, rosy-cheeked and grinning widely. Kelsey teetered on her tiptoes to hug him. The whole team was assembled. Lukas was squeezed into the far corner seat inside the inglenook nursing a nearly empty cider glass and Myrtle and Valeria were sitting opposite him, very close together and beaming at the happy couple.

'Hello, beautiful,' said Will in a low voice from behind Kelsey's back, nudging her arm as he jostled past, carrying a huge bottle of bubbly in an ice bucket hugged close to his body and six champagne flutes clutched miraculously by their stems between his fingers.

As Kelsey was busy rescuing the glasses one at a time from his precarious grip, she leaned in towards Will and impulsively kissed him on the cheek. She suddenly felt so very pleased to see him. 'Long time, no see. Where have you been, Will?'

As the chattering group half-watched Will peel the golden foil from the cork, he surreptitiously leaned close to her ear and spoke in a low monotone. 'Oh, you know: auditions, open calls, Bristol, Manchester, you name it. I even got a call back for a film in London, but no luck, unfortunately. Anyway, now's not the time for licking wounds. I'll tell you later.'

Even when crestfallen and defeated, Will looked like a movie star. His lovely dark auburn hair had grown over the summer and was now skimming his jawline, and a much longer set of recently manscaped sideburns jutted across his cheekbones, making them even more well-defined than they had seemed before. Kelsey appraised him slyly as he worked the bottle open. She wasn't used to seeing him out of uniform. As usual, his dark sunglasses were perched on top of his head, but tonight he was wearing dark jeans and a slim khaki T-shirt that was tucked in only at the front, revealing a glimpse of leather belt.

Something in his demeanour suggested that the summer of rejection – from the auditions, but maybe also from her – had cowed him a little. He had certainly needed to rein in his ego, but now that his spark was dimmed she felt sorry for it; he'd lost the cockiness that had ignited her brief crush on him.

'That is a shame, sorry, Will.' Having placed her hand gently on his arm, she hastily withdrew it at the sensation of his muscles tightening at her touch. He looked flustered for a brief moment. Kelsey tried to laugh it away. 'You're not blushing, are you, Will?' she teased, as he met her eyes and expertly eased the cork from the bottle to the loud cheer of their happy circle.

Soon, they were all squeezed around and inside the inglenook, laughing and chatting and toasting the bride and groom to be. Kelsey arranged the group taking lots of shots, amazed at how liberating the new camera felt. She didn't have to count the number of photographs she took, worried that she'd reach the end of an expensive roll of film too soon if she wasn't economical and judicious with the shutter button. Instead, she clicked away, shot after shot, and there were her pictures, showing up instantaneously on the clear, bright screen, hers to keep or dispose of with the press of a button. 'I could seriously get used to this,' she remarked to no one in particular.

It felt thrilling to see her handiwork there and then without having to wait days or even weeks for film developing and mail delivery. And the lighting was so easy, the flash just did its own thing automatically, capturing perfectly lit image after image.

When Kelsey had finished she sat down with a happy sigh on the pub stool next to Will, who immediately refilled her glass to the brim.

'Cheers,' he said, raising his glass to hers and taking a long drink, all the while looking into her eyes.

It was apparent there was something on his mind that he was building up to saying. Kelsey took an appreciative sip of bubbly and waited.

'So, how are things going with Laurence Olivier?'

Genuinely perplexed for a second, she cocked her head. 'Who? Oh, Jonathan? Now, don't be mean.' There was a warning tone in her voice, and she added with a weariness that she couldn't suppress, 'He's nowhere to be seen, I'm afraid. It turns out I interrupted something pretty complicated with his co-star Peony.'

Will nodded slowly and looked genuinely sorry as he mouthed a long, 'Oh!' before adding with suspicion, 'Hold on, you mean he's with that gorgeous American bird? The one that plays Titania? I'd never have guessed, they had *zero* chemistry when I saw them.'

'You saw his play?'

'Of course, I see everything that comes to town.'

'Hmm,' Kelsey mused. 'Well, whatever's going on with those two, I'm just glad nothing actually happened, and I didn't make a complete fool of myself in front of the entire town.' She tipped her head back, downing the champagne. 'Fill it up again, Will. I'm in the mood for drowning sorrows.'

'I might just join you.' He filled both their glasses. 'This theatre life isn't as easy as you think. I felt sure by now I'd be in a leading role, but here I am, tour guiding for the eighth summer running.'

'Eight years? Wow! You must be sad to see Norma leaving town.'

Hearing her name mentioned, Norma's ears pricked up. 'What's that, my dear?' she called out from only a few feet away, but still using the top of her voice.

'I said we'll all be sorry to see you go. I can't believe you're getting married, selling your business, and sailing off into the sunset all at once.'

'I know, lucky old me. I can't quite believe it either.' Norma beamed, turning her head to meet Gianfranco's gaze. The two looked into each other's eyes like teenagers before Norma snapped out of her trance, turning her hawk-like eyes back to Kelsey.

'But, I'm not *selling* up, darling, I'm closing up. There are plenty of other tour agencies around and with the downturn in tourists coming from Europe and the States, I doubt I'll be missed. *All* the offices are closing: Oxford,

Bath, London, Cambridge, Windsor, the lot. Did you know I employ thirty-seven people?'

'We're all going to miss you terribly, Norma. And you too, Gianfranco.'

'Oh, darling,' Norma replied with a dismissive wave of her hand. 'You young people will all be off on your adventures again by the end of the summer, you don't need me or the agency.'

Kelsey felt like throwing herself across the table and wrapping herself in an octopus grip round Norma's waist, screaming, 'But I *do* need you! I *really* bloody do. Don't leave, I don't want to go home.' But instead, she looked down at the bubbles popping in her glass.

Norma leaned across the table and whispered in a surprisingly hushed voice, 'Worry not, little one. Summer's not over yet. I'm sure it has plenty more surprises in store for Kelsey Anderson.' And with a wink and a pat on her hand Norma turned back to her fiancé and the loud chatter of the rest of the group.

Feeling strangely removed from the noisy, jovial scene all of a sudden, Kelsey took a moment to look around at her summer family, unaware that Will was watching her and smiling affectionately by her side. Everyone was joined in one joyful accord of celebration. Gianfranco was making Lukas howl with laughter at some barely audible story he was telling, and Valeria and Myrtle were whispering to each other and holding hands tightly across their thighs. That's when it struck Kelsey for the first time. Turning to Will she whispered, 'Oh my God, they're a couple too? How could I not have known?'

Will laughed, shaking his head. 'Oh, come on, woman! You really are hopeless. They've been together for years.

You *really* cannot see what's going on right in front of your nose, can you?'

Kelsey was about to agree with a self-effacing laugh when she noticed the earnest look in Will's eyes. He stared straight at her, willing her to understand. Hurriedly reaching for the bottle she spoke in a slightly higher than usual voice, 'More champagne anyone?'

★

Just as she had downed enough bubbly to entertain the idea that Will resembled a long-haired Prince Harry, though even posher, if that were possible, Kelsey realised that she might actually be very drunk indeed. The bell rang out from the bar as she attempted to stand up and found her legs wobbled beneath her, making her laugh to herself.

'Right, I'm off to my ivory tower. Night all. And congratulations again, Georma… I mean… Norma and Gianfranco.' *Oh shit, I'm pissed.*

Norma was at Kelsey's side in an instant. 'Goodnight, my dear. Get straight home now. No dawdling, yes?' Norma pointed a red fingernail into Kelsey's arm, her authority slightly diminished by the collection of multi-coloured cocktail umbrellas sticking out of her skew-whiff scarlet bob. 'Are you sure you'll be safe walking home alone with your fancy new camera equipment?'

Will, who had been shaking hands and saying good-night to the gang, sidled over. 'Don't worry, Norma, I'll escort her safely to her door.'

'Hmm, yes. Good, good,' their boss replied. She leaned close to Kelsey and spoke as quietly as she could manage. 'You know, Kelsey, it's a shame you're planning on leaving town. I'd feel so much happier going to Italy if I knew my Stratford properties were in safe hands.'

Kelsey squinted drunkenly at Norma and replied with a baffled laugh. 'Safe hands? Me? What would I do with an office, or a ticket barge for that matter?'

Rolling her eyes, Norma delivered a smudged lipstick kiss to Kelsey's forehead in what she possibly conceived of as being a motherly way, but to Kelsey, in her dizzy state, felt more like the touch of a fairy godmother's wand. 'Goodnight, dearie,' Norma said, as Kelsey and Will staggered towards the door, giggling at the realisation that they were as unsteady on their feet as each other.

Out in the street Will held out a crooked arm, pulling a stoic, gentlemanly face, inviting Kelsey to loop her arm through his, which she did, giggling at his comical expression and the lovely old-fashioned gesture.

'You don't have to walk me home, honestly, I'm fine. A few breaths of fresh air and I'll be as sober as a judge.'

'I don't think I can let go now without falling into the gutter,' Will replied, with a hooting laugh.

'I've never seen you tipsy before. You're a lot sillier and funnier than usual. Do you need a few drinks to shake off that too cool for school vibe you've got going on?' Kelsey was laughing, her eyes barely open.

'You can talk. You're a regular ice queen, Kelzey Anderzon,' Will slurred.

Laughing wildly, the pair stopped to steady themselves against the tall, dark glass windows of the Willow Studio. The evening performance was just letting out, and the street was suddenly filled with people. Will leaned against Kelsey for support. 'This is ridiculous. We're as bad as each other. What kind of chaperone am I supposed to be?' he said, removing his arm from her grip and placing it around her shoulders, kissing her softly on the temple, which she accepted with the blissful smile of the closing-time drunk.

They didn't notice Peony behind the dark glass posing for pictures with members of the audience and signing programmes. But she saw them. Her eyes narrowed, sharp, and brooding.

The pair staggered to the end of the road before making the turning up the long lane to Kelsey's house. She could just see Shakespeare's house with its flag flying high above it and the row of gleaming Victorian lamps forming an avenue outside it. They walked on until they were in the quiet residential street leading to St Ninian's Close, well away from the tourist centre and shops.

With no word of warning, Will suddenly stopped dead, pulling Kelsey to a halt outside the porch of a smart terrace. Leaning back against one of its posts to get his balance, smiling all the while, he brought Kelsey in towards his body, his hands around her hips. Kelsey's head was spinning so much that she needed to rest her forehead against Will's broad, hard chest in the hope that the world would stop moving around her.

'Kelsey?' His low voice carried to her across see-sawing horizons. 'Did I mention how ravishingly sexy you look this evening?'

Kelsey dragged her head off Will's chest to look into his face. Amused, she slurred her reply. 'What? In my crumpled clothes and no make-up?'

'You always look hot as hell, Kelsey, to me.'

Still struggling to bring Will's face into focus, Kelsey became aware that it was getting closer to hers, much closer. Her mind was completely still as their lips touched.

The alcohol had silenced any reservations she might have had about getting involved with Will, and their first touch burned intensely through her body as she let herself be kissed, standing limply, leaning into Will. For all the champagne he'd downed he now seemed strong and steady, absorbing her weight into his.

Kelsey was aware of her hands making their way, without her express permission, up towards his biceps which were solid and full of flexing, moving knots. She waited for the explosion, the moment when lips gently touching turned into ravenous kisses and searching hands and breathless gasps. But it didn't happen. The alcohol had numbed all her nerves and she just couldn't feel it. Or maybe something else just wasn't right?

Pulling away from Will's tight embrace, she tried to fix her wildly telescoping gaze on his, by now, perplexed, frustrated expression. The world spun cruelly around her and nothing was still. Then, inch by inch, her vision faded to black. As though through deep underwater currents she heard a shocked cry of, 'Jesus, Kelsey!' as her knees weakened. Will's arms slipped around her, lifting her off her buckling legs. She drifted in and out of sleep, dreaming of her dad carrying her back to her own little bed in the middle of the night after she'd sneaked across the landing and climbed into her parents' big cosy bed. The sensation was exactly the same; that of flying through the air, cradled close against a warm chest, safe and peaceful.

The delightful sensation was cut short as she felt the world's axis suddenly rotate with a sickening gyre. She was being put down onto her own two unsteady feet while Will worked her key in the lock, still supporting her with a muscular arm around her waist.

'You seem steady enough now. You can take it from here, Ms. Anderson.'

Kelsey knew she was nodding and pulling a petulant face at her knight in shining armour, though she was struggling to keep her eyes open.

Kelsey took the keys from his hand, curling them in her palm and bringing them in tightly towards her chest. 'Night, Will,' came out in a garbled slur as she passed through the open door into the dark hall.

'Night then,' was his doleful reply as Kelsey slammed the door closed with an insouciant kick that had in it all the unintentional force of someone who's drank near-on a full bottle of bubbly and countless sloe-gin chasers and had to be carried home by a very sexy, very put out work colleague.

Chapter Twenty-Eight

'There is a tide in the affairs of men, which, taken at
the flood, leads on to fortune'
(Julius Caesar)

Please forget that kiss happened! Also, I'm usually
much better at it than that, well not much better,
to be honest, but I don't usually pass out. Cringing.
Your mate, Kelsey.

Her fingers had been hovering over the send arrow for
two whole minutes as she weighed up the impact of the
words on the screen. *Just send it. I have to contact him soon,
he'll think I'm avoiding him, which, of course, I am. But he'll
be a bit crushed. Won't he? That's why he hasn't called me, he's
off sulking about it.*

It had taken twenty-four hours of bed rest, trashy
American reality TV streamed onto her new tablet, a
multi-pack of crisps, and a large bottle of ice-cold nearly
flat cola – very important that it was not fizzy – for the
sickening fug of the hangover to shift, only for the queasi-
ness to be replaced with something else: crushing shame
and embarrassment. She'd missed work. She'd let Norma
down. And she'd kissed a colleague.

'Ugh, why doesn't life have a delete button for memories?' Kelsey shuddered as she sent the text message on its way and slid down under the covers again, replaying what she could remember of the drunken snog. Within seconds her phone buzzed into life.

Don't worry about it. Pretty girls swoon in my arms all the time. Drink plenty of water, W x

'Will's got his swagger back? Oh well, that's that then. Dealt with. I am never, not ever, drinking again. Ever!' Chastising herself out loud, she sank back into a fitful sleep. The hangover had claimed the last days of July. Soon she'd be back at work, herding the late summer crowds and steering clear of devilishly handsome workmates.

★

High season. The words 'no vacancies' shone out in red lettering from every B&B window and the theatre billboards were pasted over with 'sold out' banners. The pavements were perilously busy as visitors in search of some culture, clotted cream, and classical acting shuffled along the kerbsides next to end-to-end traffic on the main routes into the town.

Kelsey allowed herself to become immersed in all the hustle and bustle, just another bit-part player in tourist town life, totally at ease in her now familiar role as a tour guide. The days were long and the frenetic energy of the school holidays had a fun all of its own.

Over the course of the first half of August she managed to meet Lukas and Valeria for lunch on the ticket barge one Saturday and Myrtle and Gianfranco for iced coffees at the main theatre bar, but Will was nowhere to be seen again. In passing, Gianfranco had beckoned her into the barge for a conversation, whispering in his thick accent.

'Will is in London. He got a call back for the film he hoped for. The actor who got the part originally, he did not want it.'

'Will's got a second shot at that movie he's been mooning over? Wow! Has anybody actually asked him what film it is, or which part?'

'He said he swore to be secret… and he would not tell us anyway… in case it does not work out. He is a man with proud feelings.'

Kelsey nodded, thinking of how robust Will had been when she'd rejected him, twice, but how fragile his feelings about his acting career were. So far she'd managed to keep the secret of their drunken snog to herself and had no plans to spill the gossip to Gianfranco.

'I guess we'll have to wait and see, won't we?'

Even though she wanted him to come back to town with news of his big break, for now, she was glad of the respite from Will's attentions. And so Kelsey's busy summer bustled on. The only thing spoiling it was her increasing awareness of its rapidly hastening end and the insistent memories of Jonathan Hathaway she'd tried to bury away.

For a while she was able to convince herself that she wasn't casting furtive glances towards the Willow Studio each time she passed, or that she hadn't gone back to the pink café where she'd first met Jonathan just so she could sit quietly and think about him for ten minutes among the chaotic August crowds. Each time she let her mind wander towards him, she would be overwhelmed by a sadness very much like grief. Writing to Mirren, she'd confessed as much.

Missing someone who's right there in the very same town as you, alive and well and just getting on with their life is much worse than missing someone on, say, the other side of the world, because if they're nearby and they still don't come and see you, then you really know all hope is lost. They simply don't want you.

★

Mid-August brought with it cooler breezes and a gentler touch than the scorching temperatures of flaming June and July. The mid-afternoon heat frequently built towards rain showers, light and warm and scented with dust and cut grass, so that the cracked earth in the town's flower beds turned a rich brown once again, and every flowering thing along the banks of the Avon prepared for the summer's grand finale, one last glorious bloom.

Planning to use both her cameras on the night, Kelsey shopped online for rolls of film for her new assignment, looking forward to the gala with a mixture of excitement and nerves. She couldn't help but tell herself that this gig could establish her reputation in town as an event photographer. Maybe she really could stay on in Stratford at the end of the season. If she pulled this off, she could get more commissions, maybe even build a career here. She had two weeks left to master her new digital camera, and so she practised whenever she could, which wasn't all that often now that she had to pick up some of Will's tour groups because he was off meeting film producers, trying to convince them he was the man for the role, whatever that role was.

Her rota for the last two weeks of August was full even before it incorporated the gala set-up hours, but there they were, in bold type to distinguish them from the tours:

August 19th – orientation on gala site

August 24th – costume fitting – performance space set-up

August 29th – dress rehearsal – final set up

August 30th – gala evening – contract terminates. End of summer season.

Those words, 'end of summer season,' terrified her. She'd have sat down and wept over them had her rota not fallen onto the doormat at St Ninian's Close with a smart cream envelope of thick parchment with her address in scratchy calligraphy. The card inside was embossed with silver bells and ribbons. It read:

Ms Kelsey Anderson, plus one guest,

is invited to attend the marriage of Ms Norma Arden and Mr Gianfranco Petrucci

Stratford-upon-Avon Registry Office

12 noon, September 3rd

Drinks reception to follow at The Osprey Hotel Brasserie

Chapter Twenty-Nine

'When little fears grow great, great love grows there'
(Hamlet)

The broad wooden door was studded with metal buttons like a Christmas ham pierced with cloves. Kelsey rapped on the brass knocker. 'Anybody home?'

Gnarled and brittle twists of wisteria branches, now sleeping after their spectacular show in the spring, framed the door. Kelsey had only just missed their blooms when she'd arrived in town on that dry, dusty day back in June.

Still in her uniform, Kelsey had headed straight for the big Jacobean house in the centre of town where the gala was set to take place. Getting no reply, Kelsey peeped her head around the side of the house where stood wide wrought-iron gates shining with silver paint and adorned with ornate theatrical masks of comedy and tragedy. A step ladder blocked Kelsey's entrance into the gardens beyond. A workman was fastening a rainbow arched sign to the tops of the gateposts. It read, *Pretty Follies: Gala of Theatre and Music.* As he climbed down to let Kelsey past she thanked him, remarking jokingly, 'The last thing I need is to walk under a ladder and be cursed with even more bad luck.'

The gates opened onto an orchard where the grass had been left to grow long and wild all summer. It was dotted here and there with tough little violas and bee orchids. The low trees were laden with pears and crab apples that already had the mellow scent of autumn on their skins. There was something else in the air too, something unmistakeable that prickled Kelsey's nostrils the very moment she walked into the quiet enclosure of the orchard.

Mulberries. But where are they?

Through a blue slatted gate in the near distance, she could just make out a single mulberry tree standing in the centre of a mossy lawn. Kelsey inhaled deeply, revisiting her memory of Will and the spice of the fruit on his fingertips. Shaking the memory away, she headed through the blue gate and onto the lawn, immediately slipping off her pumps so she could spread her toes in the springy moss.

The flower borders frothed with simple white camomile and tobacco flowers shining out like white stars. The pin-cushion heads of scabious nodded on thin stems above their spreading mounds of green foliage and scatterings of Wedgwood blue forget-me-nots mingled with Kelsey's favourites, the cornflowers. At the backs of the borders were the roses bursting out everywhere in colourful explosions like frilled flamenco skirts. On every rosebush swelled the last budded heads of the summer, pursed like lips waiting to be kissed. All they needed was a light summer rain and a blaze of sunlight and they too would reveal themselves. This was indeed the perfect spot for the gala evening. Even before it was decorated, Kelsey was enchanted.

People buzzed to and fro like hoverflies. Trestle tables were being set up, tents and marquees of all shapes and sizes were being erected and long ropes of fairy lights were being strung up so that each footpath and discovery space would be illuminated on the night.

No one had noticed her yet, except the figure approaching quickly from the back door of the big house, striding across the lawn towards her.

'You're here?' Jonathan called out.

She watched him approach in his Converse and crumpled sky-blue shirt tucked messily into dark jeans. He had his sleeves rolled up, his silver watch glinting in the sun. She hadn't set eyes on him since that night in the theatre. There'd been his text and the awkward phone call when he'd told her about the gala photography job, but actually *seeing him* in the flesh again brought back a flood of feelings, indignant, defensive and, against her better judgement, longing and warm.

'How are you?' he asked in earnest, leaning close and kissing her cheek, his eyes full of light.

Kelsey had forgotten how beautiful his smile was, and how open and expressive his face, but he was far paler than he had been on the June day they'd met at the pink café, testament to how confined to the indoor theatre he had been all summer.

'It's nice to see you again.' Kelsey couldn't help but smile for him, his presence was so invigorating. Inwardly, she rankled. *How can he be such a phoney? Just remember, he's the jelly to Peony's peanut butter. Yuk.*

'I'm showing you around today. Did you know that?'

'Nope. But I do now.' Kelsey wondered if it was a coincidence, or had he requested to be the one to do her orientation? Surely not? Hadn't Norma helped the director out by putting together the rota? She didn't even know Jonathan.

'So, where do we start?' asked Kelsey, trying to be business-like and drawing out her notebook. 'I want to recce the grounds and make a plan of all the things I need to photograph on the night. It'll require some carefully choreographed timings in case I miss something important.'

'This way.' Jonathan gently touched his fingertips to her elbow as he directed her towards the big house. It lasted only a fraction of a second but it was long enough for Kelsey to have to bite her lip to stop herself melting into a dew.

Kelsey knew the house well, she'd guided her groups through it many times that summer. She couldn't help but share her enthusiasm for the beautiful old place. 'Hey, Jonathan? You see how the house is all wonky? It's leaning out over the street?'

'Uh-huh.' He nodded, looking up at the buckling slate roof and warped leaded casements with their grainy, greenish glass panes.

'That's because the wall facing the street was built with timber beams and wattle and daub but the back of the building is just made of brick. Bricks were a lot less expensive than timber when the house was built four centuries ago. The weight of the wooden frontage has made the whole building lean over.'

'You don't say? You know, the oldest buildings in Okie are only a couple of hundred years old? That's why I love England. This stuff blows my mind. And it's not just the material stuff, it's the poetry that gets me the most.' Jonathan seemed to collect himself before turning to point towards a low stage that two engineers from the main theatre were constructing on the south lawn to the other side of the house. 'That stage is for the court masque performance. Have you heard of it? It's called *Love Restored?* I hadn't. Anyway, some actors from the local college are going to perform it. You'll definitely want to shoot that. They're on first, at around seven.'

Kelsey scribbled a note in her book. 'Ben Jonson Masque. Got it. I studied masques at university. I love their quirkiness. I remember this one being short and sweet, like most masques, and full of jokes and love songs and poetry. It's a defence of true love against greed and money, if I remember correctly.'

Jonathan smiled down at her bowed head as she wrote. 'Next stop, the treehouse. Ladies and gentlemen, please follow your tour guide, Jonathan Hathaway.'

He was already striding ahead towards a tall oak tree on the farthest side of the south lawn. Kelsey watched him go, smiling in spite of herself, even as she thought of Peony's tell-all interview for the local rag. Given that he was as good as engaged and so prone to flirting with other women, Kelsey felt remarkably safe and at ease with him.

She followed him to the treehouse, stopping at the wide steps constructed around the tall trunk. Sweeping his arm, Jonathan let Kelsey pass up them first and in through the wooden door. It all looked at least a hundred years old.

'This is gorgeous, isn't it? Get up here.' She smiled to see him standing at the foot of the steps, arms folded, seemingly just watching her with a grin. He bounded up three steps at a time.

The little wooden house was wreathed in variegated ivy and had a door high enough for Kelsey to pass through without lowering her head, but Jonathan had to crouch a little to get inside. As he closed the door, the dark enclosed them, save from the diffused light from the coloured glass panes of a small leaded window.

His voice broke the silence. 'You know the Italian company that brought *Romeo and Juliet* to town this summer? They're doing the balcony scene here. One of their company musicians is going to play the lyre down there on the bottom steps, and Juliet's going to appear at this window.'

Giddy with the feeling of being alone with this beautiful man, Kelsey lifted the window clasp, letting the light in, and sticking her head out the window, called out in the broad Scottish accent of a scolding Edinburgh Ma. 'Romeo, Romeo, where aboots art thou Romeo? Yur tea's ready. Get in here now!'

She heard Jonathan's throaty laugh and turned round in the hopes of catching his smile. The excited exchange of energy between them was there again, like electricity galvanising them into higher and higher spirits. Kelsey tried to pull the window closed, but found the ancient clasp was jammed.

'Oh no, I haven't broken it, have I?'

Jonathan reached out to try the clasp, brushing Kelsey's hand with his own, his body so close that Kelsey's imagination played delightful, suggestive tricks. *You could just slide your hands over that taut stomach… run your fingers across that broad back. We're close enough to kiss… if he weren't taken, that is.*

'Got it!' Jonathan freed the mechanism and pulled the window closed. The soft light through the coloured panes lit their faces in soft pinks, blues, and greens. She had never wanted to touch anyone so much.

'Jonathan?' she said, not knowing quite what she would say next.

'Yeah?'

'I… wish I'd gotten to know you better this summer,' she heard herself say, as she reached tentative fingertips towards his hands which were hanging by his side.

Jonathan said not a word, slipping his arms around her waist and slowly spreading his fingers out, pressing his palms into the small of her back, drawing her whole body into him. She rested her head against the soft cotton of his crumpled shirt and there in the dark they each let out a slow suspirating breath.

He held her tight, just for a moment, exquisitely, but with economy. No sooner had he lowered his face to let his lips gently brush her forehead, than he stepped back, holding her at arm's length, looking into her eyes. 'Kelsey… your friendship this summer has been so important to me. Thank you.' There was deep affection and longing in his voice, but Kelsey heard only formality and restraint.

He leaned forward once more and kissed her forehead, before taking her hand and leading her towards the little door and out into the sun and heat again. The sudden light strained their eyes, and they separated once more so they could each search pockets and bags for sunglasses.

The effect of having been in Jonathan's arms had stilled and calmed Kelsey. She didn't even want to entertain the bewildered thoughts at the back of her mind about what that clandestine embrace had meant. Instead she walked down the steps making some notes in her book.

'All right… so… balcony scene. Got it.' Tapping the pen against her bottom lip as Jonathan watched her through dark shades, she thought through her assignment. *I'll get some shots from the back of the audience if they're all going to be clustered around the steps. I might need a chair to stand on though.*

'Next up, someone's doing a sonnet reading from that little hill over there, but I've been sworn to secrecy and I'd have to kill you if I told you who it is. OK, you win, it's Patrick Stewart,' Jonathan blurted out with a sudden hearty laugh.

'Oh my God, he's a legend! My brother will kill me if I don't get a photo with the *Star Trek* guy.'

All around the garden, Kelsey scribbled her notes as Jonathan talked her through the schedule, revealing surprise after theatrical surprise. He led her onwards towards a huge yew hedge that was formed in the shape of a hollow box with one wall missing so you could step right inside and discover a garden bench against the deep, far wall. The yew was thick, forming a solid shelter-like structure, so solid in fact, that barely any light passed through it at all, and it was noticeably cooler inside. It was just high enough for Jonathan to stand upright in, though his hair brushed the red-berry-speckled branches above him.

'This is our *Midsummer Night's Dream* space. We're going to light it up inside with Christmas lights. Let me see, what else? We'll take out this bench and we're bringing in our swinging bower from the show – you know, the one you saw on the stage? It'll just fit inside.

We're going to cover it in real wild flowers and... uh... green stuff?' Jonathan shrugged.

'Ah yes, green stuff. I see.' Kelsey's eyes sparkled as she pretended to note this down.

'Hey, I'm an actor, not a botanist,' he drawled.

Jonathan lowered his rangy frame onto the bench deep at the back of the bower and Kelsey threw herself down beside him, smiling. Jonathan's legs stretched out before him, his ankles crossed. There it was, that effervescent feeling again. *Maybe we can be friends. This doesn't feel all that bad.* Kelsey looked up above them at the thin green needled leaves and the red jelly-like berries, like tiny pitted olives.

'You know yew berries are poisonous?' she stated, matter-of-factly. 'Back in Shakespeare's day they only planted them inside enclosed land, like churchyards, to protect grazing cattle from eating them.'

'Yeah? Is that another one of your tour stories?'

'Certainly is. You're dealing with a professional here, you know,' she answered primly, indicating the name badge on her work shirt with a wink.

Letting their laughter settle into smiles, the pair sat still and silent, until Jonathan gently nudged her arm and spoke in a low murmur.

'I always feel real comfortable with you, Kelsey. You're great to talk with... or just... sit with, even. Sometimes on tour I get kinda lonely, but you...' He shrugged his broad shoulders, nodding to himself, and letting his thoughts take over.

Kelsey suppressed a sigh, thinking of Jonathan's devotion to Peony. She would *not* like him saying these things to her, but Kelsey found them exhilarating. *Why couldn't*

I feel like this with Will? Or Fran, for that matter? Or anybody that's actually bleeding single? Kelsey cast a furtive glance at Jonathan who seemed lost in thought. Someone had to break the silence.

'So... you're doing a scene from *A Midsummer Night's Dream* in here... with Peony?'

'Mmm, that's right. Hey, how's... um... how's Will doing?'

'Oh, he's fine thanks. Same as always, really,' she said with a shrug.

The light dimmed in his eyes. 'Come on. I'd better show you where you're doing your living picture thing.'

She followed him over the sun-drenched lawn to a round, paved area. It was nothing more than a circle of flat grey paving stones, speckled with dry yellow lichen and about fifteen feet across.

'You mean the *tableau vivant*,' Kelsey attempted a Gallic flourish with a sly laugh.

'Yeah, the *tableau* whatever it is. It's the last performance of the evening, the big finale. So no pressure or anything.' The wink he gave her cast little crinkles at the side of his nose. Kelsey looked away.

'The finale? How do I get myself involved in this mad stuff?'

'It'll be great. Some of the crew from *Dream* are supposed to be setting up its curtain rigging next week. It's on a huge loop kinda thing supported by poles in the earth. The whole curtain will enclose all you guys, then it will be lowered to the ground, the musicians will start to play music behind you... it'll be awesome. You'll be perfect.'

Kelsey was nodding and making the occasional 'uh-huh' sound but, thinking about how she wanted to kill Norma Arden for getting her inveigled in this damned thing, she wasn't taking in one word. Jonathan talked on.

'You'll be lit by spotlights. Can you see they've already rigged them in the chestnut tree over there? No, over there, by those stone things.'

He directed Kelsey's glazed stare over to a set of squat, square stones sunk into the lawn in a star pattern a couple of metres wide.

'The Nine Men's Morris, you mean?'

'Nine men's what now?'

They spent the next half an hour leaning over the stones as Kelsey explained that it was a giant game, a sort of mixture of chequers and noughts-and-crosses. He let her guide him as they moved their black and white pebble playing pieces around the stone stations, it quickly becoming clear that Jonathan was winning. But their fun was to be curtailed.

Too soon Jonathan was called away by a technician to help set up the lighting for his bower scene with Peony. He kissed Kelsey politely on the cheek and, with a dramatic low bow and a daft smile, wished her good night.

'I let you win that one, Jonathan,' she called to him as he walked away.

'Sore loser? I'll give you a rematch if you like.' He grinned over his shoulder with a quick wink.

As Kelsey walked home that evening she couldn't help smiling at the thousand memories she was processing. If this is what friendship with Jonathan Hathaway felt like, this would have to suffice. She could try to ignore the dull ache in her chest if it meant she got to hold on to memories of his smile, his goofy sense of humour, his passion for Shakespeare, and the hard, blazing-hot feel of his body as he hugged her.

She pulled her work rota from her satchel. It would be five days before she was due to meet him again in the knot garden, and she was already wishing the hours away. There would be ten demanding tour groups in the interim and some sleepless night too, but the whirligig of time wound on.

Chapter Thirty

'But are you so much in love as your rhymes speak?'
(As You Like It)

Days later, checking her mail before heading out for her early morning swim at the local baths, Kelsey found three items in her compartment. One a plain white envelope, the second a large manila padded package, and the other, a postcard from Edinburgh with a picture of the statue of Greyfriars Bobby – the loyal Skye Terrier who wouldn't leave his master's grave unattended. People came from the other side of the world to pat the dog's head, just as Kelsey did each time she passed it on its Edinburgh street corner. She read the postcard as she walked out of St Ninian's into the cool of the morning.

Hey you, how are things? Did you get back on that horse like your Auntie Mirr said? Hope so! Looking forward to hearing all about it. As promised, I'll be back in town for some amateur dramatics on the 30th. Train gets in at 6, so I'll come straight to the gala. You know I got a hotel room this time? See you in two Shakes(peares). Hugs, Mirr.

Shoving the postcard and the unopened letter into her satchel, Kelsey remarked under her breath, 'She's really coming. Good old Mirren. I knew she wouldn't let me do the scene with Peony by myself.'

With her hands free to rip open the seal of the big envelope, she found inside the 35mm films she'd ordered for the gala shoot. *OK, now I have everything I need for my first public commission.*

Her plan was to start the evening using her old camera and then switch to digital as it got darker and harder to gauge light levels. Lost in imagining herself drifting unnoticed through the theatrical in-crowd, surreptitiously snapping candid shots of all the celebs, by the time she arrived at the pool, she had entirely forgotten the unopened letter in her bag.

After swimming, the day was a busy one. Kelsey expertly guided her two tour groups around town, fitting in a quick lunch with Myrtle and Valeria in the back of the ticket barge, while Gianfranco manned the ticket desk.

'Did you hear Will's on his way back to town? Nobody knows how his try out went, but if it was good news, wouldn't we be the first to know?' Myrtle wondered.

Kelsey worked hard to show only collegial interest in Will's whereabouts.

'If he didn't get the part, he's going to need some serious ego massage when he gets back,' Myrtle joked.

Kelsey bit into her sandwich nonchalantly, part of her wondering if she'd imagined Valeria casting a wide-eyed warning at her girlfriend. *They can't possibly know what happened after Norma's engagement bash, can they?*

That afternoon, her copy of the *Sonnets* stuffed with tips in dollars and sterling, Kelsey watched the coach pull away from the riverside as she waved off the noisy rabble inside. She'd count through the notes when she got home tonight. Right now, she was in a rush to meet Jonathan at the knot garden for another shift setting up the gala.

As she walked down the quieter back streets she loosened her plaits, letting her hair fall in thick, tight waves down her back. Her summer in the sun had lightened its darker streaks to a burnished gold, even turning the softer baby hairs around her temples to a pure white. Slicking on lip gloss and unknotting the neckerchief, she calculated that if she walked in through the back doors of the town's big chemist's she could grab a free spritz of perfume on her way through to the front, and it would also take her in the direction of the knot garden. So she did exactly that, choosing a simple rose scent from a granny-chic bottle. *OK, now I'm ready.*

Passing into the orchard she instantly spotted Jonathan bent over the long planting troughs that ran along in front of the yew tree bower. His ancient-looking faded grey Led Zeppelin T-shirt clung tightly across his broad shoulders. She watched from afar as he delved his hands into an open bag of compost, his frame hot and sweating from the exertion of setting up the performance spaces all afternoon. He'd be on stage again later this evening so Kelsey knew she had to make the most of her brief time with him.

He looked up with a broad smile and a friendly 'Hey!' before handing her a trowel. They set to work planting the earth with strawberries.

'These'll separate the performance area from the spectators' area on the lawn,' he said as he worked. The afternoon heat was building into a sticky closeness and Jonathan's brow glistened. He looked tired. Kelsey didn't mention it but she knew it must be exhausting doing two or three shows a day and rushing around setting up for the gala too.

They weren't the only ones pulling double shifts today. All across the garden there were actors, technicians, artists, directors, and seamstresses from the companies that were visiting town for the summer, all setting up their own spaces. The gala director from the main theatre company, who Kelsey knew only from their phone conversation about the shoot, was drifting between each group of workers amiably overseeing the whole thing, bringing his vision to life.

'So are you ready for your big night?' asked Jonathan with a smile, as he stopped to rest, sitting back on the lawn.

'I think so. I never properly thanked you for telling the director about my photos. You know, you really pushed me to try it out... you and my friend Mirren and my mum, and I'm grateful. I got a new camera and everything.'

'Awesome! I'm glad you're going for it. So, is this what you're going to do come fall?'

'I hope so.' She looked thoughtful for a second. 'If I go home, I could try to rent out Mr McLennan's old shop – he's my old boss.' Even as she said it aloud, she wondered why the thought hadn't occurred to her before, but it didn't appeal to her quite as much as the idea of simply staying put in Stratford and living in her beautiful little box room of a flat. 'To be truthful, I wish I could stay here and work from home. I've just extended my rent for another month so I can be in town for my boss's wedding,' she went on, while setting an upturned strawberry plant loose from its pot and planting it firmly in the soft earth. 'I have this gorgeous little terrace up on the roof above my room. It's weird because nobody ever uses it, just me. In fact I've never even met my neighbours. I think the flats next to mine are empty, I haven't heard a peep from either of them.'

'Could you rent one of those, turn it into a studio? Then you'd have the shortest commute of all time?' Jonathan's voice lifted with its lovely upwards inflection. It made everything he said sound so full of inquisitive wonder. 'You'd wake up, fall out of bed, and mosey into the next room to work.' Jonathan had stopped working altogether. He sat cross-legged with his arms out behind him supporting his weight, directing his full attention at Kelsey.

'Yeah, maybe.' Kelsey entertained the notion for a moment. 'Meanwhile, you'll be commuting from here across the Atlantic, then from Canada to... where? LA?'

'Yeah, I guess,' he shrugged, smiling through thinned, blanched lips. 'But... I *am* coming back to Stratford, you know?' He shifted his weight, bringing him closer to Kelsey, his voice, rich, deep and tentative.

'You're coming back?' Kelsey struggled to contain the sensation that rushed up her spinal column making her scalp hot and tingly. She stared at him in amazement.

'I'll be back with the whole company for a few days at Christmas to block out our new play for the Willow Studio next year. And I'll be back again in February for the actual run. I'll be in town for the whole of the spring season. We just signed the contract today.'

Delivering this news, and Kelsey's obvious delight, made his smile beam brightly and his eyes shine. Kelsey tried to slow her heart's wild drumming, barely able to hear her own voice over the racket it made in her ears. Clearing her throat, she managed an exaggeratedly casual, 'Uh... wow... so... what play is it?'

'*Love's Labour's Lost*. Do you know it?'

'Do I know it? I just finished reading it! It's so good. What part are you playing?'

And so they went on talking theatre as the heat built and a summer storm gathered in the hills surrounding the town. Jonathan was amazed to learn about Kelsey's English and theatre history degrees and wondered aloud that she'd been too modest to tell him sooner. He talked about how, come the spring, he'd be playing Berowne, a king, who's trying to swear off women completely and devote himself to his work.

'Is Peony in it?' Kelsey had eventually asked, knowing what the answer would be, and, yes, of course, she was going to be the queen, Berowne's love match. *Naturally. Who else?*

The revelation cooled the connection between them as Kelsey withdrew slightly, feeling abashed. It was a timely reminder of her banishment to the friend zone. The planters were now beautifully arranged with strawberry plants and they had spread straw thinly underneath them to keep the berries from touching the soil.

Feeling the change in mood, Jonathan said, 'I gotta go warm up soon, or rather, cool down, before tonight's

Dream. I'm usually at the studio a lot earlier than this.' But he didn't look like a man in a hurry to leave.

'I have some water, if you like?' Kelsey was already unbuckling her satchel and handing him a bottle. As she did so, the films, Mirren's postcard, and the unopened letter spilled out onto the grass beside her. Distractedly, gathering up her belongings, she watched Jonathan tip his head back and drink the water, long and slow, his shining throat moving as he satisfied his thirst. As she took him in, she ran her finger absent-mindedly through the fold of the envelope and pulled a single sheet of paper out. Finally, looking down, expecting a letter from Mirren or her mum, she found unfamiliar, neat handwriting.

How's things, Ms Kelsey Anderson? Hope you finally shook off that hangover. I'll be back in town for the gala night. The producers here are still making up their minds about me. It's a toss-up between me and some double-barrelled Oxbridger. I'd really like to pick up where we left off before you fell into a coma. So save the last dance for me on the 30th.

Doubt thou the stars are fire,

Doubt that the sun doth move,

Doubt truth to be a liar,

But never doubt I love.

Yours, Will

She looked blankly at the note. *Is he quoting Hamlet at me? My God, is this an actual love letter?* Kelsey knew she was meant to be thrilled, but she was left cold. *Hmm, isn't a declaration of love supposed to inspire… something in a girl? Maybe he's taking the piss and it's just Will being playful?*

She was roused from her confusion by Jonathan getting to his feet. Quickly slipping the note back into her satchel her cheeks burned crimson red.

'I'd better make tracks,' Jonathan drawled. 'Thanks for the water. I won't be at your dress rehearsal since it's just you gals, but I'll see you on the night.'

'OK.' Kelsey struggled to her feet, hoping he would kiss her forehead again, like last time, but he was already stepping away from her, throwing the leather gardening gloves off onto the grass. *Why did I have to open that stupid letter? Did he notice? Will's the last person I want butting in right now!*

'Coo-ee!' called a shrill voice from over by the main house.

OK, he's the second last person I want butting in.

Jonathan and Kelsey turned to watch Peony crossing the lawn holding up a scrap of white material and what looked like delicate wings. She appeared to be surrounded by her own, cool micro-climate. Kelsey groaned inwardly, feeling every bit as grimy and frazzled as Peony looked poised and immaculate, but she still managed something approaching a friendly smile.

Jonathan didn't wait for Peony to get over to them, instead he waved once in her direction and walked off towards the orchard gate, not even realising he hadn't said goodbye to Kelsey. He was lost in his own brooding thoughts.

Kelsey helplessly watched his back as he made his way out onto the street. She knew Peony's eyes were fixed upon her so she couldn't call out to him.

'I have to follow Jonny to the show,' Peony was saying in the exact same accent as Jonathan, but it sounded brash coming from her perfect rosebud mouth. 'This is your *tableau* costume. The alterations girl is in the kitchens if it needs letting out.'

With that, she handed the wisp of white to Kelsey and floated past her in pursuit of her leading man.

Chapter Thirty-One

'Is there no play, to ease the anguish of a torturing
      hour?'
(A Midsummer Night's Dream)

Kelsey hadn't really understood what a stoic she was, but
each evening she'd retreat to her little sanctuary, eating
sandwiches or salad that she had little appetite for, alone
up on the terrace, and feel amazed that she'd survived the
two set-up days where she'd been in Jonathan's presence,
or the days she'd spent waiting to be back in his presence,
without dying away entirely.

Maybe losing her dad as a teenager had toughened
her up without her really noticing, she mused. Resilience
was a wonderful quality for a woman to have. Kelsey
thought about her mum and Mirren and Norma, and all
the other women she'd ever met, even Peony. She didn't
know a single one who wasn't fortified with reserves of
quiet strength and patience, and thank goodness for it,
the things they'd all been through. She told herself it was
this resilience that would see her through to Jonathan and
Peony's departure.

Another thought intruded upon those pensive,
exhausted moments up on the twilit terrace; that there

was still time to take Mirren's advice. It might do her bruised ego good to land gorgeous Will Greville before he headed off for Hollywood stardom. But, no matter how flirtatious and sexy he was, there was one serious impediment to surrendering to his flattery: namely, that although she fancied him in the abstract, and she did really like him in spite of his brazen cockiness, all her affection was directed elsewhere, at a man bound up in a long-term love affair, a man who was living, working, and seeing the world with another woman. Yes. Resilience is a wonderful quality in a woman.

★

The last day of the season arrived. Kelsey had only one tour group booked in for that morning; twelve French-Canadian theatre fans in town on the dramatic pilgrimage of a lifetime, and it was hard to get through her usual spiel without her throat tightening with emotion. She couldn't help reflecting on her time in Stratford. She'd worked so hard all summer and learned so much. As she led her final group into the cool, silent church, she caught a glimpse of Myrtle and her own group leaving at the chancel door and the two exchanged a sad, knowing smile.

The end of the summer season hung in the cooling air with a strange melancholy. Across town, each company was packing away props, scenery, and costumes, some being loaded onto lorries for the next stage of their tour in faraway countries, while some were on their way to storage. Kelsey marvelled at the thought of all of the season's expended energy, the passion and power of all those performances, each gesture and phrase played to perfection under bright spotlights: they were all over for the summer. The playhouses fell dark once more.

At noon, Kelsey gathered her tour group about her on the steps of the main theatre, their coach's engine already running noisily by the kerb. She held the sunflower casually over her shoulder, her summer staff of office. It had come to feel so familiar in her hand.

This is going to be hard. She took a deep breath.

'My friends, it's been my honour to be your guide today. Thank you for listening so attentively. I really hope you enjoyed your visit to Stratford. Before you go, I want to say a few words.'

The group was silent, some tipping their heads to one side in polite assent, others smiling warmly. Kelsey pressed on, looking into each face in turn as she spoke.

'You have been my last ever tour group. I arrived here at the beginning of summer without really understanding the importance of this job. I didn't appreciate how privileged I was to be your host in this wonderful place. Visitors have been making their way here for near-on three hundred years to see the place where Shakespeare was born, to trace his footsteps through the streets, to visit his school, or put flowers by his grave. I hadn't understood how important these things are to people, not really. But everyone understands the language of love, and loss, and hope, and we look to Shakespeare to find expression of those things. We come to this town looking for ourselves, and we leave here enriched, having found the home of so many of our deepest feelings. I certainly have. I hope you found everything you were looking for, dear friends, and I hope you carry these memories with you wherever you go.' Kelsey knew she had to stop before the floods came.

'So, I'll let Shakespeare have the last words. They're from Julius Caesar who said, *fare thee well, the elements be kind to thee and make thy spirits all of comfort. Fare thee well.*'

Standing on the street, ringed round by men and women whom she would never meet again, Kelsey placed one hand on her stomach and another behind her back and took a long, low bow to resounding applause.

Chapter Thirty-Two

'Most auspicious star'
(The Tempest)

Kelsey wandered alone to the agency office, the rustling bag in her hand crammed with her name badge, the neckerchief, and the dreaded gilets. She grasped a large posy of irises and roses in shades of lilac and purple and tall spikes of Cotswold lavender. At last, she'd had a reason to walk into the florist's shop in the posh shopping arcade. She'd handwritten the note right there by the cash register.

Dear Norma, thank you for taking a chance on me. You gave me the start I needed. I will be forever grateful, with love, K x

Making her way towards the office she saw ghosts of her summer at every step along the busy streets. Pressing the door buzzer she noticed for the first time the 'To Let' sign in the windows up above her.

'Come up, dearie, I've been waiting for you.' Norma's voice crackled through the speaker.

Kelsey picked her way carefully up the stairs which were cluttered with black sacks of shredded paper. The landing was piled high with dusty travel guides ready for delivery to the charity shop. Norma was kneeling barefoot on her office floor surrounded by lever-arch files and folders, diaries and ledgers. A noisy shredding machine whirred as she fed it from a tall pile of papers.

Norma's satin jumpsuit wasn't the only thing that was purple; her eyes were circled with dark rings. She'd been weeping. She looked up as Kelsey walked in. For a second, Kelsey was taken aback. She'd never seen Norma without make-up, or without her high heels. When she stood up to greet her, Kelsey was amazed at how tiny she was, but also by how young she looked without the thick layer of foundation and harsh red blusher. Norma smoothed down her red bob, which was just as bright as ever, and reached out to kiss Kelsey.

'Sweetheart, are those for me? Oh, they are glorious, thank you, darling. Coffee? Yes, of course, it's time for a cuppa.' Norma was off, chattering ten to the dozen as always. 'I'm glad you've popped in, my dear. Sit down, sit down.' She poured filter coffee from a glass pot adding milk and sugar without even asking if that was how Kelsey took it, which it was. 'Here you are. Don't worry about a coaster, they've been packed.' Norma settled herself behind her desk. 'I have a proposition for you, my dear. You see the thing is, I'm leaving next week and I haven't found a tenant for the office yet. And the truth is I didn't want to find one, not just *anyone*. I've owned this building for twenty years and it was my mother's before that. I have no intention of letting it go quite yet. That's why I think you should take it.'

With that, Norma nodded her head decisively, sat back, and interlaced her fingers, waiting for Kelsey's reaction in total silence. Kelsey put the cup down on the window ledge beside her, waiting for Norma to start up again, but for once she said nothing.

'I'm sorry, Norma. What are you saying exactly? I don't need an office.'

'No. But many little birdies about town told me you *do* need a studio.' Norma's eyes gleamed as she leaned forward, drumming her sharp red fingernails upon a document on the desk.

It had only taken ten minutes. Kelsey found herself out on the street again in a bewildered shellshock. The tiny peppercorn of a rent had been agreed, and fixed for six months before it would increase to market value in order to allow Kelsey time to establish her photography business, and the lease had been signed. Her tenancy began on the third of September, Norma's wedding day. Kelsey was already reaching for her phone as she left Norma's office, desperate to tell her mum the bewildering, exciting news. Mari would be over the moon for her. Norma waved her off down the stairs, her eyes twinkling as she called out, 'And we'll talk about the ticket barge in the autumn, darling!'

Kelsey just caught the words as the door closed behind her.

'The *what*?' she'd shouted back, incredulously, but Norma was shredding paperwork again, her machine devouring documents noisily. Kelsey could just make out a satisfied cackle over the racket.

Chapter Thirty-Three

'Lord, what fools these mortals be'
(A Midsummer Night's Dream)

'I'm coming to you live from Stratford-upon-Avon, reporting on a spectacular night of music and drama, industry schmoozing and celebration. Everybody who's anybody is here this evening. This year's theme is Pretty Follies, and industry insiders tell me it's going to be the biggest night in the theatre calendar...'

Careful to avoid being caught by the rolling news cameras, Kelsey squeezed through the gates and down the red carpet. The news anchors and autograph hunters assembling in the street paid her no attention although she looked every bit as glamorous as the starlets expected to arrive as dusk fell over the town. She was giving her silvery maxi dress its second ever outing and wearing subtle shimmering make-up that gave her a soft, dewy complexion and rosy-pink cheeks. *Not bad at all*, she'd told herself as she caught sight of her reflection in the shop windows on her way to the gala.

The first of the dignitaries were arriving. Crate loads of champagne flutes were still being unloaded from a lorry and carried in through the back of the house to the kitchens which had been taken over just for the night. There was a buzz of excitement and activity.

The box-office staff from the main theatre were standing at the gates, dressed from head to foot in black, ticking names off the list of invited guests. This was strictly an industry party, a grand showcase for the town and its theatrical achievements, and one last chance in the year for companies to steal the latest hot stage actors before they became famous on the screen.

Kelsey had her favourite old camera in her hands already. She'd been given an ID badge on a lanyard at the dress rehearsal and she flashed it at the staff who wordlessly let her pass, taking up her first position just inside the gates to get shots of the guests as they arrived. The long grass of the orchard all around her was ablaze with hundreds of tiny iridescent lights in the shape of dragonflies supported on thin sticks shoved into the earth so their glowing wings seemed to sway and dip gently in the breeze. They would look wonderful in the dying light in a few hours' time. Clearly, the professional event scene-setters had been on site all morning adding glamorous finishing touches.

The Mayoress pulled up in a black limousine and the artistic directors from every major theatre in the country were lining up in black cars ready to make their entrances. Just arriving was the party from the tourist board and some MPs in black tie. Kelsey framed and focused shot after shot. Some of the guests smiled or waved as they walked past the camera; others, mainly the celebrities in their couture gowns or actors in dark shades and various quirky styles of relaxed tuxedo, spotted, then patently ignored, the star-struck Kelsey. They were happy, however, to slow their pace and turn their best side towards the lens as they passed.

Kelsey could hear jaunty medieval music playing over a PA system. First pipes, then a drum and something else, a lute maybe? Then the sounds of women's voices intertwined with them like mystic chanting and spread across the gardens. She grew suddenly aware of a presence by her side.

'Don't stop. I'll talk to you as you work,' an excited voice whispered in her ear.

'Mirren!' Kelsey let her camera fall on its strap around her neck as she threw her arms around her best friend. 'You're a sight for sore eyes. Are you all right? When did you get here?'

'A couple of hours ago. I've been working the room, well, working the garden. And I tried my little white fairy costume on. It doesn't leave much to the imagination, does it? Even by my standards.'

'I know.' Kelsey grimaced. 'Mine is so skimpy, I'm glad it's only a quickie pose then curtain-up again or I might freeze to death. They are lovely though, aren't they?' Kelsey took a quick glance at Mirren's red sequined dress and matching heels before raising the camera to her eye and turning back to the ever-increasing crowds meandering past. 'God, Mirren, you look amazing.'

A waiter joined them at the other side of the gates proffering tall glasses of champagne on a silver tray to each new arrival. He was wearing emerald-green velvet breeches and stockings with a black satin sash tied tight around his waist and a short bolero-style jacket, also in green velvet, over a bare muscular chest. Mirren eyed him as she replied.

'You did say I might meet Benedict Cumberbatch so I thought I'd better get a new frock. Is Bene on the guest list tonight, by any chance?'

'I've no idea, sorry.'

'If he is, I won't be held responsible for my actions, Kelse.'

'I'm pretty sure he's married, Mirr. Got babies and everything.' Kelsey hurriedly changed her film. She'd grown so practised, it took only a few seconds.

'Fair-do's,' said Mirren with a breezy shrug, casting her eyes around the garden. 'In that case, I'm off to see that lovely wee bullfighter with the tray over there. The bubbly *is* on the house, isn't it?' Mirren smirked, adjusting the clingy dress over her knockout hips.

Dresses like that were made for figures like Mirren's, tall and voluptuous. Kelsey could see the men openly gaping at her friend. Mirren was in her element as she called over her shoulder to her. 'Toodle-pip! See you for the flashmob, or whatever it is.'

'It's a *tableau vivant* and I *hope* you're going to take it seriously,' Kelsey called after her, but Mirren was already on her way, swinging her long black hair behind her.

Kelsey sighed, wishing she'd had the chance to tell Mirren about Norma's office and her plans for September. That would have to wait. It was time to move on. The moon was already high in the sky and Polaris was clearly visible in the north. The first of the performances would be starting soon. Eager to see how everything looked after the team effort of planning, setting up, and dress rehearsals, Kelsey passed through the blue gate onto the north lawn.

Immediately before her on the freshly mown grass was pitched a striped lilac and yellow maypole with a huge floral crown at its pinnacle bursting with gaudy dahlias and spreading stems of barley and corn. There was a pile of matching flower garland headdresses and delicate sashes available on a nearby table so partygoers could dress the part as they tried their hand at dancing with the twisting pastel coloured ribbons. A troupe of dancers in long white smocks like something from a Thomas Hardy novel stood by the maypole ready to offer a demonstration. Kelsey spent a few moments capturing them as they smiled for photographs.

All around her were pop-up performances and side-show attractions, obviously hired in for the night by the gala director. Stilt-walkers, tumblers, sad-eyed Pierrots, satyrs, goddesses, and Elizabethan zanies and antics of all kinds paraded past. A wandering minstrel in a long gabardine cloak with a huge white plume in his bonnet sang a sad lament. Kelsey caught the words, 'for bonnie sweet Robin is all my joy,' as he walked on. Over the course of the evening Kelsey managed to catch each one of these performers for a moment or two, asking them to pose with the revellers, who were scattered across the lawns chatting in small groups, which everyone, even the most famous actors on the guest list, were happy to do, perhaps assuming the pictures were for *Vanity Fair* or *Harper's* society pages.

I'm actually doing it. I'm a photographer at a big event. Everyone here thinks I'm a professional, and I actually feel like one.

Kelsey's heart was full as she packed her manual camera away in its case and heaved out the new digital machine.

Checking all its settings were correct, she set off on her way around the party again, ready to capture the rest of the action. A flurry of activity caught her eye. The catering staff dressed in pristine chefs' whites filed out of the house in uniform ranks each transporting a silver salver to the long row of banqueting tables draped in white linens. Kelsey knew she had to capture the dishes before the crowds descended upon them.

She shuddered at a huge jellied dish of something meaty and mosaicked in clear aspic as it dawned on her that tonight's menu was Elizabethan-inspired. She captured the head cooks as they proudly placed their centrepiece on the table: a giant pie, its golden crust formed in the shape of an incredible peacock, its tail feathers spread in full display. A reassuring notice placed beside it read 'summer vegetable pie'. There were several gigantic salad dishes sprinkled with bright orange edible nasturtium flowers, and countless other smaller dishes of blue-veined cheeses, poppy-seed crackers, and rich, crumbly oatcakes. She smiled to herself as she photographed a dish full of something resembling white marshmallows with stained pink tips labelled 'maiden's nipples', before framing the many colourful dishes of chocolate truffles, whole walnuts and cobnuts, huge black hothouse grapes and cherry tomatoes, and sweet syllabubs in crystal glasses bejewelled with pomegranate seeds. She caught each delicacy on film; or rather, on a digital SD card, which wasn't quite as romantic. She had to suppress a squeal of delight as she captured Dame Judy Dench picking up one of the 'maiden's nipples' between her fingertips and popping it into her mouth with a naughty smile of satisfaction.

Everybody's here. Literally everyone. Stay cool, Kelsey, stay cool!

Looking around the lawn for someone to tell – Mirren, Norma, anyone, she was caught off guard by the sudden appearance of a host of fairy children in glittering gossamer costumes skimming across the lawn on bare tiptoes, whispering wickedly in strange tongues, and waving their wands at the revellers. Her camera caught these fairy children too, though a quick look through the images on the screen showed they were a little blurred. She hadn't had time to adjust the settings for an action shot.

'Dammit! If I'd had Dad's camera in my hand, I'd have caught them. I *must* be better prepared for surprises,' Kelsey chastised herself under her breath.

'Well, he-llo! How's Scotland's answer to Annie Leibovitz this evening?' drawled a lascivious voice behind her. She spun round knowing precisely who it came from.

'Will! Will... what are you wearing?' She took in his emerald-green costume, the same as the waiters but he'd acquired a matching half-mask from somewhere, and he was holding a tray of champagne glasses. 'You look like a really camp Zorro. Why are you waitering?'

'Kick a man while he's down, woman. After all that bloody rigmarole with the producers I didn't get the bloody part, and because I didn't get the part they didn't pay any of my expenses! So, I've resorted to my original plan of surfing the autumn away. Frankly, I need the extra cash. And I don't want any of the film bods who auditioned me to recognise me. They're probably here somewhere.'

He set his tray down on the banqueting table, now crowded round with guests. Handing Kelsey a glass of champagne, he grabbed a glass of his own and quickly downed it.

'Err, should you be drinking that?' Kelsey asked. As he swallowed the last drops from the raised flute, Kelsey couldn't help but glance at his open bolero jacket and his tanned, smooth skin beneath. His stomach was deeply muscled and brown.

'Who gives a shit?' he shrugged, capturing the last millisecond of Kelsey's gaze over his torso and smiling slyly. Emboldened, he spoke again.

'Listen, after you've done your turn as a fairy princess tonight, come and meet me up in the treehouse. I'll save us a bottle of pop.' He raised his eyebrows and grinned his most winning grin.

Kelsey looked around, worried that someone might have overheard. She was startled to find Peony standing on the other side of the table. She'd been pouring water into a glass but now seemed frozen to the spot and she was glaring daggers at Kelsey. Looking away quickly, Kelsey collected herself. It didn't feel great being hated by Peony, but she knew she deserved it; she was after all trying to distance herself from her feelings for her boyfriend. She offered Peony a weak smile, but the actress scowled and rushed off in the direction of the yew tree bower.

Kelsey heaved a sigh and turned back to Will only to find he was making his way across the lawn, failing to stop to allow a single guest to take a drink from his tray. Kelsey watched him go and smiled despite herself at his sheer cheek and his terrible skills as a waiter.

Poor Will, he'll be feeling that audition badly. He got so close. Got to hand it to the guy, though, he doesn't give up. 'Meet me in the treehouse' indeed. He's too much. She knew, deep down, that she wouldn't be joining him for a midnight tryst in the treehouse, but she was flattered he'd asked and glad that he'd been true to form to the very last. It struck her that she was still smiling after him and watching him swagger across the lawn helping himself to another glass of champagne. His bravado had kept her laughing all summer and he didn't really take himself too seriously, it was quite endearing really. She found herself wishing he was staying put in town for the autumn. She really would be all alone as she got to grips with Norma's office and her plans for a photography studio of her own.

Thoughts of the future had to wait. She had a job to do. She put the champagne glass down on the linen tablecloth and walked away. Just then Kelsey heard a shrill laugh that she recognised as Mirren's. Peering into a quiet topiaried corner of the garden, Kelsey spotted her friend secreted away with an attractive young actor she recognised from the cast of the *Othello*. Mirren had a hand on his bicep and they were perilously close to one another. *Maybe Mirren hasn't changed at all. Or maybe she's out for one last fling before really settling down?* Either way, she didn't want to know. Kelsey thought of sweet, devoted Preston back home with a heavy heart.

Turning her back on the pair she walked off towards the yew tree bower which was ablaze inside with lights. The *Midsummer Night's Dream* scene had just begun. She supposed she had to face it at some point, but she'd been dreading saying goodbye to Jonathan. She might never see him again after tonight and she doubted they could keep up their friendship by email or social media. Why prolong the agony of quietly, secretly pining for him?

He was heading off to Canada in a few days and the thought of living on in the town without him all winter made her queasy and weak at the same time. Of course, he'd be back at Christmas, but she'd be heading home to visit her family for the holidays, and yes, he'd be back in February for *Love's Labour's Lost* but she knew she couldn't see him then either. She didn't know what was worse, the thought of him leaving, or knowing that he was coming back for another run and bringing Peony with him. She knew that if she didn't make some serious efforts to avoid him next year she'd have to go through all this pain again. It was so hard to avoid people in a small town like Stratford where everybody knew everyone else, but that's what she'd have to do, and the sad realisation stung.

It was growing darker by the minute and the strings of twinkling lights all around the garden came into their own, gleaming out in the twilight. There was a large audience crowded around the yew tree bower and Kelsey could just make out Jonathan using Oberon's English accent as he spoke words of love and reconciliation to Titania. Kelsey bided her time, forcing her brain to record and preserve the lilting cadence of Jonathan's voice, before politely working her way to the front of the crowd.

'Excuse me. Sorry,' she whispered as the final row of spectators parted to let her in.

Raising the camera to her eye, she was greeted by the sight of Peony reclining in the swinging seat which was decked in real ivy, white dog roses, honeysuckle, and the glossy green leaves of enchanter's nightshade. Jonathan was leaning over Peony and pressing his lips to hers in a slow, languorous kiss. The masochist in Kelsey pressed the shutter button and her camera caught the moment. *One for the road, I guess. I suppose that's as good a reminder as any why I shouldn't spend the winter mooning over Peony's boyfriend.* Her heart sank deep and heavy.

As Kelsey emerged gloomily from the crush of clapping people, she saw the gala director pacing on the lawn with Mirren by his side.

'Ah, there she is!' Mirren called out, pointing to Kelsey. 'Come on, we've got to change, it's time.'

'Already?' Kelsey asked, alarmed. It had been a long, strange evening. Looking at the counter she saw she'd taken nearly three hundred shots on the digital camera alone, and the image of that very last shot was now seared in her memory. She allowed herself one last sigh for Jonathan Hathaway.

'Ms Anderson? *Tableau vivant* in twenty minutes,' called the director to reinforce the need to hurry.

Chapter Thirty-Four

'Some Cupid kills with arrows, some with traps'
(Much Ado About Nothing)

Mirren gripped Kelsey's hand and the pair rushed across the lawn towards the big shed which had been requisitioned as a changing room for performers.

'You all right?' she asked with concern in her voice. 'You're not still suffering over that Fairy King are you? Oh, come here.' They had rushed inside the shed doors and Mirren held her arms out wide for Kelsey who willingly stepped in close for a hug. 'Only half an hour to go then you can leave, OK? It's almost over,' Mirren said close to her ear.

Kelsey thought about heading home to her soft bed in her little sanctuary. Then her mind flitted to Will. Would he really be waiting in the treehouse for her after the gala? If he did, he was going to be very disappointed. She ought to tell him not to expect her but there was no time now.

'Right, where's our costumes?' Mirren rummaged through the packed clothing rails.

'Aren't you leaving after the *tableau* too?' Kelsey asked.

'Erm… maybe,' Mirren squirmed a little, looking uncomfortable.

'Oh.' Kelsey knew exactly what that meant. She'd arranged to meet Othello. She was about to tell Mirren she really, really ought to talk with poor Preston back home and not just jump into bed with some luscious actor, but Mirren was sorting through their costumes and looking agitated. It could wait until after the show.

'Here's yours.' Mirren shoved Kelsey behind the white sheet that had been suspended on a rope across the far end of the shed for making quick changes. 'Don't forget your wings,' she added, before diving behind the makeshift curtain herself.

As the pair slipped out of their party dresses, Mirren asked, 'I missed the dress rehearsal yesterday. Is there anything I should know?'

'You didn't miss much. Titania – Peony I mean, wasn't even there, but the director showed me where we're supposed to stand. There'll be a chaise lounge thingy in the middle of the circle for Peony to recline on, like the queen bee that she is, and we all cluster around her. You and me are at opposite sides of Peony. I'm at her toes; you're at the head end. Watch out for her crown, it's very tall and sharp. We hold the lanterns up above her, and we do *this*.' Demonstrating the pose they were both to strike required her to stretch her body upwards as though reaching for the stars, holding the lantern at arm's length, while extending one foot behind for support.

'Very pretty, Kelse. You look like a ballerina.'

By now, they were in their costumes and appraising themselves in the long mirror that leant against the far wall.

'And how long do we hold the pose for?' Mirren looked nervous now.

'Thirty seconds after the curtain drops. Then it'll come up again. Just long enough for the crowd to get a peek at us. Any longer and they'll see me wobbling about on tiptoe.'

'I didn't realise this was the evening's big finish, Kelse. It's a good job I love you.'

Mirren leaned into the mirror inches from her reflection, wiping off her red lipstick and replacing it with a delicate pink, which she then expertly applied to Kelsey too.

'I know.' Kelsey arched an eyebrow. 'Norma Arden has a lot to answer for.' She blotted her lips with a tissue and gave her fairy wings a final check. 'It's hard to believe the Victorians were so into this kind of thing. Living pictures, I mean. It's amazing what the aristos got up to before Netflix was invented.'

'Oh God, I'm nervous,' said Mirren, wrapping her hands around her bare arms. 'It's a long time since we did anything like this, and it's a far cry from the school drama club panto.'

Kelsey thought how strange it was that she'd never noticed before how, underneath all her bravado, Mirren didn't have a lot of confidence. She was reminded of Will and his delicate feelings about his acting career.

'You look amazing, Mirr. Just follow my lead and try to enjoy it. It'll be over in a flash.'

'That's what I'm worried about,' Mirren joked, rearranging her ample bosom which was threatening to spill out from the delicate costume. It had little more to offer in the way of support than a simple ballet leotard.

'*Tableau Vivant* cast assemble,' called the director's assistant into the shed where Kelsey and Mirren had been joined by many more fairies, including Peony and the little children Kelsey had seen rushing across the lawn earlier.

'Positions please,' the assistant called again.

Every fairy fell into two neat rows as the director bossed and bustled. Kelsey slipped her hand into Mirren's and offered her a reassuring wink. Mirren smiled back with misty eyes. 'I'm glad we're doing this, I've really missed you this summer. Listen, you know your hot red-head, Will whatshisname?'

'Silence please. And… go! Hold your positions all the way to the circle please,' commanded the assistant as the group filed past into the cool evening air.

'Never mind, tell you later,' Mirren fell silent.

The two rows of fairies led by Peony in her glistening crown, who had been glaring at the whispering Mirren and Peony, were flanked by the box-office staff holding up sheets of white voile so no one could get a glimpse of them. They tiptoed in silence the short distance across the lawn and made their way inside the huge round curtain of white velvety material that had been expertly constructed by the technical crew. It hadn't been there for the dress rehearsal the day before and it was far bigger and sturdier than Kelsey had imagined.

Peony took her place on the chaise longue and was taking care to arrange her long white costume to maximum effect. Her décolleté was painted with shimmering silver and green floral patterns just as it had been for the performance Kelsey had seen at the studio theatre. She really did look breathtaking. Three fairies arranged themselves behind the chaise, and the tiny fairy children draped themselves picturesquely on the flagstones in front.

Kelsey and Mirren were the last to take their positions. Mirren looked beautiful with her wings spread out behind her and her lantern held aloft. She raised herself up onto a tiptoe and assumed an angelic demeanour. Kelsey struck the same pose attempting to mirror Mirren's posture to achieve a symmetrical affect. The director cast his eye over the group before rearranging the children. He gave everyone an ecstatic thumbs-up, mouthing the words 'break a leg,' before leaving the silent scene.

The PA system on the south lawn crackled into life. 'Esteemed guests. The highlight of this evening's entertainment is about to commence. Members of various touring companies, including the Oklahoma Renaissance Players, as well as Stratford's Tinkerbell Ballet Group, will present a *tableau vivant* in imitation of the golden age of French ballet-theatre.'

Kelsey caught a glimpse of Mirren's widening eyes and incredulous expression, and the pair burst into giggles.

'Ssh,' Peony hissed, with a sharp glare at Kelsey.

Behind Peony's perfectly poised head, Mirren rolled her eyes dramatically with a wicked grin on her face which made Kelsey smile all the more. The opening in the curtain through which they had passed was being clipped closed behind them. They could hear the expectant chatter of the crowds gathering outside and the musicians shuffling their sheet music on the stands behind the curtain.

'And… three, two, one,' someone counted down from outside and a slow, baroque sounding violin began to play a spellbinding melody.

Everyone in the group took a deep breath and exhaled simultaneously, readying themselves for the fall of the curtain. Except someone was moving, suddenly and frantically.

Peony had raised herself to a kneeling position, placing a bare foot upon the ground. Reaching out with one hand she grabbed the ribbon sash around Kelsey's waist, bringing her face to face with her.

'Are you proud of yourself?' Peony hissed through gritted teeth.

The curtain around them began to slowly sink to the ground as Kelsey gasped in shock. Her lantern fell and a loud crack rang out as it hit the stones.

'What?' Kelsey gaped, her eyes wide in panic.

'One minute you're making eyes at Jonny at a photo shoot and slobbering over him at the pub, the next you're kissing that tour guide guy outside the theatre. Don't think I didn't see you! But I never told Jonny. He doesn't need any more heartache.'

Shaking her head in confusion and fear, there was nothing Kelsey could do but try to struggle back into her pose. In the last second before the fairy dell scene was fully revealed Peony let go of the sash and settled herself on the chaise again but Kelsey couldn't regain her balance and tumbled down onto the flagstones at Peony's feet.

All she could do was pull her delicate costume over her thighs and shake her hair back over her shoulders. Staying how she had fallen with her forearms flat on the stones and her head and shoulders raised, she fought hard to assume as fairy-like a pose as she could manage in spite of the shock.

What the hell is she playing at? Kelsey's face blanched from livid pink to bloodless, horrified chalk as her heart pounded wildly.

The curtain continued its slow descent. The crowd began to gasp and raise their phones to capture the scene. There was nothing Kelsey could do but freeze.

A moment of absolute silence fell as the gathered crowds took in the scene: a regal fairy queen at the centre of her majestic court, her underlings all around her. It was a magical sight. There in the still summer air under the full August moon fluttered four hundred years of memories, echoes of every gossamer wing-beat, and changeling child to have graced a stage. The dusky night sky was pierced with tiny stars, each one recalling centuries of dramas performed by the flare of lime lights and tallow candles and bright roving spotlights, a strange and powerful moment of connection between the past and present. But all Kelsey could feel was the burning in her cheeks and shame in her chest.

What's she implying? I've been carrying on with Will and causing Jonathan heartache? His heart was never mine to hurt!

Her mind raced on as she gradually became aware of Jonathan's presence out there in the crowd. She didn't want him to see her like this. If she was honest with herself, she had been looking forward to the *tableau* just so he would have a chance to see her in the spotlight for a change, so he might carry with him memories of her posing, serene and beautiful, when he moved on. When she examined her feelings she was ashamed. No wonder Peony was furiously territorial and insecure; Kelsey *did* wish Jonathan was hers instead.

Before the *tableau*, Peony had told her co-star exactly where she wanted him to stand to get the best view of her on her chaise, and her eyes were fixed upon that spot, her chin raised in a majestic pose. Jonathan Hathaway was there, but he wasn't looking back at Peony. His gaze was transfixed somewhere down by her feet. He was watching Kelsey, utterly unaware of Peony's fixed stare. Peony witnessed it all, unable to look away. She saw his lips parted in wonder and desire and a smile of amazement playing at the very edges of his mouth. And he had tears in his eyes.

The music swelled to its height as Jonathan took in the supernatural scene, enchanted. His chest was rising and falling heavily, but he stood stock still, as fixed to his spot as Kelsey was to hers. Kelsey's eyes were trained straight down at the ground, wishing it would open up and swallow her. She had no idea that Jonathan was taking in her delicate white costume, just a sheer slip of white material over her pale skin. He saw her hair falling over her shoulders and shining like gold in the spotlights. He studied her eyes, sad, dignified, and suffering.

The applause began, wild and enthusiastic, as the curtain slowly rose again, concealing first the fairy children, then Kelsey and Peony, and finally Mirren who, once safely hidden, immediately tore at Peony's crown, knocking it from her head, but she froze again as the director burst in through the back of the curtain demanding to know what the hell had just happened.

'It's OK,' Kelsey said sadly. 'I fell.' She looked at Peony, expecting to see a smirk of triumph, but instead she was weeping.

The crowd were still applauding as the two friends ran back to the shed, shivering now in the evening air that had more than a hint of September in its falling.

'I don't get it,' Mirren raged. 'She pushed you, didn't she, the nutter?'

'No she didn't, and if she had, I'd have deserved it. I've come between her and Jonathan and caused them both so much pain. I see it now.' Kelsey's eyes widened. 'I have to get out of here.'

'Don't go,' Mirren implored. 'Let's have some champagne and celebrate the end of the season and you can tell me all about what's been happening with Jonathan since I last saw you.'

'That's just it, nothing *has* happened, other than me wishing he'd leave Peony for me, which is ridiculous and just plain wrong. Please just stay here, enjoy the party,' Kelsey said, slipping her shoes on and kissing Mirren on the cheek. 'You enjoy your hotel tonight and I'll meet you for breakfast in the morning, yeah?'

After putting up a protest, Mirren eventually hugged Kelsey in dismay and watched her friend gather up her cameras and run away down the garden. When Kelsey was out of sight, Mirren sighed and reached for her red lipstick. The night was still young. Why waste the moonlight?

Chapter Thirty-Five

'Ladies, sigh no more, men were deceivers ever;
One foot in sea, and one on shore, to one thing
    constant never'
(Much Ado About Nothing)

Out on the lawn, the partygoers formed quiet huddles, some were talking contracts and plans for next season while some were in amorous pairs making quite different kinds of plans. Kelsey ran all the way to the orchard gate until her cameras became too cumbersome. As she passed the yew tree bower, she could make out a deep, drawling American voice in the dark, and it was angry. Jonathan and Peony were deep in a tense exchange of words.

'You have no right interfering,' he was hissing.

'I'm trying to protect you, but if you're too dumb to see she isn't going to leave him, then you're a bigger jackass than I thought you were.'

Kelsey could barely make any of it out over the music filling the garden and it didn't matter, anyway. Their lover's tiff was no concern of hers and she'd finally learned her lesson to leave them well alone.

At that moment she caught sight of Will in his emerald-velvet costume and mask sneaking up the steps of the treehouse holding Mirren's hand as she tiptoed behind him. Kelsey's thoughts spun wildly. What should she do? She wanted to get out of there as quickly as possible but should she go back and drag Mirren out of that treehouse? When had the pair of them even had a chance to meet tonight? *God, Will's a fast worker!* Mirren's problems with Preston were obviously coming to a head if she could arrange a midnight rendezvous with a man she didn't know from Adam. Before she had time to resolve that Mirren was a grown woman and she was going to leave her to it, Kelsey heard a loud 'Fine!' shouted in an irate voice. Turning, she spotted Peony running in her direction, mascara streaks down her cheeks. Kelsey quickened her pace but Peony's strides were so long she had caught Kelsey by the elbow in seconds.

'Kelsey, stop! Please!'

Kelsey raised her hands in defence and ploughed past.

'How many times do you have to prove to me that Jonathan's your man? I get it, OK! But nothing ever happened, I swear, except in my head. Just go back to Jonathan, forget I ever existed, please.'

'No, you *don't* get it,' cried Peony through heavy sobs, pulling her to a halt. 'You don't get it at all. I love that dumbass like a brother, he's the only family I have and watching you parading around with that Will guy has been killing him. Why didn't you just leave Jonny alone if you don't want him?'

'*What*?' Kelsey snarled in disbelief. 'Peony, please, just let me go.' She wrenched herself free of Peony's grip and raced out of the garden, heading for home.

Norma was by the gate getting into a taxi with Gianfranco when she stopped open-mouthed at the sight of

Kelsey in floods of tears. 'Kelsey, dear. Let us drop you off,' she called out in her claxon voice.

'Not tonight, thanks, Norma.' Kelsey came to a halt by the open door. 'Although… can you take these until tomorrow? Safe keeping.' And with that, she handed Norma her precious cameras and ran into the dark night. Norma watched her go before calmly raising a finger to the waiting cabby. 'One moment please, driver.' She slipped through the gates into the garden.

Chapter Thirty-Six

'I would not wish any companion in the world but
    you'
(The Tempest)

By the time Kelsey reached St Ninian's Close the sobbing
had stopped and she was panting heavily, exhausted from
running, her mind a cacophony of questions and unhappy
memories.

*What the hell happened tonight? Norma was right. The
Midsummer Madness got me. She warned me about it. Be wise,
she said. Well, we can chalk this up as a big fat failure for wisdom.*

Closing the door behind her, she climbed the stairs in
the dark. Walking straight past the entrance to her flat
she clambered up the steps onto the roof terrace. The
multi-coloured fairy lights she had strung up in honour
of Mirren's first visit were still twinkling away in the dark.
Throwing herself down on the hard iron chair, she drew
her knees up to her face and the tears fell all over again.

Kelsey shivered as her adrenalin ran out, making way
for tiredness and heartache like she'd never felt before.
Tonight was supposed to have been special, the night she
worked the room and made a name for herself; the night
she let Jonathan slip away while being all dignified and

stoic. Instead, she'd been bawled out by Jonathan's girl-friend in front of everyone and she'd made a fool of herself. *And what was Peony going on about? She loved Jonathan like a brother? Her near fiancé?* All she understood was that she'd hurt them both and it felt dreadful.

In the back of her mind she heard a low rumbling and gradually became aware of lights flashing, and something else. *What is that?* There was a low voice calling out in subdued tones.

'Kelsey! Down here!'

Shuffling to the edge of the terrace's low wall, she saw a taxi in the street below. The driver was flaring the headlights again and again while a figure stood on the pavement, arms aloft, waving to her. Kelsey could make out Norma and Gianfranco in the back of the cab gazing up at her. Gianfranco's face was all concern but Norma was smiling placidly.

Jonathan waved his arms frantically, trying to get her attention without waking the entire neighbourhood. 'Kelsey, let me in.'

Without knowing where the strength came from Kelsey found herself racing downstairs and reaching for the lock. As she heaved the door open, the taxi pulled away into the night and she and Jonathan were left alone face to face on the doorstep. He burst into passionate speech the instant he saw her.

'Kelsey, I am so sorry about Peony tonight. She's always been like this, looking out for me, but she shouldn't have interfered. I've asked her a hundred times not to. I guess tonight she couldn't help it.'

'I get it, she's your girlfriend, she has every right to be mad given the things I've been thinking about you this summer… the things I've been hoping.' Kelsey looked down at her feet.

Jonathan seemed to become breathless at hearing this. He gasped imploringly, 'But she's *not* my girlfriend. I told you that, that night at the Yorick?'

'Yeah, and then you ran off and never told me why and the next thing I know I'm reading about how you're as good as engaged to her.'

'Huh?' he spread his hands, dumbfounded.

'You're the jelly in her peanut butter sandwich?' Kelsey looked accusingly at him.

'Oh! You saw that? I didn't think anybody read that tacky rag,' he smiled as his shoulders dropped in relief.

'What are you so pleased about? It isn't funny, finding out that the guy you had the best date of your life with, at least *I* thought it was a date, is actually in a long-term relationship with his co-star.'

'Everything they printed in that interview was bullshit. Peony didn't say any of it. I mean… it is true about our nicknames, PB and J, but that's all.'

Kelsey's eyes widened as she scrutinised Jonathan's face. 'You're not getting engaged?'

'No. And she didn't even say that. Wait until I get my hands on that sleazy old reporter!' Jonathan's jaw worked and flexed as he spoke through thinned lips. 'She's given enough interviews to know the amount of lies these losers print so now she records every one she does. She made me listen to the whole thing, not that I didn't believe her. Peony's no liar. I told you we're like brother and sister, through thick and thin… granted, this appears to be a particularly thin bit, but she always has my best interests at heart.'

'If you're not together, and she's not jealous, why's she so angry with me?'

'She's frustrated with *me* because all this time I thought you were with Will and it was killing me. She told me to just stay away from you, but I couldn't. When I heard your crazy boss lady was in charge of the gala set-up schedule, I asked her if she'd put us together, even though Will had told me you two were an item, and then I saw you reading the poetry he sent you, so I tried to just be a friend to you and I tried to fall out of love with you, but I couldn't. Norma just told me in the cab that she wasn't so sure at the time, but she's certain you and Will aren't together now. Is that... is that true?' Jonathan held his breath, not daring to hope for too much.

'Of course I'm not with Will. We flirted a bit and he's a bit of a dog on heat but... Hold on.' Kelsey slapped a hand on Jonathan's chest. 'Go back a bit. You tried to fall out of love with me?' She sounded out each word in slow amazement.

'Yes. And it's been killing me. I'm sorry I let Will scare me off so easily. I was holding back, trying not to get in the way. Peony's had to deal with my moping around like a love-struck Romeo all summer and I guess things blew up tonight because she's sick of watching me wanting you. And, man, I want you *so* much.' His pale eyes closed as he forced the words through his gritted teeth.

When he raised his eyes to meet Kelsey's again they were clear and earnest. 'I'm sorry you've been hurting, thinking Peony was my girl. But most of all I'm sorry for being an idiot and leaving it too late to tell you that I am completely, ridiculously in love with you.'

'Stop, stop, shh shh, I get it now,' she soothed, reaching out for him in the moonlight and slipping her arms around him. 'Jonathan,' she spoke into his warm chest as he circled his hands across her shoulders. 'I've been in love with you since the day we met.'

Stepping up onto tiptoes, she lifted her face to his, closing her eyes. Jonathan inhaled deeply. She felt his chest expanding as he tightened his arms around her, raising her off her feet. The touch of their lips when it came contained the entire summer's longing within it.

Chapter Thirty-Seven

'Are you sure that we are awake? It seems to me that
yet we sleep, we dream'
(A Midsummer Night's Dream)

It had started slowly at first. Kelsey led Jonathan from the
moonlit doorway upstairs to her flat where they had fallen
onto her little white bed in the dark and kissed all night,
his hands cradling her face, their eyes open even as their
lips met, relishing the sensation of being so close at last.

They were still wearing the clothes they had left the
gala in as the sun came up and their kisses slowed. Kelsey
shivered in the dawn light from the window, the lacy
curtains waving in the breeze. Jonathan reached out and
pulled the window shut while Kelsey drew the covers up
over them. Lying back on the pillow, warm in each other's
arms, they wordlessly fell asleep.

It was full light when they awoke to a fine September
morning. Jonathan stirred first and was stroking Kelsey's
long hair and running his fingertips over her temples,
watching her as she slept. As she opened her eyes and
looked into his, the electric connection between them
sparked into life. Pulling him closer, Kelsey pressed her
body against his. Jonathan rolled his head back, his heart

beginning to pound in his broad chest, before bringing his mouth down to meet hers.

Every movement had been perfect, from his tender hands undressing her, to the endless mouthy kisses he had pressed into her flesh, to the first exhilarating movement of their hips together and the slow, languorous rhythm of their bodies.

It had been difficult to drag themselves out of bed on that first morning, but they were both ravenously hungry. Kelsey's face was flushed and she was smiling to herself in a dopey post-sex glow, feeling like the most gorgeously womanly woman in the whole world. She watched from beneath the covers as Jonathan made the coffee, heating milk in the microwave, and popping bread in the toaster. There was next to nothing in the fridge, but they still managed a decent breakfast up on the terrace. Kelsey dragged the duvet up the narrow steps and they sat snuggled up and warm as the sun shone in a watery sky.

In the gardens below, the rowan trees were thick with red berries but their green leaves were tinged with gold and brown at the tips. Autumn was on its way and soon Jonathan would be gone.

'So what do we do now?' Kelsey asked with a shrug.

Jonathan wrapped the covers tightly around her, kissing her forehead before he replied. 'Well, if you want to be old-fashioned about it, I'd ask you to wait for me. Would you do that?'

'I can do that. I'll be right here when you get back.'

'It's not *all* that long until Christmas, right? And I can try to extend that visit by a few days so we can spend Christmas Day together? And then I'll be back for *Love's Labour's Lost* mid-February.'

'In time for Valentine's Day?' She broke into a broad smile.

'I'll do my best.'

'I wish you didn't have to go.'

'Hey, don't worry, I'll call you every day. Besides, you *are* going to be pretty busy.'

Kelsey thought of the tenancy agreement she'd signed and the office on the town's busy main street lying vacant. She had no idea what to do first. *Some new signage for the front? A website? Adverts in the local papers? Would Mr McLennan be able to sell her some reflectors and a backdrop so the office actually resembled a real studio?* There was so much to think about, and with everyone leaving town, she really would have to do it all alone. But something told her she'd manage. It had been a hard summer, and she'd learned a lot of lessons about trusting her instincts and knowing when to take action. This was her time now. And she was ready.

'Stay there, I've got something to show you,' Kelsey said, as she wriggled out from under the warm covers.

'Don't be long.' Jonathan smiled as he watched her slip down the stairs to her apartment.

Once in her room, Kelsey made a beeline for the pile of big cardboard envelopes under the bed. She was looking for one photograph in particular. *Now where was it?* As she searched she caught sight of a flash from her phone. It was a text from Mirren. She was on her way home.

Believe me when I tell you I'm not proud of myself. I got the early train this morning. I'll be home in an hour. I'm going to tell Preston that it's over. I think we both deserve better than this. I'll just have to follow your example and be brave. See you in a couple of days. Love Mirren, xxx

Kelsey sat back on the floor, her legs crossed, looking down at her phone.

'I got lonely up there,' came Jonathan's voice from the doorway. He had the duvet over his shoulder. He threw it over the bed and climbed in. 'And it's kinda chilly on the roof too. Are you OK?'

'Yeah. Mirren's gone home to break up with Preston. He'll be devastated. He worships the ground she walks on.'

'But she couldn't love him really, could she? And cheat on him like that? Poor doofus deserves better than that.'

'That's what Mirren said, sort of. They've been together since we were all at school. I think that's part of the problem. She's tried to fight it but the romance has been gone for a long time. Maybe it was never really there in the first place?' Kelsey suddenly cocked her head and allowed herself to laugh. 'Doofus? Really?'

'Get over here.' Jonathan held the covers open for Kelsey and she slipped in beside him.

'I'll ring her and Preston tomorrow, see how they're both doing,' she said. 'You know, Mirren still thinks I'm going home tomorrow. I didn't get a chance to tell her about Norma's office.'

'You mean your studio,' said Jonathan, proudly, letting his fingertips explore the side of Kelsey's face and her hair.

'Yeah, my studio,' Kelsey chewed her bottom lip with excitement. 'My studio! It sounds weird.'

'It sounds perfect. I can't wait to see it up and running in December.'

Kelsey shuddered as a thrill of nerves ran up her spine. She took a deep breath and exhaled slowly.

'What was it you wanted to show me?' asked Jonathan, seeing that Kelsey was anxious and wanting to save her from it.

'Oh yeah.'

Reaching down to the pile of photographs on the white carpet, she grabbed one by the corner and handed it to Jonathan.

'This. I took it the day we met. You'd just been dragged away by Peony.'

Jonathan inspected the bright image of two white chairs on either side of a café table under a pink striped awning.

'Wow! You took this that day? It's beautiful. Peony was so mad because I'd taken a two hour lunch break just so I could talk to this incredibly beautiful woman when the show was opening in a few days and we hadn't managed a single tech run-through.'

Kelsey smiled at the memory.

'But that was nothing compared to the argument we had when you came to photograph me at the theatre when I should have been working with the technician on the lighting for our scenes! Wow, she was mad. I just couldn't concentrate on anything but you.'

'At least somebody was trying to be professional. Poor Peony,' said Kelsey, thinking of how she's misread her completely. She handed the picture of the pink café to Jonathan. 'You should hang on to this. That's where you should meet me, when you come back again.'

'You got yourself a date.' Jonathan reached his hands around her back, pulling her close. 'But I'm not leaving town just yet,' he grinned, looking hungrily at her lips.

Chapter Thirty-Eight

'Love comforteth like sunshine after rain'
(Venus and Adonis)

On the third day of September Kelsey was behind the camera lens again.

'By virtue of the authority vested in me, I take great pleasure in pronouncing you husband and wife. You may kiss your bride.'

Gianfranco smiled his broad, gappy grin as he bent his head to kiss Norma. His lavender-grey jacket strained across his biceps, his neck muscles bulging against the white shirt collar. Norma, in a deep purple skirt suit and tall red stilettos, let him dip her backwards as they kissed like movie stars to the delight and applause of their friends. Her severe red bob was tucked back behind her ear and secured with a cluster of tiny lilac roses and slim pheasant feathers, echoing the small posy she held in her, now bejewelled, ring hand. Kelsey had never seen them so happy.

As the wedding party made their way out of the registry office, Kelsey led the way, shuffling carefully in reverse with her dad's camera held to her eye, the scent of freesias and clouds of pastel confetti blowing in the breeze, her camera clicking with each backward step.

'Easy now,' Jonathan murmured in a low voice, his hands cradling Kelsey's hips. He nuzzled his face into her hair as he helped guide her backwards, keeping her from stepping into the long flower beds that lined the path.

'How do the paparazzi manage this? And their subjects are usually trying to run away from them.' Kelsey laughed as she bumped clumsily into Jonathan's long legs. She turned to face him, tall and elegant in his dark suit.

The newlyweds were now on the registry office steps surrounded by friends and family taking their own snaps of the happy couple.

'I think that's my duties as official wedding photographer discharged, don't you?'

Now she could focus on Jonathan again. Holding each other tightly with the dopey smiles of the newly in love, Kelsey saw the flicker of passion light Jonathan's eyes and a sudden serious look of intent. They gazed at one another frozen and breathless for a second, before he kissed her hard and long, unseen by the cheering crowd facing the wedding party.

'I will never stop wanting you,' breathed Jonathan in his deep drawl, his eyes closed, still slowly brushing his lips over Kelsey's.

'I hope not,' she sighed.

★

'I didn't even know you could get purple Rolls Royces,' exclaimed Kelsey in surprise. Norma and Gianfranco were saying their last farewells to the wedding guests outside the Osprey Hotel, making their way through the crowd one by one. Norma was weeping and talking at one hundred miles an hour to each person in turn. Myrtle and Valeria were by Kelsey's side.

'Don't forget this,' said Jonathan, handing Kelsey the silver horseshoe ornament suspended on delicate lilac ribbons.

Myrtle leaned in and whispered in her ear. 'So, no Will then, hon? Is it true? I heard he'd set off for America this morning? An audition somewhere? Was it Iowa?'

'No,' Valeria butted in. 'It was Oklahoma, wasn't it? I heard he left with an actress from one of the visiting companies.'

Kelsey gaped at Valeria. 'You're kidding?' She looked up at Jonathan, anxious to see his reaction.

'Well, the Oklahoma Players *do* need a new male lead. I've told them I'm leaving after *Love's Labour's Lost* in the spring. I'm going to try out for some British companies, see if I can get some work that lets me stay here.'

'What? And you're telling me this now?' Kelsey gasped, her eyes filling with happy tears.

'I only told the director late last night. You were sleeping, and then the wedding kinda took over this morning. You've got to hand it to the guy, your buddy Will is a fast worker.' He laughed, before adding, with a quizzical expression, 'Peony *did* send me a message about some guy she met the day after the gala. He's already declared his undying love for her, apparently. I haven't heard from her since, which is probably a good sign.'

Despite knowing the role he had played in keeping her apart from Jonathan this summer, Kelsey tried to think generous thoughts of Will. He was finally getting the break he had worked so hard for. She looked hopeful for a moment. 'You know, maybe he really does like her. He did say she was hot, come to think of it. He can't only be interested in the acting job, right?'

Jonathan placed his arm around her shoulder, pulling her close to his side with a wry smile, his eyebrows raised. 'Who knows?' he said.

'Shouldn't you warn her?'

'Hmm, I think we've learned to butt out of each other's love lives from now on. And you saw how she can take care of herself when she needs to.'

'Maybe just have a quick brotherly word?'

'All right, I'll see her in a day or two for the *Hamlet* rehearsals, I'll talk to her then.'

'OK, but be gentle, Peony's had a hard time this summer.'

They exchanged a slow kiss before Norma and Gianfranco finally got round to saying goodbye to them.

'Well, dearie, we're off!' Norma extended her arms to Kelsey for a tight embrace.

Knocked off balance by Norma's whirlwind energy, she steadied herself before speaking. 'Congratulations, both of you. Have a lovely honeymoon. Have a lovely life! And thank you, Norma, for everything.' Her eyes flooded again as she handed the horseshoe over.

'Now, no crying, my dear. This is the happiest day of my life, and yours too, I think.' She held her purple gloved hand out to Kelsey. In her palm was a key. 'I'm not the only one getting a good luck charm today.'

Kelsey took the key in one slow, deliberate action, curling it up tightly in her palm as Norma leaned in, whispering as best she could when it didn't come naturally. 'It's yours now. You can let yourself in. The alarm code is the year Shakespeare was born.'

Within minutes, the bride and groom were being driven away by their smart chauffer, heading for the airport and a new life in Italy. Norma waved a hankie out the open window before turning away and falling into Gianfranco's arms in the back seat.

'Yorick?' said Valeria decisively with a hand clap.

'You wanna go, Kelsey?' asked Jonathan. 'It would be nice to drink some champagne. My flight's not until five a.m., I can take my hangover with me.'

'You go ahead,' she ushered in a calm voice. 'I just want to check something out, OK?'

'OK, I'll see you there.' Jonathan wrapped his arms around her and kissed her tenderly. 'I'll be waiting.'

Kelsey nodded and watched as he crossed the street, running to catch up with Lukas, Valeria, and Myrtle.

Walking slowly to the end of the street, Kelsey turned left and crossed the road at the busy little roundabout by the bank and the fancy shopping arcade. Turning her back on the River Avon, her pace quickened as she approached the street where Shakespeare once lived and there on the corner stood the tall building which had, until a few days ago, housed the Norma Arden Historic Tours Agency. There was a 'LET' sign in a second-floor window. Her window. Looking down at her fist she unfurled her fingers. The key glinted in the September light.

'Fifteen sixty-four,' she muttered under her breath. 'The year Shakespeare was born.'

Climbing the steps, she looked at the door buzzers to her left. Norma had removed the little card with her own name on it and replaced it with a new one, written in neat purple biro:

Kelsey Anderson. Photographer.

Breathing deeply, she turned the key in the lock, pushed the door open, and punched the number into the alarm system. For a second she stood still, trying to take it all in.

It would be a long autumn ahead, full of change and learning new skills and waiting for Jonathan to come back to her, but she was ready, and for now she was contented, standing sure and steady on her own two feet at the threshold of her new life.

A Letter From Kiley

Thank you so much for reading *One Summer's Night*. It's the first of two books following Kelsey Anderson as she embarks on an exciting new life in beautiful, theatrical Stratford-on-Avon.

If you loved reading *One Summer's Night* I'd be so grateful if you'd leave a review. Reviews can really help new readers discover my books. And thank you again for reading my debut novel and for your support, it's hugely appreciated.

I began writing *One Summer's Night* a few days after hearing the campus where I've taught English Literature for the past decade was closing down. I'd always dreamed about writing this book, ever since I was a tour guide living and working in Stratford. As one door closed, another opened and I finally had the opportunity to go for it, my dream job as a writer, and tell the story I'd been carrying around in my imagination for so many years.

At first I told myself I was writing this book just for me, to see if I could do it, but by the time I had a first draft I knew I wanted to share it with readers.

One Summer's Night is written straight from my heart and is wrapped up in the many happy memories I have of arriving in Stratford aged twenty (a baby!) and finding friends, adventure, and fun – not to mention my husband and my home – there.

One Summer's Night follows Kelsey on a similar journey to mine as she leaves Scotland with only her beloved vintage camera, and finds her feet, and her true career path as a photographer, in the theatre town. Her new life isn't picture perfect though. Two gorgeous actors are vying for her affections and there's confusion and heartache in store for her. Will she find true love before the summer ends?

You'll find the Stratford that Kelsey discovers isn't always a *strictly* faithful rendering of the town – there are secret gardens and inglenook fireplaces in cosy pubs, a tour guide agency and a studio theatre that only exist in Kelsey's world - but you're not after a guide book, I hope. Hopefully you're here for a heart-warming and uplifting romantic comedy to chase away the last of the winter blues.

I've always voraciously read romantic novels – and I always will. My firm favourites are Jenny Colgan and Rowan Coleman's Scarlett Bailey novels, and right now I'm obsessed with Holly Martin and Jeevani Charika's books. But until I started writing myself I had no idea what an amazing community of readers, bloggers and reviewers there was out there, just waiting to make me feel welcome! I'm always up for romantic book chat on Twitter – try stopping me! So please, come meet me for a chinwag @KileyDunbar

One Summer's Night has embedded within it my love of Shakespeare, which began in Mrs Marr's English class in high school and was nurtured whilst sitting, goose bumped and open mouthed, in the cheap seats at Stratford's Royal Shakespeare Theatre.

I hope my love for the poetry and the place shines through in my story, and you enjoy reading *One Summer's Night* as much as I enjoyed writing it, and I hope you love Hera Books too.

I knew as soon as I heard that two kickass women, already publishing legends, were launching their own company I wanted to be on board, and it's my dream come true to work with Keshini Naidoo and Lindsay Mooney. Your interest in our book means the world to us. I'm excited, not to mention terrified, to be able to share it with you. So, thank you, for being here right at the beginning, supporting us.

Lots of Love, Kiley x

Twitter: @KileyDunbar
Facebook: https://www.facebook.com/Kiley-Dunbar-Author-Book-Page

Acknowledgments

I started writing *One Summer's Night* whilst on holiday with my little family in August 2017 and it's their awesomeness I acknowledge first. Thank you Nic and the babies for loving me, for giving Mummy some peace to write and for all the cups of tea. You are my best people and my wee world.

Michael McGill always thought I could do this and he showed me how. Thank you so much for cheering me on every step of the way, Angel. I love you.

Keshini Naidoo, my editor, and Lindsey Mooney at Hera Books have my gratitude forevermore for just 'getting' me and my writing, for inviting me on board and taking my life in a whole new exciting direction. Thank you Keshini for the thoughtful, careful edits and for making *One Summer's Night* an immeasurably better book. I hope it makes you and Lindsey proud.

Thanks also to Jennie for those meticulous copy edits and for saving me from a lifetime spent cringing about sneaky mistakes and glaring oversights.

I'm so grateful to the *Romantic Novelists Association* and specifically to my New Writers' Scheme 2018 reviewer and all of the committee. The RNA's insight, support and feedback changed my life.

My friend Liz read an early draft of the opening chapters of *One Summer's Night* and gave me valuable notes. She came with me to my first ever writers' conference when I didn't have the bottle to go alone and patiently replied to my many messages asking for advice. She also selflessly drank all the wine with me. Thank you.

Mark Stay and Mark Desvaux helped me in a million practical and inspiring ways. They reassured me and made me laugh when I was flailing, and they brought me into a supportive community of writers. They are also responsible for my Hobnobs habit.

Thanks Mum and Dad and all the family. I love you lots and hope you enjoy my book. And thanks Amos for all the cuddles and nose boops.

Sara, Laura, Kelly, Kirsty, Joanne, Barbara and Angi never once raised an eyebrow when I told them I was writing this book, and they are sweethearts the lot of them. Thanks also to my completely brilliant students and the colleagues and friends at uni who kept me going as I worked the day job whilst writing half the night.

The Dream Team, big and small, were always there for me, and I love them all.

Thank you too, most of all, lovely readers, for coming with me and Kelsey on our summery, Shakespearean adventure to Stratford. I hope you adore this book, it is yours now.